KENNEDY SLOANE GETS SCOOPED

CAILA KLAISS

Helping talented writers publish exceptional books

Kennedy Sloane Gets Scooped

Printed in the United States of America. For information, address
Acorn Publishing, LLC
3943 Irvine Blvd. Ste. 218, Irvine, CA 92602

www.acornpublishingllc.com

Interior design by Kat Ross
Cover design by Damonza

ISBN-13: 979-8-88528-138-6 (hardcover)
ISBN-13: 979-8-88528-137-9 (paperback)
Library of Congress Control Number: 2025914261

For my parents.
Without your love, support, encouragement, nudging, and
occasional shaming, I never would have started writing this chapter.
I'm endlessly grateful and hope you know that all my "chapters"
have begun because of the two of you.

One

Kenny started her day just before sunrise like most other mornings, mentally pumping herself up for the hours to come atop the saddle of her Peloton, powering through a forty-five-minute hill climb that was sprinkled with motivational pep talks. Rushes of adrenaline from the Snoop Dogg playlist and the high five emojis that lit up the scoreboard on the upper right corner of *KennyNYC*'s screen had a way of physically waking up her still sleepy body.

For inspirational and aesthetic purposes, the stationary bike occupied one of the front-facing bay windows of Kenny's spacious three-bedroom apartment on the fifteenth floor of the high-rise, doorman building on Riverside Boulevard.

There was no energy like waking up on the Upper West Side of Manhattan. On the days Kenny couldn't muster the enthusiasm to sign into a vigorous instructor-led class, she'd at least sit on the bike and peddle at a leisurely pace while preparing for the day. Those mornings she'd allow herself to get lost in the sight of activity along the Hudson River.

Flashing lights cruising up and down the West Side

Highway would make her wonder. Was there an accident, a fire? Or was the president or Taylor Swift in town? The congestion on the George Washington Bridge. Were these commuters who transplanted out of the city to make their Jersey housewives happy? Or was a Yankees game bringing traffic to a screeching halt?

The barges that moved at glacial paces through the current. What were they carrying? The occasional paddle boarder or kayaker. Were they wearing wet suits? Who would risk falling into that murky water? The Circle Line cruise ships that glided by several times a day. Were they filled with awestruck tourists or native New Yorkers falling in love with their city all over again?

The endless air traffic shuttling airbuses of passengers to and from JFK and LaGuardia. Who were on those planes and where were they going? Would one of those aircraft hit a flock of birds and descend on the congested river? Captain Sully and his crew made that miraculous landing in this exact location.

Kenny was endlessly curious. As a journalist, she was trained to be keenly aware of what was going on around her. Born a news producer, she was inherently interested in people's stories.

Today Kenny didn't have time to let her mind wander. She pulled her feet out of her cycle shoes, hopped off the bike and flung her sweaty tank top over her head and into the hamper. She glanced in the full-length mirror, assessing if she could ever be one of those girls who was confident enough to workout in just a sports bra.

She slid into her slippers and shuffled through the kitchen to plug in the percolator. Kenny always filled the pot with water and coffee grinds the night before. Accustomed to working and living on deadlines, she valued every minute of her day, especially the mornings; and the three minutes it took to prepare the coffee pot were best allotted to the night-time routine.

She grabbed the remote and turned on the living room television which she could see through the open window of her galley kitchen. She turned to Channel 7 and tuned in just in time to catch Joe Gold's last local forecast before the network morning shows started.

"Well, folks, it looks like it's going to be a beautiful summer day in New York! The tropical storm that was making its way up the coast all week has changed course and is spinning back out into the Atlantic. We have a perfect ten on our hands. A balmy seventy-eight degrees with ample sunshine. Get out and enjoy this Wednesday!" exclaimed the jovial weather man.

Kenny smiled, pulled out the seasonal coconut crème Coffee mate from the refrigerator, and whispered, "Thanks, Joe."

James had been on the West Coast for business trips for the past two weeks, and Kenny and the twins couldn't wait for him to get home. His flight was due to land at LaGuardia Airport later that evening and the couple planned to surprise Jimmy and Rosie with a weekend trip to Long Beach Island to close out the summer before school started. Every New Yorker knew that even a black cloud hovering over the borough of Queens would wreak havoc on air traffic, and Kenny hoped any weather-related flight delays wouldn't dampen the get-away. The clear, dry forecast was a welcome prediction.

While most Manhattanites would jet out to the Hamptons for a quick escape, she had always preferred to head to the Jersey Shore to find peace and relaxation away from the hustle and bustle of the city. An easy trip down the Garden State Parkway took city-dwellers to some of the oldest and most storied beaches in the country in less than two hours.

August was the favored summer month among beach-goers on LBI, how locals and longtime vacationers referred to their beloved eighteen-mile island off the coast of New Jersey. It was considered late in the season, and most tourists had evacuated for the fall months and back-to-school routines. August was when the bay and the ocean waters reached their warmest temperatures of the year. Sidewalks and running paths were sparse of pedestrian traffic, making for lackadaisical bike rides and unhurried walks. The notoriously long lines for ice cream at The Skipper Dipper and Ship Bottom Ice Cream Co. were minimal. Seafood markets were amply stocked with the freshest selections of the daily catch, but you didn't have to pick up the scallops or crab legs you planned to boil for dinner, before lunchtime. Farias and other surf shops hosted their year-end tent sales offering discounted rash guards, sunscreen, and OluKai sandals. It was the last hurrah for the once-again sleepy beach town before it went into hibernation.

The clock turned 7:15 a.m., and Kenny braced herself. It was the last day of summer camp for Jimmy and Rosie, and she was chaperoning their field trip to the Central Park Zoo followed by a picnic lunch in Sheep Meadow. At any minute, the twins would burst through their bedroom doors with more enthusiasm than the sea lions in the Polar Circle at feeding time.

She was excited to spend the afternoon with her two six-year-olds and their playmates, but an important work dinner at Tavern on the Green that evening lingered over her head. She was meeting with Luke and Lonnie Locke, two hot-shot attorneys from Connecticut. They were brothers from a lengthy line of legal minds and the duo was a force to be reckoned with both inside and outside the courtroom. They represented a defendant in a high-profile, salacious, and scan-dalous murder story that gripped the nation's attention.

Clinton White, branded by the media as Dr. Love, was a Harvard-educated, uber wealthy, world-renowned cardiologist with movie-star looks. He stood accused of murdering his runway model turned immigration power-attorney wife. The pending trial had taken the true crime world by storm and the courtroom drama would be covered gavel to gavel by television stations across the country, if not the world. It was poised to reach the same level of infamy as OJ Simpson, Casey Anthony, and Alex Murdaugh.

In news speak, Kenny "owned" the story. She had built a strong working relationship with the Locke brothers, who trusted her with extremely sensitive and confidential details and documents about the case. The knowledge they shared enabled her and her network, WBS, to be the first to break and report news on all things Dr. Love. The story was a rating's dream. The access and exclusives she'd secured had viewers tuning into WBS in droves. It was only a matter of time before the Locke brothers allowed their client to speak directly to the media; and when Clinton White finally granted an interview, it would be to Kenny and WBS.

Luke, Lonnie, and Kenny met over breakfast meetings, lunch meetings, and held meetings in the parking lot of Dunkin Donuts down the street from the Hartford courthouse in the wee hours of the night if news warranted. They took boxing classes together at a studio in Midtown and she went to Marc Jacobs and Canada Goose sample sales with their wives. They even had a meeting *with* Clinton White in his home, in the kitchen where the murder allegedly happened. What eventually was deemed by the authorities to be the murder weapon hung on the wall over the kitchen island.

She and the attorney brothers had gotten to know one another well but her nerves still set in before big meetings with them. Landing the interview with Clinton White would catapult her to senior producer status and make her a household name across the news industry. Between the field trip, Jimmy's soccer practice in Riverside Park and Rosie's piano lesson at Lincoln Center, there would be no time to stop at home or at the office to change or freshen up before the meeting. If there was a minute to spare, the frazzled news producer would make a stop at Sephora to boost her hair with dry shampoo and spritz a sample perfume to mask the inevitable stench that would linger from the Penguin House inside the Central Park Zoo.

There was a lot at stake today that required her to remain laser focused, but she couldn't help looking ahead to tomorrow when her happy, little family would be reunited. No extracurricular activities, no work commitments, no cross-country plane rides. Just James, Kenny, Jimmy, Rosie, and the Jersey Shore.

Two

Ring.

Startled, Kenny sprung up from her bed, fumbling to find her phone on the nightstand. In a half-asleep state, she knocked over a glass of water and pulled the charger from the wall, but managed to turn off the ear-piercing alarm. She flopped her head back on the pillow, held her phone overhead, thumbed the clock icon, and turned off the subsequent three alarms she had set. She couldn't remember a time she overslept and rarely hit the snooze button, but she set four morning alarms for every five minutes out of an abundance of caution.

"I cannot believe this! Again? Really? *Come on!*" She lamented as she lay flat on her back, staring at the high white ceiling.

She had the same dream—or cruel nightmare, as she perceived it—*repeatedly.* As soon as she fell asleep, a vivid, picture-perfect glimpse of what her life was supposed to look like emerged. It was a beautiful life. A life others envied. She loved that life. Living that version of her life for five hours every night was the best part of her day.

Then she would wake up. And it wasn't her life. She knew people who had that picture-perfect life, and she didn't like to think of herself as a jealous person, but she'd be lying if she didn't admit she harbored a few resentments.

This was the type of self-reflection Kenny vowed to work on with the help of Marilyn, the therapist she had been seeing since breaking off her engagement to George three years ago. Recently, Marilyn directed Kenny to engage in a new "rise and shine" ritual. She was to complete three simple tasks before stepping a foot out of the bed. With her eyes closed, she would describe an emotion she felt, choose a color she identified with, and read aloud a passage from *Meditations from the Mat*, a daily reflection book the therapist had given Kenny when she learned of the journalist's yoga practice.

Kenny leaned over the side of the bed, pulled the book out, and flipped to Day 298.

"Today I am feeling frustrated, and I'm seeing black," she defiantly mumbled to herself. "Who wouldn't be miserable and seeing darkness with these recurring night visions, Marilyn?" she complained to the therapist who wasn't there. "This whole rise-and-shine ritual is a bunch of bullshit, by the way."

She blinked open her eyes, sighed, and redirected her attention back to the meditation book.

"Day 298: 'Thoughts are energy, and you can make your world or break your world by your thinking' by Susan Taylor."

Despite the bitterness Kenny woke up with, these words made her smile. First, she was a huge fan of Susan Taylor. Every female in the media industry knew her. Taylor was a renowned, respected, and groundbreaking journalist. She was also a fellow Fordham alum. Kenny had a soft spot for all Rams, especially those who helped pave the way in the cutthroat business they shared a passion for.

She knew she needed to change her attitude.

Grinning and shaking her head, she said, "Okay fine, Marilyn, you win. Today I will see yellow. Like an orangish-yellow over the ocean at sunrise. Not that obnoxious smiley-face emoji yellow. And I will *try* to be optimistic."

She rolled out of her red down-feather duvet cover, slid into her slippers, and glided across the parquet floors of her two-hundred-square-foot apartment to plug in the percolator, reflecting on how strange dreams could be. So much of the life she had just woken up from *did* hold true. The coffee was made before she went to bed, Joe Gold was delivering a fore-cast for a perfect August day, and she was one murder trial away from delivering an exclusive interview with Clinton White, which would clinch WBS the top spot in the Nielsen ratings.

Then there was the significance of the twins. Kenny's bloated belly that looked like a 3D dart board from the dozens of hormone-filled needles served as a reminder that she didn't have them. Someday she would have children but, for now, they sat in a freezer in a storage unit in the basement of a warehouse in Bayonne.

At her gynecologist's urging, Kenny recently completed a cycle of IVF so she could retrieve and preserve eggs that disappeared with each birthday she celebrated. It was all the rage among women in their thirties, living the single life, and focusing on their careers rather than motherhood. She was grateful for science and being able to swing the costly proce-dure but was still bitter. The weeks of daily invasive ultra-sounds, blood work, and multiple injections made her fat and crazy.

On her last visit before the retrieval procedure, as Dr. Lee struggled to count the number of follicles and measure the lining of her uterine wall with the transducer, the fertility specialist said, "Kenny, you need to relax and let go. Open up, girl! You just completely closed your vagina."

"Tell me something I didn't know, Doc! Maybe if I relaxed, let go, and opened up, I wouldn't be here with you with my legs in stirrups for the fifteenth day in a row!" Kenny barked back.

She took this directive as an insult to her thirty-two-year-old, lonely, single, self-loathing self. Was Dr. Lee saying that Kenny's vagina was like her heart and soul? Closed-up, hopeless, resistant to anyone trying to get in? How offensive. *And could vaginas really close?* she wondered.

But today was not a day to relive the poking and prodding of the last few weeks, figuratively or literally. She was going to see yellow, think optimistically, and discuss her encounter with Dr. Lee at her next therapy session with Marilyn. Although, after Dr. Lee successfully harvested a dozen eggs and gave Kenny the clearance to start working out again, her disgust toward "The Baby Whisperer," as the woman of *The View* famously called her during an interview, began to wane.

Since her five-foot-three-inch frame was carrying around twelve extra pounds, Kenny's physique wasn't anywhere close to the svelte body in her dreams. She pulled out her "fat" pair of stretchy black leggings and dug around the back of her activewear drawer for the loosest fitting tank top she could find.

She dressed, washed her face, brushed her teeth, pulled her hair back in her favorite silk blue scrunchie, and scrolled through the sixty emails that came in overnight as she sipped her coffee and filled her Swell bottle for yoga.

Subject: Record temperatures sweeping the country
Subject: Tom Brady returning to the NFL-again?

Subject: Clinton White in court tomorrow-did we know this?
Subject: POTUS to Middle East to broker peace talks
Subject: Air travel at record high since COVID

Sandwiched between the president and Brady was the inevitable Clinton White message.

"Does no one read their emails?" Kenny balked. "For the hundredth time, yes! We know that Clinton White will be in court tomorrow," she shouted, banging her head against the wooden block of furniture that served as a dining room table, writing desk, and ironing board.

She pulled out her laptop and crafted *another* email to the entire news division about the status of Clinton White, the case of the prominent cardiologist and head of the FDA during George W's presidency who stood accused of murdering his former model, and now legal immigration lawyer-wife, Ada White.

Kenny had been covering the case since the previous September when Ada White, the beautiful and equally successful wife of Clinton, didn't show up at her parents' Yom Kippur gathering in New Canaan. Clinton was a Southern Baptist from Georgia, but Ada was a devout Jew and would never miss the high holy holiday without explanation. Her body was never found, but Clinton White was arrested and charged a few months later after police said they had mounting evidence against the disgraced doctor.

Kenny didn't mind being the point person on the story. She was getting exposure and gaining credibility among the higher ups and executives at WBS. Her reporting had been spot-on, and she was the first to break every detail when news emerged. She was positioned to land the exclusive interview with Clinton White when his lawyers gave him the clearance to speak to the media, but the day-to-day was getting old and taking a toll on her patience and sanity.

She spent more time working out of the Stamford Courthouse lobby than her own cube at the office. The servers at Dunkin Donuts on West Broad Street had her large iced coffee, two Splenda, and cream prepared before she placed the order, and she logged countless hours halted in traffic on the Cross Bronx Expressway commuting up north. A small silver lining was racking up an abundance of Emerald Club points at National Car Rentals where she achieved Executive Status and had a new plastic green card in her wallet to prove it.

She needed to hold on a bit longer. Her career had steadily escalated since she started at the network as an intern twelve years ago, but this "get" would be monumental. Landing the Clinton White interview would mean huge things for her professional life. She would be able to write her ticket to any position within WBS or at any of the network's competitors.

From: Kennedy Sloane
To: WBS News
CC: WBS Executives
Subject: Clinton White Coverage

Hi Team,

Reminder that Dr. Clinton White (aka Dr. Love) will be in court in Stamford tomorrow. He will appear in Judge O'Toole's courtroom (Courtroom 1) at 9:00 a.m. Local news station Channel 4 will be pool camera. WBS will plug in, and feed footage live back to the studio. White will be permitted to dress in civilian clothes for this appearance but will be shackled at the hands and feet. We expect that White will be taken in the back entrance of the courthouse, so we'll have a crew staking-out that door to try and catch video of him coming and going.

This is a status hearing and won't last long—ten minutes tops. The biggest news we are hoping for is that a trial date will be set.

I'll be in the courtroom and plan to overnight in CT. Please reach out to me with any editorial questions and DO NOT reach out directly to anyone in the White family. They are tired of the media, and we do not want to burn any bridges.

Side note: O'Toole is a real character on the stand. Made for TV, a sound bite machine.

FOR GUIDANCE ONLY: I am meeting with White's attorneys (Luke and Lonnie Locke) tomorrow evening. WBS is in position to get White's one and only sit-down (fingers crossed!!). Remember, the judge has issued a gag order so the interview will happen post-verdict. If White's convicted, the interview will happen in a room at the courthouse before he is hauled back to prison (no cameras are allowed in Connecticut prisons). If he's acquitted, the interview will take place at his home.

Thanks!
Kenny

She hit *Send* and pulled out her daily planner and pad of neon pink Post-it notes to begin her ever-growing daily to-do list. She realized she was behind the times by not relying on one of her many electronic devices to keep life on track, but she was old school that way. She liked to physically write things on paper, read things from a hard copy book or newspaper, and felt immense satisfaction when crossing tasks off her lists.

Every Black Friday, Kenny ordered the following year's case-bound daily planner from Papyrus. This year's version was black with pink flowers and the words *Wildest Dreams* scrawled across the front in gold. Each day of the year a half page was allotted in the journal, and that's where she would stick her daily Post-it note.

<u>To-Do Wednesday, August 30</u>

- Book travel for CT trip—rental car and hotel (National @ Columbus Circle + Courtyard Marriott on Summer St.)
- Make a reservation for dinner with White's attorneys (Bartaco Tapas or Capital Grille)
- Raid supply closet at the office (Post-its, pens, notebooks, highlighters)
- Connect with crew to discuss meet-up plans for courthouse (Jim, camera operator + Sam, audio)
- Journal today's tasks for therapist
- Research illustrators for *Armchair Detective*

Kenny ripped the square pink paper off the pad and stuck it over the box labeled with the corresponding date, grabbed her gym bag and yoga mat, and bounced out the door, down the steps of her *prewar* brownstone.

Three

Kenny *tried* to be present during the walk down Amsterdam Avenue to her Vinyasa class. Her head was usually buried in a phone or notebook. She made it exactly two blocks before getting distracted by September's Feature Author poster in the window of Amsterdam Books, the quaint family-owned bookstore that had been a staple of the neighborhood for decades. The small shop was known around the city for their popular book clubs, story times, and author signing events. Being selected as a month's feature author was a one-way ticket to the top of The New York Times Best Sellers List.

Kenny desperately wanted to see her name and the cover of her book on the poster in the display window. That desire becoming reality was so close, she could envision it if she shut her eyes. She had recently submitted the manuscript of her first novel, *Armchair Detective*, to a publishing house for consideration. The novel was a compilation of unsolved criminal investigations that had gone cold and was narrated by the prosecutors, detectives, as well as local, state, and federal law enforcement officials who resurrected the cases and pulled out all the stops trying to crack them. The story offered firsthand accounts from victims' families and highlighted the work of genealogists, hypnotists, psychics, therapists, and bounty hunters who threw their hats in the ring using their respective areas of unconventional expertise to solve the crimes that baffled more traditional investigation techniques.

With the world's obsession around true crime and real-life murder mysteries, everyone in Kenny's sphere told her *Armchair Detective* was going to be an instant hit. She agreed. At the very least, it would be talked about on the countless crime podcasts that spread like wildfire after *Serial* tapped into the untouched market in 2014. There was an excellent chance it would be picked up by the Friday night news-magazines *20/20* and *Dateline,* and maybe it would even catch the eye of filmmaker Joe Berlinger. He was so riveted by a Ted Bundy novel that he directed a multi-part series for Netflix *and* a major motion picture starring Zac Efron and Lilly Collins. The possibilities were endless.

After peering into the window of the bookstore for too long, Kenny reeled in her wandering mind. She wasn't sched-uled to hear back from the publishing house about the edit and publication process until next week, and she still needed to find an illustrator to design a catchy cover.

Kenny noticed the city was happy this morning, people were smiling. The workers rotating the bouquets of flowers in the tubs outside of the corner bodega; the bussers spraying down the sidewalks and facades of restaurants, bars, and cafés; the dog walkers herding gaggles of canines; the public works crew emptying the always-overflowing garbage cans in front of Grey's Papaya. Even the commuters who rushed to catch the downtown 2 train that rumbled below ground somewhere between Seventy-Second and Seventy-Third Streets seemed to be less aggressive than usual.

Maybe Kenny wasn't the only one seeing yellow. Or maybe these people were always this pleasant and she was too distracted, every day the last ten years of her life, to notice or pay them any attention.

Steam Hot Yoga Studio was on the third floor of a dingy building in the middle of Seventy-Second Street, sandwiched between bustling Broadway and a more peaceful Columbus Avenue. A walk across the lengthy Seventy-Second Street was like a journey from one world to another. Broadway was commercial and chaotic with Duane Reed, Trader Joes, and four major banks in a one block radius. Columbus was comfortable and familiar, lined with coffee shops, wine bars, boutiques, and family-owned pizza joints that served up slices for generations.

Kenny pushed through the revolving door of the nondescript building and instantly sensed the serenity. The first floor was occupied by a physical therapy practice and the second floor was a photography studio, but the scent of sandalwood and eucalyptus that emanated from Steam Hot Yoga wafted through the entire building. She climbed the six flights of steep, narrow, brown steps that desperately needed to be swept and mopped, readjusting her unfolding mat at each landing. The ungraceful ascent was a reminder she needed to invest in one of those fancy bags that keeps the unruly six-foot cut of textured rubber securely in place.

The door to the studio was propped open, and Kenny quietly entered. She liked to be the first one in the hot room so she could get her favored spot in the back corner and avoid unwanted chit-chat with other yogis. The space was also known to be the hottest, most challenging. The sweatier, the better. Kenny was out of breath after scaling the steep steps for the first time in weeks, twelve extra pounds in tow; she didn't want anyone to see her huffing and puffing.

She kicked her flip-flops into the cubbies that lined the wall under the street-facing windows and checked her phone one last time before silencing it for the next hour, hoping that nothing earth shattering happened during her ten-minute walk to the studio that would prevent her from practicing.

From: David Greene
To: Kennedy Sloane
CC: WBS Executives, WBS News
Subject: RE: Clinton White Coverage

Kenny, thank you for your valiant efforts. Please keep me directly in the loop on the status and logistics of the White interview. It's the get of the decade. We'll finally close the gap between us and the competition. We can't lose this one. Keep doing what you're doing. You are a rising star here at WBS. DG

David Greene
President and Executive Director, WBS News

Beaming with confidence and pride from the accolade, Kenny tossed her phone in her red drawstring sack and grabbed her oversized Swell bottle. She took a deep breath and peered out the window, admiring the rays of sunshine popping between the buildings on the other side of the street. It wasn't a sunrise over the ocean, but the sun coming up over her city was a close second.

$$Four$$

"Breathe in, two, three, four. Hold two, three, four. Out two, three, four. Breathe in two, three, four. Hold two, three, four. Out two, three, four," Yogi Marah hummed as she glided around the candlelit room, incense stick in hand while the class settled into their mats.

Marah was a pint sized, raspy voiced spiritual guru. She seemed timeless, but Kenny thought she was much older than she presented given her experiences of the universe. Marah traveled to India to master her practice and met the Dali Lama when she was exploring Tibet. While she was in Stanford's Ph.D. program, she moved to Germany and wrote her thesis on the correlation between yoga and the philosophies of Immanuel Kant. Her Vinyasa style focused on the mind just as much as the body, and she believed that humans had the supernatural power to *breathe* through any difficult or adverse situation. Classes revolved around breathwork. Kenny hadn't bought into the faculties of inhaling and exhaling, but she mostly took to heart everything that Marah preached.

Marah's deliberate, yet effortless guidance filled the

studio with an energy that was palpable from all corners of the room. As the heat and humidity rose so did the audible breaths from the room of yogis who filled and emptied their lungs in rhythmic unison.

For the first time in a while, Kenny slowly started to feel connected with her body as the community moved through a fast-paced series of Sun A and Sun B Salutations.

"Top of mat. Rise up. Forward fold. Halfway lift. Forward fold. Hands to mat. Chaturanga. Upward facing dog. Downward facing dog. Breathe in. Breathe out," Marah hypnotically repeated.

Although her body was heavy and her swan dive wasn't as graceful as it was a few weeks ago, Kenny felt her limbs elongate and strengthen with each flow. The sweat poured off her face and body like a faucet that someone forgot to turn off. It was a rapid detox. The movement and positions were invigorating and freeing. Except the forward fold. The position that had her bent in half, face to feet, was a glaring reminder of how badly she needed a pedicure. Her toenails were chipped and misshapen, and she could not remember the last time she had a tootsie tune-up. Memorial Day? Easter?

"Mental note: Add pedicure to to-do list," Kenny quietly whispered to herself between breaths. "Throw in brow wax and Brazilian, too."

A good brow wax was like an instant face lift, especially when Kenny had a spare fifteen minutes to enjoy the under-eye gel masks her esthetician started adding to the service. She wondered if the treatment was offered to all loyal clients or only to her out of pity because she always looked so stressed and tired.

The hour-long class approached culmination, and she took pigeon pose on the right side. And then pigeon on the left side before reclining into Savasana.

"Namaste," Marah cooed as she firmly placed a chilled lavender towel across Kenny's shut eyes, her body sinking fully into corpse pose.

Kenny laid, completely still, in the pool of her own sweat for longer than the traditional two minutes a yogi stays in the final resting posture. She wasn't ready to give up the quiet and 105-degree temperature of the room or to begin tackling her ever-growing to-do list. She was also self-conscious about standing up, knowing that her soaked, oversized tank would cling to the rolls of her midsection.

She gingerly pushed herself up to a seated position, rolled up her mat, and made her way out of the hot room. After grabbing a bottle of guava goddess Kombucha from the cooler in the hall, she sat on the cubbies to cool down. She reached under the bench for the red drawstring bag and pulled out her flip-flops, sliding ten grimy toes into them. While she sipped the raw tea drink with one hand, she dug around for her phone with the other, and when the screen lit up, mid-gulp, she almost regurgitated the liquid that was halfway down her throat.

Fifteen missed calls. Five voicemails. Thirty-seven emails.

All with the subject line *URGENT: Dr. Love.* Flagged with the red exclamation point of dread, the symbol that noted exceptionally high priority messages.

Kenny's heart rate was still elevated from the workout, but she physically felt the blood-pumping organ drop inside her. It had been exactly sixty-eight minutes since she received the glowing email from David Greene singing her praises. And now this.

From: David Greene
To: Kennedy Sloane
CC: WBS Executives, WBS News
Subject: RE: Clinton White Coverage

WHERE ARE YOU????????? CALL ME NOW.

David Greene
President and Executive Director, WBS News

Oh my God. What could have happened in a little more than an hour?

There were no fewer than one million thoughts going through Kenny's head and breathing certainly wasn't one of them. In fact, she may have forgotten to breathe altogether. Before she had time to process what was going on she could hear David Greene's voice coming at her from the other side of the phone. She wasn't sure if she dialed him, or he called her. But she knew she needed to regain her composure to verbalize something, anything.

"Clinton White sat down with NBC!" the usually docile executive barked. "He gave them *hours* for an interview. He gave them access to the homestead—a tour of the house where the murder happened! He gave them old home videos and family photographs. He even gave them his children's report cards and homemade Father's Day cards they crafted when they were students at Sidwell Friends School! For Christ's sake, Kenny, what the hell happened?"

Alarmed by the delivery, but mildly relieved by the absurdity of it all since Clinton White was incarcerated—and it would have been *impossible* for even the most stealth reporter to contact him—she confidently asserted, "David, I apologize for any confusion but that's not possible. White has been sitting in a cell since his arrest last year, no media can get to him. Where did you hear this? *The Daily Mail*? It's probably just that tabloid trying to stir drama. You know they'll conjure up anything they think will drive viewership."

"In fact, Kenny, yes, I did read it in *The Daily Mail*," David scolded in a stern tone that was unfamiliar—and scary. "And on *Page Six*. And in the *Daily News*. And in *People*. It's even in the goddamn *New York Times*!"

"I . . . I . . . I don't, I don't under . . . I don't kn . . ." she sheepishly stammered, again grasping for words.

The only thing she knew for certain was that now she *was not* breathing, and her heart dropped further down her insides like the ball at Times Square on New Year's Eve. The drop was fast and slow, at the same time. The only thing missing was the ten-second warning.

"I don't know what you do or don't know or understand, Kennedy. But understand this: I want to know how this happened, and I want to know that you will never lose a big interview like this *ever* again," David chided with emphasis on the word ever. *Click.*

Find out what happened. Okay. Find out what happened? What? How the hell am I supposed to find out what happened?

None of it made sense. The relationship and trust she built with Luke and Lonnie Locke over the months, was any of it real? Or was it all one of those crazy dreams that she mistook for reality?

Before calling the Locke Brothers to attempt to piece together the career-killing events that were unfolding in front of her, she scrolled through her emails. The contents were nauseating. Headline after headline and links to articles about the get of the decade. The get that was supposed to be hers.

The Daily Mail: "Dr. Love's NBC Interview Will Leave Viewers Blushing"
New York Post: "Harvard Hottie Gets Intimate in NBC Exclusive"
New York Daily News: "NBC Woos the Love Doctor"
People: "Dr. Love Spills All to NBC"
The New York Times: "Clinton White Breaks Silence in Primetime Exclusive Interview"

Kenny began to get lightheaded. Her stomach turned and head pounded. Her hands were clammy and eyes stung as they welled with tears. She had to get in touch with the Locke Brothers to try and fix this mess. She launched an aggressive communication outreach assault. Both of their cell phones went straight to voicemail and Helen, the office manager, didn't pick up the landline. Emails were met with out of office replies. Text messages weren't read.

Kenny found the "Send Read Receipt" phone feature stalkerish and creepy but liked that Luke and Lonnie always had theirs enabled. Until now, when she knew they weren't reading her texts. Not only did the Locke brothers promise her an interview and give it away without warning, but now they were blatantly ignoring her.

WTF.

She chucked her Kombucha bottle in the trash can; her ability to swallow disappeared with her ability to verbalize a sentence. She collected her belongings and, this time, shuddered when she looked out the window. The glass, fogged up from the heat and humidity still pouring out of the hot room, was like the state of her head. The golden rays of sunshine had given way to swirling, angry gray clouds that blanketed the city. The skies looked like they would open at any moment.

Mental note: Add "Buy umbrella" to to-do list.

Five

By the time Kenny reached Amsterdam Books, the rain was driving down in sheets. Yoga mat under arm and drawstring bag strapped to her back, it took every ounce of focus to not slip out of her flip-flops, breaking an unpolished toe or twisting an ankle. The weather had taken a complete one-eighty in the last ninety minutes, and she seemed to be the only New Yorker who didn't get the memo. The rest of the city was outfitted in wellies, rain slickers, and heavy-duty umbrellas—not the cheap, disposable ones vendors peddle on street corners. They were dressed for the Whirlpool Jet Boat Tour at Niagara Falls, not a walk on the beach like she was.

As she rounded the corner onto her block, a yellow cab cruising north on Amsterdam Avenue was nearly swallowed whole by a crater pooled with water, and the liquid that spun around the tires sprayed her like a garden hose nozzle on the soaker setting. Defeated, drenched, and unscathed—except for her ego, reputation, and career—Kenny peeled off her clothes before she even had both feet through the door. Stripped down to nothing, she rummaged through her closet to find a medium-weight plush, microfiber robe that accidentally ended up in her suitcase after a stay at the Four Seasons in Houston a few years ago. She wrapped herself up in the cozy security blanket, grabbed her computer, and plopped down on the couch.

From: Luke Locke
To: Kennedy Sloane
CC: Lonnie Locke
Subject: Word travels fast, huh?

Hey Dear,

Saw I missed you. Dr. Love created a real mess for me and Lonnie this time. Before you get yourself all in a tizzy, we didn't know about the interview until the Daily Mail *broke the news this morning. Which means we weren't present and have no idea what he said. As you know, this could have major implications for our case and trial.*

Clinton's sickly father took a turn for the worse yesterday and Judge O'Toole called an emergency hearing just before the courthouse closed for the day. He released Clinton from prison with an ankle monitor until his trial so he could spend time with the old man who is on his deathbed.

We haven't spoken to Clinton since we dropped him at home after court yesterday and that's where things get murky. But this is what we've pieced together.

Clinton went to visit his father last evening and Clinton White Senior's doctor was there. The doctor has a daughter who is in the page program at NBC and has her sights set on on-air reporting (Blonde hair, blue eyes, big boobs. Sounds more like FOX material, right? LOL.). Anyway, Clinton invited the father-daughter duo over to his house and around 1:00 a.m. neighbors saw camera crews loading into the garage.

Judge O'Toole is PISSED. He immediately sent a warden to Clinton's house to pick him up and haul his ass back to prison. He continued tomorrow's hearing indefinitely, so we won't be back in court until October at the earliest.

Sorry if this throws a wrench in your plans.

Lonnie or I will call you in the next few weeks.

—Luke

Kenny's blood boiled.

"Don't you dare 'Dear' me, Mr. Luke Locke!" Kenny screamed. "I'm a professional and deserve to be addressed as one! And *throw a wrench in my plans*? This is a hammer—no, a chainsaw. This a chainsaw cutting right through my career and my whole life's happiness." She continued her tirade.

"And don't even try the media jokes with me! Better suited for FOX, don't ya think, ha!" She growled, now flailing her arms in the air, and pacing back and forth in her one room rectangle, affectionately called The Dollhouse. "What I do think is that you're a lousy attorney who lost all control over your wife-killing client because he has the hots for a glorified intern!"

She collapsed on the couch, exhausted after her second spontaneous one-sided rant of the day. *This is another topic I should broach with Marilyn*, Kenny thought. Yelling at people who aren't there can't be a healthy habit. When she finally closed her mouth and regained awareness of her surroundings, she heard muffled sounds coming from the couch.

"Kenny! Kenny! Earth to Kenny," the words whispered, becoming clearer with each pillow and cushion she moved.

"Oy! I'm coming, Colby! Hold on. You fell somewhere between the arm of the couch and mattress." Kenny yelled at the floor as she wrestled to find the phone that was lodged in the frame of her pullout sofa.

Still breathless and exhausted, she squeaked out a weak, "Hey, Colby. Sorry. I must have butt-dialed you when—"

"During one of your meltdowns?" Colby interjected. "Yeah, I figured. I heard the whole thing. At least now you won't have to recount the saga for me over Margarita Wednesday tonight."

"I don't think so, not tonight. It's been a day, and it's not even noon. You don't know half of it. And Margarita Wednesday isn't a 'thing.' You're like freaking Gretchen Wieners trying to make 'fetch' happen."

Before Kenny had time to rile herself up again, now that she had a captive audience, Colby stopped her dead in her tracks.

"You're right, hon, I'm sure I don't know half of it. And guess what, I really don't care, love," Colby purred in his sweet, condescending tone only he could pull off. "I don't have the mental capacity to ponder network booking wars today. You know this month's self-care project is freeing up space in my head. As is making Margarita Wednesday a 'thing.' My shrink says midweek pick-me-ups are vital for sanity."

Colby Jackson and Kenny had been best friends since the pair met on treadmills in the gym at the West Side YMCA on West Sixty-Third Street the summer after they both graduated from college. He was the Stanford Blatch to her Charlotte York. She was the Grace Adler to his Will Truman.

Kenny worked down the street as a desk assistant at WBS and couldn't afford membership at one of the fancy, boutique gyms or high-end sports clubs most of her colleagues belonged to, so she took advantage of her parents' family plan package. They were lifelong members at the Y in her hometown in Pennsylvania.

Colby moved to New York from the Midwest to accept an entry level gig at Bound Books, a powerhouse publishing company, and was squatting in one of the Y's dorm-style rooms until he became acclimated to the city and found an apartment and roommates.

He was a husky, not too tall, not too short build with strawberry blond hair, fair skin, and almond-shaped deep brown eyes. He was born and raised in a small town in South Dakota and went to the University of Madison–Wisconsin for agriculture. His father was furious, nearly disowning him and threatening to pull tuition money, when Colby switched to journalism—a major his father deemed for sissies and liberals.

"How will you ever find a girlfriend or support a family with those credentials?" Colby's father demanded.

Kenny and Colby quickly became thick as thieves. They knew everything about one another. The good, the bad, and the ugly. They always had one another's backs. She flew to Deadwood over the Fourth of July one summer to offer moral support and function as a buffer when Colby decided to tell his father he was gay. *And* had fallen madly in love with a Puerto Rican named Paolo *who* was twenty years his senior.

Colby planned and executed an intimate, yet lavish, bridal shower for Kenny at a swanky wine bar in the West Village that even caught the eye of a photographer from *New York Bride Magazine.* The next week, he drove her home to her parents' house two states away and helped Mrs. Sloane ship back all the gifts after Kenny called off the engagement to George. He also tracked down the editor-in-chief of *New York Bride* and threatened a lawsuit if there was any mention or visual of the spectacular celebration in upcoming issues. Though deep down, he wanted nothing more than his event planning skills to be flaunted on the glossy pages of a widely read magazine.

Their relationship knew no bounds. There were no secrets. It was built on brutal honesty and trust. And even though there was never any physical attraction or chemistry between them, it was the most intimate relationship either ever knew.

"You have such a way with words, Colby Jackson. I don't have the mental capacity to deal with *you* today," Kenny shot back. "I think your shrink probably meant going for a jog around the lower loop of Central Park as an outlet for a midweek pick-me-up, not promoting Wasted Wednesdays. But fine. I'll meet you for one drink. *One*. The minute you utter a word about your Labor Day plans for Fire Island or try to talk me into a nightcap at Flaming Saddles, I'm out the door. I'm not kidding."

"Calm down, Queen," Colby hissed.

She could practically hear his eyes rolling.

"I'll have one Jose Cuervo original, on the rocks, no salt with a pink umbrella ready for you upon arrival. I'll be at our usual high top in the back corner," Colby said in a satisfied tone.

Before she could respond, he continued. "Love you, mean it, bi-yee."

Kenny shook her head and smiled. In their decade-long friendship, she couldn't remember a conversation that didn't end with this affectionate farewell. He even ended texts with *LYMIB*.

She knew that neither David Greene nor anyone else in the industry would care about Clinton White's ankle monitor or dying father; NBC's young, hot page whom Dr. Love gave the interview; the mess he made for the Locke brothers; or Judge O'Toole's reaction to any of it, but she forwarded Luke Locke's email to the network. The only thing worse than being scooped is cobbling together a rationalization for why it happened. She wasn't sure if sharing this email would be perceived as a feeble attempt to defend herself or elicit some degree of pity, although that's exactly what she was doing. But she figured the explanation was better coming straight from the horse's mouth, leaving nothing open to interpretation or lost in translation. Without contemplating the pros and cons of distributing the message to the masses any further, Kenny hit the *Send* button and felt the tiniest bit of relief.

She was so focused on reeling from her crisis that it was 1:30 p.m. before she realized she hadn't eaten a morsel of food all day and was still soaked from the sweat session and subsequent monsoon she waded through. Shivering and soaked, she trudged to the refrigerator. The fridge had the staples of any thirty-two-year-old single female living alone in New York. A carton of eggs, a quart of egg whites, a brick of muenster cheese, a bag of shredded mozzarella cheese, a bottle of Grey Poupon mustard, a half-eaten jar of expired salsa, a can of coffee, a sugar-free coffee creamer, lemons, two bottles of chardonnay and a twenty-five cup Brita dispenser. Everything in The Dollhouse was miniature, except the refrigerator. Ironically, the place she didn't need space. Even the realtor who showed Kenny the micro studio ten years ago was surprised when he saw the normal size fridge. Groceries never took up more than one shelf; in fact, the Sunday night Zabar's order could fit on one of the shelves on the inside of the door.

"Scrambled eggs it is," Kenny sarcastically exclaimed.

She cracked two eggs into her one small frying pan that she stored on her one small burner. The oven and kitchen cabinets where most people kept cookware and appliances were stocked with shoes, towels, and offseason clothes. While her life may have resembled the lives of Carrie Bradshaw and Monica Greene from the outside, the reality of her living situation paled in comparison.

Kenny scarfed down her bland brunch and then turned on the water in the bathroom. The shower was tiny. Anyone over five-foot-six inches had to crouch to get under the shower head and complained that if they moved the wrong way, the curtain would stick to their naked body. But this tiny space was ideal for her. The water temperature was hot, and the pressure was hard. She could stay in the shower for hours.

She grabbed a plastic cutting board that barely fit between the vanity and the wall where she stored it, and placed the chopping block squarely across the sink, under the faucet. There wasn't room for hand soap, much less a hairdryer or brush, on the small porcelain bowl, and Kenny's grandmother had the grand idea during one visit to use the kitchen tool as a makeshift makeup and hair table. The cutting board never got much use in the kitchen. Kenny grabbed a bath towel from the cereal cabinet, lit her favorite white cherry merlot candle, and placed it on the makeup counter. Pandora was turned to the Billy Joel station, and Kenny slipped out of her robe and into the scorching water that shot down at her like a jet stream.

She pulled out a Tupperware bin from under the bathroom sink that contained a collection of unnecessary and overpriced bath products that she had accumulated over the last few months when Marilyn got on her case about the importance of self-care. Kenny didn't know the exact meaning of the term "self-care" but somehow interpreted it to the practice of stocking her bathroom with expensive bottles of spa and beauty aids she'd never have time to use. During this shower event, she applied it all. She opened the washes, the scrubs, the masks, the lotions, the hydrators, the oils; and used the loofahs, the sponges, and textured washcloths. After all the potions she had lathered into her hair and over every inch of her body, a different person would emerge from the shower. Either a refreshed, rejuvenated, recharged version of herself or a pruned, lobster-red creature that looked like it boiled in scalding water too long.

She turned off the water, stepped out of the tub, wrapped

her hair in a cotton towel turban, and patted herself dry. She unapologetically sang aloud to "Vienna," her recently self-proclaimed theme song, like she was on stage at Madison Square Garden, while she smothered her limbs and torso with globs of raw coconut oil. Until one line jilted her back to reality and the events that erupted that morning. The lyrics were a reminder to slow down and breathe when life gets too loud. But Kenny was never good at that.

The notion of not being completely reachable at all hours of the day and night was a foreign concept. She hadn't been on a vacation where she totally disconnected since Spring Break her junior year at Fordham, when she and her roommates did an all-inclusive deal in Cancun with a bunch of guys from Columbia who they had met at Brother Jimmy's BBQ in Midtown on a random Thursday night.

Kenny blew out the candle, turned off the music, and got ready for the rest of her day. By now it was 3:00 p.m., but she still had a good two and a half hours to tend to her to-do list before meeting Colby for that one margarita.

Six

Kenny sprinted around the Upper West Side and completed her mundane errands by the time she reached the office to raid the supply closet and replace her loot of producer essentials. She dreaded the thought of having to deal with anyone face to face, but by the time she got to her desk there was news breaking about an orchestrated prison escape that spanned several high-security prisons across several different states. It was reported that multiple inmates from lockups in Arizona, New Mexico, Texas, and Florida had escaped at the same time. All the convicts had links to the Mexican drug cartel and were considered armed and dangerous. The situation seemed dire, but Kenny selfishly welcomed the scenario knowing that the newsroom would be distracted by the escape and the coverage would headline all the evening broadcasts. Meaning Clinton White would not. At least for tonight.

Trying to maintain a low profile, she slid into her fancy, ergonomic desk chair on wheels without making direct contact with anyone. She wanted to use the time to research illustrators for the cover of *Armchair Detective*. Each month when Amsterdam Books announced a new Feature Author, Kenny filled with excitement and anticipation for when her own book would be on a poster in that window.

The publishing world was a tricky business, but Kenny was fortunate that Colby could help her navigate it. He had risen in the ranks at Bound Books as quickly as she'd climbed the ladder at WBS. He had a direct line to Muffin Evans, the head honcho at Bound. Muffin was unequivocally the most powerful woman, the single most influential person, in the publishing world.

Known inside and outside the industry as the Manuscript Eater, Muffin was revered, idolized, respected, feared, and hated by all who knew her. Or knew of her. She was the antagonist in the story of any aspiring or published author. Her name didn't fit her personality, demeanor, or looks. There was nothing sweet or savory about Muffin. Which is likely why she embraced the name Manuscript Eater. She referred to herself only as M.E. If the role of Muffin were cast in a movie it would be handed to Meryl Streep a la Miranda Priestley in *The Devil Wears Prada*. She *was* the Anna Wintour of the literary world. Little was known about M.E.'s personal life, although she was rumored to have had a years-long fling with Donald Trump that spanned the Ivana and Marla years. She also made headlines when she sued the co-op board of her luxury apartment building on Billionaires Row after they rejected her proposal to knock down an interior wall and expand her kitchen.

Promptly at 6:00 p.m. every evening, Muffin had an extra dirty vodka martini—shaken not stirred—with three olives at the bar of the Mandarin Oriental at Columbus Circle. It was a widely held belief in the writing community that if an author was invited to join M.E. for a drink, his or her manuscript was going to be published. If an author was requested to dine with her at Per Se or Eleven Madison Park, the book was being made into a movie.

Muffin Evans expected manuscripts to be submitted at a level of perfection. Since *Armchair Detective* was going to end up in M.E.'s French manicured hands, largely because of Colby's access to her, Kenny went to great lengths to ensure the manuscript was stellar and worthy of the woman's keen eye. She had no less than twenty people read the draft prior to nervously releasing it into the hands of the experts. She solicited critiques from her circle of family and friends to her network of coworkers and beta readers. Feedback across the board was overwhelmingly positive with the biggest criticism being that the novel didn't end with a preview to the sequel.

The last piece to the publishing puzzle was designing a catchy and visually alluring illustration for the cover of the book. Colby said that having a vision for the cover and a few vetted illustrators who could bring the vision to life would score credibility with M.E. Kenny was determined to compile an impressive list of concepts and artists ready for presentation and was cautiously optimistic she'd be sharing that list while choking down a dirty martini at the Mandarin Oriental within the next two weeks. She *hated* olives.

It was approaching 5:00 p.m., and Kenny wanted to make a swift exit down the back steps of WBS before the producers who worked on the evening broadcast started to hustle around the newsroom and edit bays in their nightly race to deliver the most recent and current version of global events live at 6:30 p.m. The rush was as exhilarating as it was terrifying, but today she didn't want to feel either of those things. She took one last look at her to-do list and inconspicuously slipped to the stairwell.

<u>To-Do Wednesday, August 30</u>

- ~~Book travel for CT trip—rental car and hotel (National @ Columbus Circle + Courtyard Marriott on Summer St.) NO NEED~~
- ~~Make reservation for dinner with White's attorneys (Bartaco Tapas or Capital Grille) NO NEED~~
- ~~Raid supply closet at office (Post its, pens, notebooks, highlighters)~~
- ~~Connect with crew to discuss meet up plan at courthouse (Jim P camera operator + Sam S audio) NO NEED~~
- ~~Journal today's tasks for therapist~~
- ~~Research illustrators for *Armchair Detective*~~
- Pedicure/Wax (move to Thursday's list and add manicure)
- ~~Buy new umbrella~~
- Colby @ Hole in the Wall Mexican, 5:30 p.m.

Seven

Colby sat perched at a high-top table behind two blue glasses the size of fishbowls filled to the brim with freshly shaken margaritas. Kenny wasn't sure if the condensation dripping down the side of the glass was because the liquid was overflowing, or the glass was sweating due to the sweltering temperature inside the Mexican joint. The rainstorms that lingered earlier in the day finally passed through and allowed the sun to shine over the city again, but the thick air that accompanied it was suffocating.

Neither Kenny nor Colby knew the name of the Mexican place. They weren't sure it even had one, like the many other ethnic establishments they frequented in Hell's Kitchen. The restaurants that dotted the West Side neighborhood weren't known for their ambiance, prestige, size, or popularity. They were known for their authentic cuisine and cheap drinks. A double win for anyone who didn't know their way around a kitchen, had a curious palate, and was living paycheck to paycheck. Kenny and Colby affectionately named their favorite haunts Hole in the Wall *Insert Cuisine*. Hole in the Wall Mexican was their favorite, but they also enjoyed Hole in the Wall Japanese, Chinese, Thai, Indian, Italian, Brazilian, Greek, and Ethiopian. They visited Hole in the Wall Vegan once, but decided they were too carnivorous for the plant-based menu.

Colby jumped off his stool and wrapped Kenny in a bear hug, giving her pecks on both cheeks.

"You look great, Kenny," he exclaimed as he took a step back, tightly clenched both of her shoulders, and scanned her up and down.

She giggled, swatted his hands down, and rolled her eyes.

"I mean it! Your skin looks flawless. I'm loving this boho chic look you're sporting, and it looks like you lost some of those pesky hormone pounds you packed on," he continued, waving his hands in tiny circles in front of her midsection.

"I spent an hour in the shower sloughing and moisturizing, head to toe, so I should look like the next Cover Girl. As for the boho look I'm 'sporting,' it's a vain attempt to mask those pounds *and* my toes that are in desperate need of a pedicure," she countered using air quotes and looking in disgust at her flowy floral tunic and tan canvas mules.

"I think you look fabulous, diva. Learn to take the compliment. Maybe some time out of your pencil skirts, A-line dresses, and pumps will do you good. Cheers to my bestie," Colby toasted, raising his glass.

Kenny sipped her margarita while he ordered a second with a floater, and guacamole and chips to split. After the rollercoaster of emotions that she rode all day, she finally found herself sitting upright and at the top of the incline again.

"Since Fire Island and my planned shenanigans for post Hole in the Wall Mexican are off the table, let's talk about *your* love life," he squealed as he winked and pointed both index fingers in her direction.

"Oh my god, Colby, we are *not* going there right now. I'm

on all the apps and every man in the tristate area is a total freak. And if they're not a freak, they're gay, married, or a serial killer. And look what happened this morning. I don't even have time to go to an hour-long yoga class without the world crashing down around me. Forget about starting a relationship."

"You are even more dramatic than me, Kennedy Sloane," he interjected. "You've only had two quasi-relationships since you broke things off with George and that was three and a half years ago. People these days get married, divorced, and remarried in that span of time. What about the hedge fund guy? The one you said you had a schoolgirl crush on. The two of you laughed until you cried and made out in the back of cabs, movie theaters, and crowded elevators. You seemed to like him."

"I don't know, I guess things just fizzled after I was sent on that assignment to Little Rock for a few weeks." Kenny shrugged.

"How about the actor-model-trainer guy? The one that whisked you away to Breckenridge for a romantic weekend. You said après-ski had a whole new meaning after that trip and the chemistry between you two was steamier than the hot tub that was nestled in the side of the ski slope—or something corny like that. What happened to him?"

"I lost his number when I misplaced my phone at the Charlotte airport. Verizon couldn't retrieve my contacts," she defensively answered.

"You lost his number," Colby interjected. "You really think that's going to work on me? The research department at WBS can pull a number for any person who's ever *owned* a phone. I bet they could track down Alexander Graham Bell's original phone number. What you meant to say is that you stopped returning Mr. Après Ski's calls and texts, and he gave up on you."

"Fine, okay!" she shouted and threw her hands up like she had gotten caught committing armed robbery. "Guilty. I dropped the ball on both of those nice guys. It's just that . . . it's just that George really did a number on me. It's easier to drown myself in work, a world that I can control. Or thought I could, until this morning."

"Enough of this, Kenny," Colby said in a sincere tone. "I'm worried about you. It's been over a year since you've been on a date; work consumes every fiber of your being; and if I ask you to go below Fourteenth Street, you act like you need a passport. We're getting you out of your drought and, for God sakes, out of the bubble of the Upper West Side."

He waved his hand to the bartender. "We'll have another round, *hombre*! One with a floater." Then he fixed his gaze back to Kenny. "I'm using the restroom and when I come back, we're making a roadmap for your life. We're even going to pick out a hot little two-seater convertible so you can see yourself driving around on it."

She sheepishly grinned, nodded in agreement and blew a kiss in Colby's direction as he strutted victoriously toward the sign that read "El Baño" like he just won a bullfight.

While her best friend made his exaggerated and detoured trek around the bar to the bathroom, Kenny's phone pinged. She glanced at the screen and then swiftly to the bartender.

"*Yo voy,*" she mouthed while darting to the door.

Eight

Kenny forlornly lay curled up in the fetal position at the bottom of her bed. Her eyes were puffy and red, and smudgy streams of jet-black mascara ran down her cheeks.

"I can't believe he lied to me," she sobbed into her pillow.

Every few minutes Kenny regained her composure long enough to inflict more torture and reread the email that pinged her phone when Colby stepped away from the table.

From: Muffin Evans (M.E.)
To: Kennedy Sloane
Subject: Armchair Detective

Kennedy,

Thank you for your submission to Bound Books. I'm sure you are aware that the resurgence of the true crime genre is dissipating. The ideas are stale, repetitive, and predictable. Your manuscript is well-written, but the content is too reactive. Though that is under-standable given the nature of your industry.

Here at Bound we look for innovators, creators, and forward thinkers who give readers something they don't know they need. Or even better, don't know they are craving. You are an impressive writer, so if you conceive an original concept in the future, do let us know.

The decision not to publish Armchair Detective *was a unanimous one by the review team, led by Colby Jackson. You can contact Colby if you wish. Please do not reply to this email as any further message will go unread.*

—M.E.

For the umpteenth time today, Kenny forgot to breathe. Thoughts swirled in her head like a cyclone. There was a full-blown Category Five hurricane decimating all the senses that her brain controlled. Her vision was blurred, her hands shook. She tried to open her mouth but wasn't sure if words or sounds came out. Her emotions were no longer on a roller coaster; they were on a free fall from the top of Kingda Ka.

The news that *Armchair Detective* wasn't going to be published by Border Books was devastating. And M.E.'s words about Kenny's creativity and profession were stinging. But knowing that Colby was aware, knowing that he *led* the team who rejected her manuscript . . . there were no words for that.

Marilyn the therapist had a colored *Wheel of Feelings* poster that hung in her office. That's what Kenny needed. She needed that wheel in front of her so she could go around it and tell Colby every single feeling that bubbled inside her. When she mentally spun the Wheel of Feelings, it felt like someone was playing roulette in her head. The little ball bounced around rejected, resentful, inadequate, embarrassed, and furious until it halted to a stop at betrayed.

Marilyn once compared Kenny to a tightly wound clock. The therapist warned that if she didn't learn how to process her emotions, she, being the clock, would be wound one too many times and her spiral springs would snap and shoot out in all directions.

This is the night, Kenny thought. *The night my springs will burst and ping and ricochet off every surface of this Dollhouse.*

Her nerves tempered as she downed a goblet of chardonnay. She decided to continue self-medicating and poured a second. Marilyn would not condone her party-for-one, but Clos du Bois was the only reliable source of sanity at this moment. The oaky beverage with hints of butter and apple kept her clock ticking rather than combusting.

Sitting in Buddha pose on her faux cowhide area rug with her back leaned against the bed, Kenny sipped her wine and stared blindly at the wall in front of her for an undetermined amount of time. She thought she should engage in a mindless activity to accompany her happy hour, so grabbed the laptop and deemed trolling social media or stress shopping to be the most viable options.

She closed out of pop-up ads as furiously as they polluted her screen when she accidentally enlarged one, instead of minimizing it. She did a double take. At first glance, the picture of the living room she saw looked like her own, in shape and size. It was as if an interior decorator broke into her studio, staged it to look like a swanky, modern apartment in Miami, posted the photos online and then quickly left, leaving Kenny with her archaic appliances, collection of hand-me-down furniture pieces and black, red, and leopard print décor.

After today, anything is possible.

She zoomed in on the ad.

PELICAN POINTE VILLA #5. SEA PINES, HILTON HEAD ISLAND. Be the first to stay in this recently renovated 1 bed/1 bath condo featuring an open floor plan and oversized Pella windows. The kitchen boasts lava stone countertops and stainless-steel appliances. The bathroom is outfitted with a His and Hers vanity and walk-in shower. Bedroom and living space open to balconies over-looking the community pool and pickleball court. Easy access to the beach and a short walk to Sea Pines Center and Harbour Town. Email Hailey at Low Country Hospitality for more information.

Kenny hovered the mouse on the carousel of images and clicked on each of the looping photos.

Photo One: The interior of a clean, sleek living space. The room gave off a personality that could be described as bright, cheery, carefree, happy. The rows of kitchen cabinets and countertops that formed an L shape were white. The bar height, rectangular table under the wall-mounted flat screen TV was white with four white leather-backed stools around the perimeter. The engineered hardwood floors were the lightest shade of oak. On the wall opposite the TV was a bright yellow block leg sofa with tufted upholstery and a matching oversized square ottoman that could serve as a footrest, coffee table or extra seating. The area rug boasted the most vibrant shades of orange, turquoise, magenta, and indigo. The pattern reminded Kenny of a painting she made with Spin Art as a kid.

Photo Two: The walk-in shower had three frosted glass sides. The fourth wall and floor were a mosaic of octagonal glass tiles in shades of seafoam green. The bamboo vanity was decorated with the same tiles as the shower and two round light-up mirrors hung on a cream wall over the sinks.

Photo Three: The queen-size bed was blanketed with a fluffy white comforter with no less than eight throw pillows of all shapes, sizes, and shades, ranging from deep purples to light lilacs. There was no headboard or baseboard, but there was a violet-colored velvet bench at the foot of the bed. The ceiling was wallpapered with a floral design that matched the purples of the throw pillows and a crystal chandelier hung from the center.

Photo Four: A panoramic view of the concrete three-lane

lap pool. The two long sides of the pool were lined with lime green lounge chairs. Small round tables and free-standing lime green umbrellas placed between every other one. On the opposite side was a large, wooden gazebo that housed dining sets and grills. At the far end of the pool was a pickle ball court.

Photo Five: A picture of the Harbour Town Lighthouse proudly towering over a fleet of yachts, clusters of red wooden rocking chairs, and the eighteenth hole of the Harbour Town Links golf course.

Photo Six: A wide angle shot of the sun rising over the ocean, golden-yellow rays of light reflecting off the water with palm trees, which appeared to have been swaying when the picture was snapped, in the forefront.

Kenny took the self-guided house tour a dozen more times. If Villa #5 had a cyber neighbor, they'd be calling the cops on a tipsy brunette stalking the place. She saw herself in each room of the villa, swimming laps in the pool, and sipping her morning coffee on one of the red rocking chairs under the lighthouse. She lingered on the last photo a little longer than all the others. *That* was the yellow, *that* was the image, of the sun rising over the ocean she so desperately wanted to see all day.

Her legs started to fall asleep, and she remembered she had to wash the day and streaky makeup off her face before the rest of her body fell asleep, too. She stood up, took a big stretch, and wobbled toward the bathroom, passing her almost empty bottle of wine and phone that was lit up like a Christmas tree. Seven texts, three missed calls, one voicemail. All from Colby.

"Leave me alone, Colby," she shouted as she removed the cutting board from the sink and struggled to remember where she put the brown bottle of Perricone face wash after the spa session she treated herself to hours earlier.

Billy Joel had it right, Kenny thought as she lathered her face and took a good, hard look at the tired face staring back at her in the mirror. *Maybe I should get away for a while.*

Kenny decided to ignore Colby for the rest of the night and polish off the bottle of wine. Then proceeded to engage in a very deep conversation with herself, dissecting the lyrics of "Vienna" and how each line correlated to her life.

"Maybe Pelican Pointe is *my* 'Vienna'?" she mused aloud.

She took a few more gulps from her goblet and went back to the ad on her computer. But instead of scrolling through the photos, yet again, Kenny waved her cursor back and forth across the screen and eventually clicked on Hailey's hyperlinked name.

From: Kennedy Sloane
To: hailey@lchospitality.com
Subject: Pelican Pointe Villa #5

Hi Hailey!

I recently came across the ad for Pelican Pointe Villa #5 and am VERY interested in renting the unit for a month. I'd like to check in immediately. It's been quite the night, so I'm leaving a voicemail on your office line, too! Please let me know a convenient time to connect.

With urgency,
Kennedy Sloane

Nine

Colby rolled over in his bed and was relieved to find he was there alone. Wednesday evenings that start with strong cocktails at any one of the Hole in the Wall joints and end with a drag show at Industry Bar often make for awkward Thursday mornings.

He popped a few Advil, chugged a Gatorade, and debated whether he should Door Dash a sausage, egg, and cheese on an everything bagel to Kenny's apartment. When his best friend went to bed angry, hurt, upset, or depressed, waking up to an H&H bagel sandwich and diner-style coffee usually helped her start the new day with a clean slate.

This situation was extra delicate though. It was unchartered territory and Colby had to proceed with caution. He wasn't exactly sure *why* Kenny left Hole in the Wall Mexican so abruptly and then ignored his calls and texts after that. A small piece of him questioned if he could have been the reason behind her Irish Exit and subsequent radio silence.

Was she angry that he'd suggested she spend more time on her personal life? Did she think he was trying to life coach her? If so, that wasn't his intention. He needed a life coach just as much as the next New Yorker. Maybe she overheard people talking about Clinton White and that threw her back into a tailspin. It's possible those hormones were still going haywire in her head.

If she's like this after a round of in vitro, what will she be like for nine months when she's pregnant? he thought. Maybe she saw a guy from Bumble she ghosted and wanted to dodge him.

Regardless of which scenario caused Kenny to bolt before the bill came, she'd get over it with time and space. He just hoped she'd bounce back before the next shoe dropped. He had every intention of telling Kenny over margaritas that Border Books wasn't going to publish *Armchair Detective*, but he couldn't bring himself to do it the same day she lost the Clinton White interview. Luckily, he now had a whole week to break the crushing news to his best friend. When he was leaving the office for Margarita Wednesday, his boss, Muffin Evans, informed him that she was jetting to her home in Bora Bora for a few days and any rejection letters in the que would be held until her return.

Thank goodness for poor cell service in the South Pacific.

Ten

Kenny squinted her eyes and pushed the red comforter down to her waist where she was then able to kick it off the bed with her legs and feet. The Dollhouse was like an oven. She forgot to close the blackout shades, which were nothing more than two black waffle-weave shower curtains that hung from a tension rod. When she started working at WBS, her first assignment was on the overnight shift, so she needed to sleep during the day. Expensive blinds for oversized windows were not in the budget for an entry level television producer. The sunlight that beamed through the window was baking her like a potato—which sounded quite appetizing since she didn't eat anything the day prior except a bland scrambled egg and few bites of guac. Whether she wanted to or not, she was literally seeing yellow.

She struggled to push herself up to a seated position while she tried to ignore her pounding head. She caught a glimpse of the wine glass and stared at it with disgust. It was on the floor next to her open laptop in front of the couch where she sat comatose for hours. She was still reeling from the events that happened the day prior and knew, at the very least, there would be a steady, dull, constant reminder in her head for a few hours.

Losing the Clinton White interview to NBC, learning that *Armchair Detective* wasn't going to be published by Border Books, and being betrayed by the only guy—the only person —she implicitly trusted, stirred up a lethal cocktail that gave Kenny the most severe emotional hangover she ever had. Marilyn told Kenny emotional hangovers were what she experienced when she was overwhelmed, overstimulated, or drowning in her own emotions. Kenny knew all the signs. She could see them coming from the Financial District. Sometimes they were manageable, but when she nursed an emotional hangover with a margarita and bottle of wine, the following twenty-four hours proved brutal.

She popped the Advil and chugged the Gatorade she left on her nightstand before bed and reached for her phone so she could turn off her five alarms before the piercing *ring* joined the drum beating in her head.

"*Oof*, too fast," she grunted as she grabbed her meditation book from under the bed and returned to a vertical position. Her pounding head was now also spinning in circles. She sat completely still for a few seconds and then began the Marilyn-mandated rise and shine ritual.

"Today, I am seeing yellow and feeling hungover," she sarcastically professed, rolling her closed eyes to the back of her head. "I wonder if *that's* on the Wheel of Feelings?"

"Day fifty-one: 'The mark of a moderate woman is freedom from her own ideas' by Lao-tzu."

Kenny burst out laughing. She was anything but moderate. Since she was a kid, it was all in or all out. The current state of her love life and the empty bottle of Clos du Bois were just two glaringly obvious examples of hundreds that she could rattle off.

The notion of being free from one's own ideas also seemed

like a ludicrous concept. Marilyn would encourage her to do things like "get out of her own head." Whose head Marilyn thought Kenny should be in, she didn't know. In stark contrast, Muffin Evans told her she didn't *have* any of her own ideas. That she reacted to *other* people's ideas.

So, which is it? No wonder I'm crazy! she thought.

The one thing making the day's meditation slightly tolerable was that Kenny would be able to dazzle Marilyn with her knowledge of Lao-tzu. In other words, try to veer the venerable therapist off her course and avoid another lecture about how Kenny should try to live by this quote.

I love Lao-tzu, Marilyn! I find Taoism very enlightening. Have you read Tao Te Ching?

Kenny had zero interest in Chinese philosophy but did remember a brief monologue Marah gave ahead of a restorative yoga class about the Old Master and his theories of harmony and balance. Unfortunately, the only thing balanced in Kenny's world was the crippling effects of her two hangovers. They were making her equally miserable.

She hastily filled the percolator with water—she hated when she forgot to make the coffee the night the before—when she was startled by her ringing phone. It was barely after 7:00 a.m. Unless the world was ending, and her life was about to blow up, she couldn't think of a reason to talk to anyone at this current moment.

Oh wait. The world did come crashing down—yesterday! And it didn't come with a courtesy phone call.

She didn't stray from the task at hand and let the call go to voicemail. She was about to dump a heaping tablespoon of grinds into the pot when the phone started ringing and startled her all over again.

"Shit," she yelled, throwing up her hands, coffee grinds flying. "I'm not buying whatever you're selling."

Area code 304? West Virginia.

Kenny knew the "304" area code very well. Three years prior she covered the case of two disgruntled, young lovers from Morgantown, West Virginia, who plotted to kill their parents because they didn't approve of the teen romance. Jack Smith and Diane Long hatched a foolproof plan that would bring them their happily ever after by the age of fifteen. The lovestruck pair combined the money they earned from their part-time jobs at Kroger, where Jack pushed grocery carts and Diane restocked produce, to buy zip ties, an aluminum Louisville Slugger, two one-way Greyhound bus tickets to Pittsburgh and a surprisingly inexpensive hitman. Things went awry when their "hitman" turned out to be an undercover cop who arrested the lovebirds and charged them with attempted murder during gym class at Mountaineer Prep where, ironically, they were playing baseball.

Kenny had been writing letters to Jack and Diane while they were in prison, hoping that they'd agree to an interview when they were released. She even deposited money into their JPay accounts, the prison system that allows inmates to communicate to the outside world via email or video conference. She thought corresponding via fancy technology would be more appealing to the Gen Z'ers than an old school snail mail letter or—*gasp!*—phone call. Jack and Diane were no Clinton White, but an interview with them would rate well. Both were coming up on parole hearings, and Kenny thought maybe they were plotting their reentry into society with a splashy interview. She could only hope.

"WBS, this is Kennedy," she confidently answered, going full speed into interview booking mode.

"Kennedy! Hey there, it's Hailey. I know it's early, but I wanted to get back to you as soon as possible. I was delighted to hear from you. I processed your credit card, as you requested, for the security deposit but wanted to chat about a few things before I go ahead with the rest of the payment," a sweet, bubbly voice chirped from the other end.

Kenny pulled the phone away from her ear and stared at it for what seemed like an eternity. She could feel every muscle of her face tightening and squinting in confusion.

Who is Hailey and why the hell is she processing my credit card?

Kenny knew she wasn't having one of her vivid dreams. The coffee grinds she anxiously started thumbing stuck to her fingers, and she could feel beads of sweat sliding down the nape of her neck. The Dollhouse was hotter than a greenhouse, and she could feel her face getting redder than a tomato with the thought of the stranger on the other end of the line draining her bank account.

"Um, hello? Kennedy, are you still there?" the voice chimed after a long pause. "I'm sorry. I should've mentioned I'm calling from Low Country Hospitality about your upcoming stay at Pelican Pointe."

Oh my God.

"Yes, yes, hi, Hailey. You can call me Kenny." She forced out a salutation, her voice cracking.

She cast another gaze of disgust toward her empty wine glass and frantically pulled up the message she sent to this Hailey girl.

A month? In South Carolina? By herself? Had she lost her mind? She couldn't swing that. Personally, professionally, or financially.

"What a cute nickname. So, Kenny, I have you all set to check in on Monday, September 4th. I'll text you the keypad for the front door when the unit is ready and will have the cleaning service leave your plantation passes on the kitchen counter. We weren't anticipating such a quick response to our ad, so the villa still has a few more renovations that need to be completed. Minor things like power washing the exterior, hanging wall décor, and patching up a few spots on the walls that got nicked when furniture was delivered. The porch furniture is on back order for another month and the cable and internet provider can't make a service trip to the unit for two weeks. *But* the owner has agreed to knock off $2,000 and throw in an additional week if you can live with the inconveniences! If the porch furniture is an issue, we can arrange to move up a few pieces from the pool deck. The grand total will be $2,500 for five weeks. You are just going to *love* Pelican Pointe! Do you have any questions?"

Kenny felt like a bobblehead figurine, nodding up and down in agreement, trying to comprehend all that the vivacious speed talker on the other end of the phone said. Hailey was the Energizer Bunny on steroids with the voice of a sorority girl. She sounded like Cher Horowitz from *Clueless.* Kenny wondered if there was a theory behind her rapid, breathless delivery. Maybe the quicker she spoke, the quicker people agreed *"Sure, OK,"* to whatever she said, forgetting they had responsibilities or budgets, because they got lost in the excitement she projected.

"Sounds great, Hailey," Kenny blurted out.

What?

"I've never done anything so spontaneous. Like, ever. But I really need this. When I emailed you last night it was because I washed down a margarita with a bottle of wine after having a terrible, horrible, no good, very bad day. You know, like that kid, Alexander," Kenny rattled.

Shut up, Kenny. What are you saying?

"But your call, so early this morning, it's like the universe is sending me a message."

Now you sound like a sorority sister on speed.

"My best friend, therapist, yoga instructor, gynecologist—even Billy Joel—have been telling me I need to relax, open up, and disappear for a while. This is great," Kenny concluded.

This is not great. This is not practical. This is the dumbest idea you've ever had. This is your clock losing its spring moment. You sound like a total lunatic.

"You know Billy Joel!" Hailey shrieked "That's awesome! The only star I've ever seen here in West Virginia is some guy named John Mellencamp. He gave a free concert in Morgantown a few years ago. Said he was trying to save the reputation of one of his hit songs because 'kids these days' were giving it a bad rap."

"I don't actually *know* Billy, that was a bit of an exaggeration, but I do know of John Mellencamp and heard about that Jack and Diane concert." Kenny laughed, feeling relieved that Hailey likely didn't hear or process any of the other ridiculousness that she just spewed. She also chuckled thinking back to all the hilarious songs, memes, and SNL skits that went viral linking Jack Smith and Diane Long to John Cougar's 1982 love ballad.

"One question, though: Why are you working for Low Country Hospitality when you live in West Virginia?" Kenny asked, finally reeling herself back in and thinking the journalist in her should ask a question or two to verify she wasn't being swindled by a scam artist.

"Random right? I'm a tourism and hospitality major at WVU and did an internship with Low Country Hospitality this summer at their Hilton Head properties. Best summer of my life. The boss said if I was able to keep up with reservation inquiries, he'd keep me on during the semester."

"Good for you! I've stayed at the Waterfront Hotel. Right there, on the Monongahela River. It's run by WVU students, right? It was always a great stay. I feel like I'll be in good hands if that's where you've been learning the ropes, Hailey."

"Thanks, Kenny. Reach out anytime you have questions. It's been nice chatting, but I gotta run. It's Rush Week. Eek! Have a great day."

Eleven

"Bella. Good morning, sunshine. What are we driving today, Miss Kenny? All your usual poisons have full tanks of gas and are ready to go," the friendly Hispanic man dressed in perfectly pressed khaki pants and a green and white striped polo shirt enthusiastically greeted.

Damien, the manager at the National Car Rental on West Fifty-Sixth Street, had been the second most constant and reliable man in Kenny's life, next to Colby. Until the recent Border Book betrayal, anyway. With all the trips back and forth to Connecticut over the last nine months covering the Clinton White case, Kenny spent more days than not picking up or dropping off cars. Damien would open the garage early or close it late depending on Kenny's schedule. He always made sure one of Kenny's three favorite vehicles to drive was available in the fleet. On the days the city was experiencing severe weather temperatures, Damien surprised Kenny with hot chocolate or popsicles.

"Good morning, friend! Let's do the Nautilus today. But there's one caveat. It'll be a one-way drop off," she said with a hesitant grin.

Kenny learned the hard way that rental car companies *do not* like when their vehicles are returned to a different garage than they were driven away from.

When the world began shutting down because of COVID, Kenny was on an assignment in Ottawa, Canada, where a blizzard dumped feet of snow and grounded all air traffic. At risk of being stuck on the wrong side of the border, Kenny decided to hop behind the wheel of her midsized SUV and made the seven and a half hour trek down Interstate 81 back to NYC. Driving through a Canadian blizzard was stressful enough, let alone wondering if patrol agents on either side of the border had been given the directive to restrict anyone from coming or going by the time she reached customs. To her relief, the agents at the Buffalo-Niagara Falls crossing allowed her to pass through and the snow had let up a bit.

It wasn't until about thirty miles into the U.S. and Kenny was on the phone with Colby, explaining that she got pulled over for driving too slowly and realized the speedometer on the rental was in kilometers. Then it struck her that she had no idea where she was going to drop off the four-wheel drive she picked up at the Toronto airport five days prior. Colby jumped into action while his panicked friend continued her odyssey back to civilization and called every National Car garage in all five boroughs begging them to accept the vehicle. The only agent who would even entertain the thought of taking a car that had been driven one-way, across international borders and didn't gauge speed in miles, was a guy at a creepy parking lot surrounded by a chain-linked fence somewhere in Jamaica, Queens that allegedly serviced JFK.

"Take your bags, leave the keys under the seat, and get out of here before my manager sees you or that car," said the guy who was wearing a black sweat suit, black skull cap, and N95 mask.

To her knowledge, Kenny never observed a drug deal but imagined she could've been mistaken for a trafficker peddling illegal foreign goods down the street from a world renown airport at one in the morning.

"Anything for you Miss Kenny," Damien said with a wink. "I'll call downstairs and have them bring up the Nautilus. Where are we headed, who should I tell to expect the drop off? Need an EZ Pass?"

"I'm taking some time off work—and heading to Hilton Head, South Carolina, for a few weeks. It's been an exceptionally rough few days, and I need to hit a reset button. Or something . . ." Her voice trailed. "I'll probably make a stop or two along the way to catch a few hours of sleep and plan to pull onto the island sometime Monday morning. Let's throw in the EZ Pass to be safe. You know, Damien, that's the first time I've said any of that out loud. And it sounds just as crazy as it seems," she nervously giggled.

"Good for you, mami. You know I worry about you and all those crazy hours you work. I almost called WBS myself when I saw you had a reservation for first thing on a Saturday morning."

"You're always looking out for me, Damien," she said with a forced smile.

"I heard that Dr. Love guy you always talk about is going to be on TV. Is that because of you?" Damien asked as he furiously pounded away at the computer keyboard. "He was all the talk at my cigar club last night. My buddies' wives think the guy is a real dreamboat."

Kenny always wondered what the agents had to record before releasing a rental car to a driver. The process seemed to take longer than going through security at an airport. And with that innocent inquiry about Clinton White, the drawn-out wait made it seem like it was the Sunday after Thanksgiving at Atlanta's Hartsfield-Jackson.

"Ugh, yea. I heard that, too. Unfortunately, NBC landed the interview. WBS lost that one," Kenny lamented.

She stopped short of admitting that the sexy, charismatic, wealthy wife-killer was the flame that started the wildfire that eventually engulfed the landscape of her life in less than twelve hours and ultimately led her to Damien's underground garage too early this Saturday morning.

The relentless promotion of said interview is what prevented Kenny from purchasing a plane ticket in the first place. With her abundance of Delta SkyMiles, she could have had a first-class seat and jetted down to Hilton Head in two hours and change. Aside from rarely flying in or out of JFK, LGA, or Newark without bumping into a colleague or competitor, Kenny knew that reminders of the Clinton White interview would be everywhere.

Although the main event, the two-hour Wednesday Primetime Special, was still five days away, NBC's publicity team would do a brilliant job of rolling it out. Every day, they would drop a sound bite or two from the interview to keep Dr. Love in the news cycle and build up anticipation leading to the broadcast. The racks at the countless Hudson News stores and stands that occupied more real estate in airports than some airline carriers would be abundant with papers and salacious tabloids boasting clever, attention-grabbing headlines that, in Kenny's opinion, were nothing more than free publicity for NBC. Whatever the Peacock network decided to leak that day would be looped into the banners that scrolled across the bottom of CNN, FOX, and News Nation. Kenny knew that there wasn't a waiting area, restaurant, lounge, or bar at any airport that didn't have at least one TV in a traveler's view at all times.

Kenny deemed any airport to be unsafe for her sanity. Driving twelve hours down Interstate 95, acting as her own pilot and copilot, in a rental car seemed to be the more viable option.

"Guess it's like any other business. You win some and lose some. Hertz has really given us a run for our money lately," Damien said as his typing slowed down, and he took one last forceful click of the mouse. Kenny knew this last click meant that copious amounts of paper would begin flying out of the printer. "But today you're back in the winner's circle. Between your Executive Status and the free rentals that you've accumulated, the Nautilus won't cost you a penny! You can drop it off on Beach City Road at the Hilton Head Airport."

Damien came out from behind the counter, dropped the keys and EZ Pass into Kenny's hand, and gave her a hug.

"Drive safe and call me if you run into any vehicle problems. Oh, and take this. Start your vacation early," the car attendant said and handed her a coconut beach scented Yankee Candle air freshener he pulled from his pocket.

Kenny hopped in the car, adjusted her seat, and smiled and waved to Damien in the rearview mirror as she pulled away.

Who just happens to have an extra Yankee Candle air freshener in their pants pocket? She laughed to herself. *I bet Damien's counterpart at Hertz doesn't.*

Kenny felt a pinch of guilt as she merged into Columbus Circle and realized the trusty car attendant was the only person she had been completely truthful with about her need to recharge.

Since she had all but eliminated her social life, she had no plans she needed to cancel or postpone. She emailed her parents a lengthy message about how she'd been deployed to South Carolina for a highly confidential assignment and was told to pack for a few weeks. Kenny loved her parents dearly, but she needed a break from them, too. Given the nature of her job, if she periodically checked in, reminded her parents that the project she was working on was top secret and couldn't be discussed, and shared just enough to let them know she was safe, they wouldn't think too much of it. She had been on the road for longer than five weeks at a time in the past and they'd find comfort knowing she was at least on the same coast.

She reluctantly sent Colby a terse text. Not because she forgave him or was even sure if she'd speak to him again, but because she was nervous Colby would show up at One Police Plaza and demand the chief send out search troops and canvass the 20th Precinct for his missing friend. She certainly didn't need that drama.

Text to Colby: Going to South Carolina on a sensitive assignment for a few weeks. Expecting poor cell service.

Kenny was semi-truthful with work since she couldn't pull the top secret assignment card on the people who were allegedly sending her on it. She hadn't taken a vacation in several years, and since all things Clinton White were on hold until October, she made the argument it would be a good time to cash in on her dozens of unused vacation days. She went a step further to say she'd be spending time with family who live in Hilton Head, South Carolina, and working on a book she's been wanting to write. The line "of course, I will be completely reachable any time of day or night by phone, text, and email" sprinkled throughout the proposition. The facts that her *entire* family lived in Pennsylvania and her book had already been written—and rejected—Kenny perceived as misguided truths rather than flat out lies. Just tiny, baby-sized fibs that didn't make her seem like the single, burned-out, anxiety driven, emotional trainwreck she really was.

She double-parked the Nautilus in the middle of West Eighty-Third Street and threw on the flashers so she could load up the luggage that was neatly stacked inside the front door of The Dollhouse. After years of being a plane hopper, the role bequeathed to junior producers who were sent on all the assignments, she was an expert at packing, unpacking, loading, unloading, navigating security lines, and reigning in her lead foot if she sensed she was in a highly patrolled speed trap. If she was flying, she knew which airports were lax about checking liquids and sharp objects in carry-on bags. If she was driving, she knew to ensure that the GPS was set to English and not a foreign language spoken by the previous renter before driving out of the rental company parking lot and onto a major highway. If she had to check into a hotel, she knew the front desk always had free toothpaste, toothbrushes, razors, and even makeup wipes for travelers who forgot their toiletry bag or, in Kenny's case, became lazy in the packing department. If she had to travel by bus or train with no seat assignments, she knew to always sit toward the front, on an aisle and pretend to be asleep under a pair of blackout sunglasses with her head tilted back while other passengers boarded. This increased the odds of getting the row to yourself as most onboarders walk past the napping passenger to the back of the bus or train, in hopes of also finding themselves alone in a row.

She made a half dozen trips up and down the steps of the brownstone, lugging a large black Samsonite suitcase on wheels that swiveled, the matching carry-on version, two giant duffel bags from the same set, and an unsightly bedazzled hot pink international sized carry-on that she was forced to purchase from an overpriced, gaudy store in the Las Vegas airport when the zipper on her suitcase busted at the departure gate as her flight was about to take off. She hated the suitcase, but the vision of it always made her laugh at the week she had been on the Strip covering the case of a debonair gigolo who went to jail for swindling smitten girlfriends out of money and love.

Kenny checked her laptop bag three times to make sure she had all her chargers. *Phone, watch, computer, iPad, mophie, electric toothbrush.* She also packed up the notebooks and pens she snatched from the office earlier in the week *just in case a creative thought popped into her head,* and she felt compelled to start writing. At the last minute, she emptied the Tupperware from under the kitchen sink where she kept her cleaning supplies and threw in the Percolator, Brita and a replacement filter. Luckily, the midsized SUV wasn't much smaller than The Dollhouse, since the contents of the studio were essentially what Kenny had packed.

Once the car was loaded, she sat back in the driver's seat, with the four ways still flashing, and reclined her head for a few seconds. She let the cold air blow through the vents to bring her nerves and body temperature down and basked in the aroma from Damien's beach-inspired, coconut-infused parting gift.

She pulled up Google Maps and began typing S-E-A when *Sea Pines, Hilton Head Island, South Carolina 29928* populated in the destination bubble. Kenny vaguely remembered taking a virtual drive down I-95 after the sixth or seventh time she virtually toured Pelican Pointe Villa #5 on Wednesday night.

Estimated time in hours with light traffic: twelve hours, six minutes.

She reached for her Wildest Dreams planner that was on the passenger seat, pulled out the day's pink Post-it, and stuck it on the steering wheel.

Ironic. Never in my wildest dreams did I think I'd spontaneously pack up my life, strategically cram the material possessions of it into a rental car and take them on a long-distance road trip in an attempt to escape the mental elements of the same life for a few weeks.

<u>To-Do Saturday, September 2</u>

- National @ 8:00 a.m.
- Finish packing
- Unplug appliances
- Empty fridge + take out garbage
- Lock windows + close blinds
- Richmond, VA (Exits 83B - 62)

It wasn't even 9:30 a.m. and she was able to cross five of the six items off her "to-do" list.

"All right, Miss B, let's go," Kenny triumphantly said as she hit the blue "Go now" button on the screen and shifted the car into drive.

The summer between high school and college, she and her girlfriends went on vacation to Ocean City, Maryland. It was a rite of passage for all the recent graduates of northeastern Pennsylvania to descend on the popular beach town over the Fourth of July for a week of partying, exploring and other debauchery. "What happens at Senior Week, stays at Senior Week," was the only rule.

Luckily, what happened at Senior Week wasn't always remembered, making the rule much easier to follow. On the girls' sleepy and sunburned drive home from the epic week, the Garmin navigation system seemed to be in a similar hazy and confused state, taking them in circles around and through the ghettos of Philadelphia. The voice barking directions became known as "The Bitch in the dashboard." The four-hour trip took seven, but The Bitch eventually got them home. Over the years and as Kenny's girlfriends started driving around their babies and toddlers, The Bitch was shortened to Miss B.

Miss B and Kenny cruised up Broadway and made a left at the Seventy-Ninth Street Boat Basin that led them up the Henry Hudson and over the George Washington Bridge.

Twelve

Kenny arrived at the shortest leg of her trip down Interstate 95 just as the multiple days of driving alone began to weigh on her focus and sanity. She played all the usual mind-distracting games she could think of that still allowed her to safely operate a vehicle. She made mental notes of the different license plates she passed on the road and then wrote them on a sheet of paper when she pulled over at rest stops for a quick leg stretch.

Somewhere around Fayetteville, North Carolina, Kenny saw a license plate for New Mexico with the image of a Chile pepper and slogan, "The Chile Capital of the World." *Who knew?*

Kenny loudly shouted, "South of the Border," each time she saw one of the kitschy, yet historic, billboards promoting the tourist trap disguised as a truck stop and theme park in the city of Dillon that straddles the border of North Carolina and South Carolina.

She moved on to a real brain twister and calculated how many hours she had spent behind the wheel of the car, versus how many hours she still had left.

It took Kenny six hours and thirty minutes to drive from New York City to Richmond. It took another four hours and thirteen minutes for Kenny to drive from Richmond to Florence. Navigation tells Kenny it will take her an additional two hours and forty-five minutes to drive from Florence to Hilton Head. How many hours will it take for Kenny to drive from The Dollhouse to Pelican Pointe?

She was so distracted by her math problem that she almost missed the direction from Miss B that she had been anticipating since she pulled out of the parking garage on West Fifty-Sixth Street.

"Take Exit 28 to SC-462 E toward Coosawachie. Keep left toward Hilton Head Island," Miss B instructed.

Kenny followed her reliable copilot and veered right off the Interstate she had spent the last two days traveling. She was laser focused on Miss B's voice for the next several miles as she took a series of left and right turns down the narrow two-lane roads through the Lowcountry before reaching Okatie Highway that put her on 278 E, the Cross Island Parkway, and the final leg of her journey.

The Cross Island Parkway looked like the typical gateway to any island. A necessary link connecting a mundane, practical, busy highway to a slice of paradise, nirvana. The seven-mile stretch was a modest glimpse of the beauty that awaited at the end of it. The four-lane divided highway surrounded by marshland was separated by a grassy divider that was landscaped with palm trees and ornamental grasses. Every few hundred feet pops of color sprung from the scattered clusters of flowering pink crape myrtle trees and blooming purple lantanas. They reminded Kenny of the wildflowers on the cover of her planner.

It was a little before 11:00 a.m. and the overcast skies slowly gave way to puffy white clouds against a backdrop of bright blue. Rays of golden sunshine peeked through, and

Kenny opened the sunroof and all four windows, allowing the warm island breeze to blow through the car. Traffic on 278 was much heavier than she expected for a Monday morning. She knew a lot of people who worked on Hilton Head lived on the mainland in Beaufort and Bluffton, but it seemed late in the day for commuter traffic.

Maybe this is what people mean by island time?

Kenny took a deep inhale as the gridlock came to a halt and had a strange, unfamiliar sensation after she exhaled. In that moment, she felt relief, at peace. For the first time in a very long time, she didn't feel like she was suffocating. Maybe this sensation, this feeling, this "awareness of breath" as Yogi Marah called it was a real, tangible, beneficial thing. She closed her eyes for a split second and envisioned sitting bumper to bumper on the Cross Bronx Expressway, wondering if she could evoke that same sensation. She immediately heard the noise of sirens and horns; she saw the angry drivers and aggressive panhandlers hoping to score loose change from drivers who were trapped and had nowhere to go.

Nope, definitely not. Breathing would never be an option when battling tristate traffic.

Congestion let up by the time Kenny reached Hudson's Seafood House on the Docks, one of the oldest restaurants on the island where the freshest catches of the day were served from the docks that they came in on to the picnic tables that dotted the banks of Skull Creek. She hadn't had seafood since she was shamed by a cameraman from Louisiana into ordering a catfish platter dinner after an interview that she and the crew produced in Baton Rouge. It was still a bit early in the day for a crab cake sandwich and hushpuppies, but she desperately needed a coffee.

The fatigue from the long, monotonous few days of driving started to set in and the adrenaline she had been running on in both anticipation and fear of the trip was wearing off. Twenty minutes out from Sea Pines and four hours until check-in at Pelican Pointe, she had time to spare.

"Dunkin Donuts near me," Kenny requested of Miss B.

As the route on the screen started remapping and shifting the aerial view it displayed, *Hailey Lowcountry* flashed on the dashboard.

Text from Hailey: (Emoji: waving hand)! Code 2 (Emoji: door) is #0830#. (Emoji: broom) (Emoji: sponge) is done!

Text from Hailey: & Savi's havin LDW celebration (Emoji: fireworks). You can prbly c from (Emoji: beach umbrella). Chck it out!

"Wow, okay, Hailey," Kenny sighed, "this is like hiero-glyphics."

Miss B immediately interjected, "I'm sorry, I didn't get that," before she started repeating, "recalculating, recalculating" after Kenny missed a U-turn, distracted by trying to decipher Hailey's message of graphics.

Kenny pulled over to silence a clearly frustrated Miss B and reset the address to the new destination, Pelican Pointe. The coffee could wait. Reading between the tiny pictures and one-letter words, Kenny interpreted the message to mean that housekeeping was finished, and she could enter the villa. The second text was more elusive. She felt like she had a bad partner for Pictionary.

Kenny solved the fireworks and the beach part of the riddle. But who was Savi? Maybe she was a friend of Hailey's and LDW was the latest fad theme party. Fordham didn't have Greek Life, but Kenny's friends who were in sororities and fraternities were forever going to parties where they had to dress like a sexy lion tamer or don nothing but strategically wrapped bed sheets. Either way, Kenny was past that phase of her life and wouldn't be attending any party down the beach hosted by Hailey's friend or anyone else, especially on a Monday night. Although she appreciated the invite and southern hospitality.

In that moment, she felt a pinch of sadness. It had been months, maybe even longer since Kenny had gone to a party or any type of social event just for fun. And the messages from Hailey were the exact type of thing she would have called Colby about to have a quick laugh and debate the cryptic language of college kids. She was lonely and missed her friend, but not enough to speak to him.

Pelican Pointe was on Sea Pines Plantation at the southernmost tip of Hilton Head, the shoe-shaped barrier island off the coast of South Carolina that stretched twelve miles long and five miles wide across the Atlantic Ocean. The shoe was developed into a series of eleven planned communities, called plantations, and Sea Pines was the toe of the shoe. Each plantation had its own identity, character, and feeling. As Kenny cruised down the palm tree lined Cross Island Parkway, she passed the Shelter Cove, Palmetto Dunes, Shipyard and Wexford plantations before dead-ending into her final stop, Sea Pines.

Kenny pulled up to an entrance labeled the Greenwood Gate where a tall, broad gentleman wearing khaki pants and an army-green short sleeve button-up shirt popped out of a tan hut and greeted her with a toothy, white smile.

"Good morning! Welcome to Sea Pines," he enthusiastically waved.

"Good morning, Derek," Kenny brightly replied, as she caught a glimpse of the friendly watchman's name badge.

When she was nine years old, her grandfather taught her the importance of addressing people by their name.

"It makes them feel special, noticed," he would say. "If

you know a person's name, use it. If you can't remember their name, call men 'John' and women 'Mary.' They might be a bit confused at first, but they'll feel appreciated and will respond."

Until that point, Kenny thought that the Irish-Catholic coal miners of northeastern Pennsylvania weren't too creative in the name game, so everyone ended up a John or Mary at birth. After she was let in on this secret, she realized that it was no coincidence that 85 percent of her grandfather's acquaintances were "named" John or Mary.

"It looks like we don't have a Plantation Pass. Will you be joining us here on Sea Pines for vacation or just visiting for the day, miss?" Derek trailed off, giving Kenny an inquisitive eye.

"Kenny, my name is Kenny. And yes, I'm here on a bit of an extended vacation. I'll be staying at Pelican Pointe for a few weeks. My passes should be at the villa when I check-in. I'm headed there now," she explained.

"Ah, Pelican Pointe, I believe that's Mr. Cunningham's newest property. The man is building quite the empire here on Sea Pines. He does many wonderful things for the community and plantation. I'll give you this temporary pass for now, Miss Kenny, until you get all settled," he said as he slid a date-stamped piece of postcard-sized flimsy pink paper stock onto the dashboard.

"Great, thank you, Derek. Have a wonderful day!" She chirped as she put her foot on the gas.

"You're very welcome. I guess I'll be seeing you around, Miss Kenny," Derek grinned and directed the car through the gate.

She couldn't help but smile. She appreciated the simplicity of that old-school, personal moment. No scanning, swiping, downloading, or tapping necessary to enter paradise. Rather, a friendly gatekeeper, who sat in a cozy guard house flanked by colorful hanging baskets, welcomed her to the island oasis. She was certain that the system hadn't changed since the plantation was developed in 1956.

The speed limit on Sea Pines was 35 mph, but Kenny found herself barely pushing the gas to 20 mph. Natural beauty was everywhere, and she wanted to take a mental picture of each frame she was passing. Streaks of sun beamed through the openings of the awning formed by the towering palm and live oak trees that draped over Greenwood Drive like a piece of fine sheer fabric. As she traveled down the windy, two-lane road she noticed the paved leisure trails that clung on either side. They were sparse and serene, nothing like the congested path along the Hudson River that she was used to running. Kenny couldn't wait to lace up her sneakers and go for a jog, with the wind in her hair and the ocean air kissing her skin.

She approached Fraser's Circle and saw a biker in the distance who would be reaching the roundabout at the same time. Unlike New York "behind-the-wheel" Kenny, she didn't power on the pedal to beat out the biker, who wouldn't have known they were racing, because she wouldn't have had time in her day to let him or her pass. As she got closer, she noticed the cyclist had something big and clunky on his back while a medium sized dog that was tethered to a leash that hung off the right handlebar ran alongside him. She always admired city food delivery guys who strapped fancy apparatuses to their bikes so they could transport piping hot pizzas or Chinese food to the doors of starving New Yorkers who didn't know a spatula from a screwdriver; but this biker was equally, if not nimbler, at balancing all he had in tow on two wheels.

The biker must have sensed she was coming because by the time she rolled to the intersection, the cyclist was at a complete stop. Her eyes immediately took to what was strapped on the guy's back. It was a bright red golf bag with the letters "JLP" embroidered in bold, red font on a white pocket. Her head cocked to the left and brows furrowed, trying to make sense of how that worked. How was the bag not slapping against the rear tire, burning a hole through the fabric from the friction? How did the biker keep the clubs vertical on his back, so they didn't T-bone oncoming cyclists or get tangled up in the dog's leash?

Kenny's inner journalist was tempted to poke her head out the window and ask all those questions. Her gaze moved forward to the biker himself who was looking back at her with a not so confused face. She was met with a "are you going to wave me on?" kind of facial expression. The one that you would expect a biker to give the driver of a vehicle when they are both stopped at the same crossroads. She gasped a quick breath, her face now heating up red with embarrassment from staring.

Oh my God. Stop staring, Kenny.

Not only was Bike Boy incredibly talented on a bike, but he was also strikingly handsome. Piercing blue eyes popped off his perfectly tanned skin from under his navy Penn State baseball hat. His defined biceps were on display from under his white Nike Dri-FIT polo and his coy, closed mouth smile released a kaleidoscope of butterflies in her stomach. Now she was staring harder, longer, and directly in his eyes. The news producer in her wanted to know *everything* about this man.

Oh my God, Kenny. Are you paralyzed? Do something. Wave Bike Boy across the street.

The dog started barking and snapped Kenny back to reality. She mustered the most juvenile and pathetic version of a smile and waved him across the street. Bike Boy chuckled, extended a strong left hand in Kenny's direction, and rode away. She hadn't had butterflies like the ones that were just set free in her belly in years, but she was certain Bike Boy and his pup were on their way to meet his tall, thin, blonde, dog-mom of a girlfriend.

She pulled onto Fraser Circle, veering halfway around the circumference to Lighthouse Road. Miss B directed her to make a left onto Plantation Drive and then another left in just a few hundred feet.

Tucked away on a tiny cul-de-sac, Pelican Pointe could easily be missed. Three rows of light brown and beige stucco villas were linked together in a U shape and protected by a canopy of moss-covered oak trees that stood tall above them. Scrub palmettos masked the façade of the units making the living quarters chameleons to the lush surroundings. The narrow driveway could be mistaken for a golf cart path or one of the miles of leisure paths that weaved throughout the plantation. A tiny, understated carved brown sign matching the trunks of the oak trees that read "Pelican Pointe" was the only indication this small sliver of the tropical paradise hid behind Plantation Drive.

Kenny aligned the rental car with a few other vehicles that were parked in the unmarked paved plot of land outside of the villas. It was instant sensory overload when she stepped out of the car. Her legs wobbly from being stationary and behind the wheel for the last three hours, she leaned her back against the driver's side door and gave her limbs a chance to regain feeling. She lifted her gaze to the sky. Behind closed eyelids she saw the bright aura emanating from the sun that was beaming down warm waves of heat on her face.

She breathed in the smell of pine needles and freshly cut grass and could taste the sea salt on her lips. The quiet and stillness was a welcome reprieve from the constant barrage of noise and chaos she had grown accustomed to. In the distance, she heard the staccato *ping, pong, ping, pong* of a tennis ball and the faint *buzz* of a leaf blower.

Kenny popped open her trunk, grabbed her big and little suitcases, and rolled them down the coastal concrete walkway to Villa #5.

"Pound. Zero. Eight. Three. Zero. Pound," she whispered as she poked the keypad on the front door with her index finger. She heard a *click* and pushed open the heavy beige, wooden door. "Welcome home, Kenny. Welcome to Vienna."

Thirteen

*Text from Damien National Car Rental: Arrive in SC,
Mami? My counterpart at the airport called and they are
low on inventory b/c of the holiday. They offered to send a
driver to your location to pick up the car and get it back into
circulation. Send me your address.*

"Labor Day! Right. Now the traffic makes sense," Kenny said
to her screen.

She had planned to make a trip to Harris Teeter or Piggly
Wiggly to stock up on a few essentials while she still had a
car. But avoiding a trip across the island to the airport and a
subsequent Uber ride back to Pelican Pointe seemed more
appetizing than any provisions she'd stock in her refrigerator.

*Text to Damien National Car Rental: I've arrived and that'd
be great! I'm staying at Pelican Pointe on Sea Pines. The
only Nautilus with New York tags in the lot. Will leave the
keys under the mat on the driver's side. Thx!*

Text from Damien National Car Rental: I'll let them know.

> *Savannah throws a Labor Day party and a lot of people rent cars for the evening to go over for the festivities and fireworks.*

> *Text to Damien National Car Rental: (Emoji: thumbs up)*

And there you have it, Kenny thought.

Civilization reached a point where the rush to convey information was so urgent that even the names of historical cities were shortened. "Savi" wasn't Hailey's friend, and Kenny wasn't invited to anyone's party. "Savi" was Savannah, Georgia's oldest city. A city that was hosting a celebration to honor a federal holiday. Since Savannah and Hilton Head were only separated by a few miles of the Intracoastal Highway, there was a chance Kenny would be able to enjoy the fireworks from the beach.

Riddle solved. Facepalm emoji.

She was a proficient unpacker, but she despised the daunting task and her nomadic career made her efficient at living out of suitcases and bags. Knowing that she'd be at Pelican Pointe for the next thirty-five consecutive nights gave her the encouragement and sense of stability she needed to hang clothes in the closet and hide toiletries in the bathroom vanity. She collapsed her duffel bags and stuffed them into the small black suitcase; she zipped up the hot pink Vegas suitcase inside the large black one; and rolled the Samsonite set into the hall coat closet, out of sight. She couldn't remember the last time she knew *for certain* that she would be staying in the same place for thirty-five nights. She did know for certain that it hadn't been any time in the last ten years.

It was almost 4:00 p.m. and Kenny had hit the wall. She was deliriously happy to be settled in at Pelican Pointe but also starved and exhausted. She thought about venturing out to explore and grab a bite to eat, but when she remembered it was Labor Day, she quickly nixed the idea. She pulled up the Instacart app and started adding a few items to her cart that would hold her over for a few meals.

While she waited for the delivery of her New York staples to arrive—coffee, creamer, eggs, salsa, cheese, lemons, and nacho chips—she plopped down on the yellow sofa and stretched her feet onto the matching ottoman. Although the open blinds let in an afternoon that was turning cloudy, Villa #5 exuded happiness. It was cheerful and bright, just like the photos that jumped off her computer screen five nights ago. Her attitude fed off her surroundings, and she didn't want this feeling, this optimism, to go away. Ever. Or at least for the next five weeks while she took her break from reality.

After years of working on serious self-assessment with Marilyn the therapist, Kenny knew she often struggled in battles that involved setting boundaries. To fully optimize this opportunity, this chance to recharge, she would have to put some conditions on herself and the situation to avoid distraction or getting "stuck in her own head," as Marilyn would say.

Kenny pulled her Wildest Dreams planner out of the laptop bag and flipped to the back of the book where there was a section of blank pages that simply had *Goals* scrawled across the top. She tore out one of the perforated sheets, crossed a solid, black line through *Goals* and under it wrote *Hiatus of Life Conditions List*.

She stared at the blank page for a few moments and reflected on the series of events that collided simultaneously last Wednesday and rocked her world to its core like a catastrophic earthquake that continued to give off debilitating aftershocks after the initial blow. Every time she'd regain her footing to stand up and face one situation, *Wham!* Another blow would come, knocking her back down. Kenny thought about what she needed in her life. Maybe more importantly, what she needed to eliminate from her life.

<u>Hiatus of Life Conditions List (in no particular order)</u>

- Exercise daily.
- Eat healthy, every day.
- Eliminate "to-do" lists.
- Restrict alcohol.
- Write ("original" ideas for novel).
- Try new things.
- Limit work emails.
- No new male relationships (straight *or* gay).

Satisfied with the Conditions List, Kenny hung it on the fridge so it would always be in view, a constant reminder that following these simple, temporary life hacks could lead her to the happiest five weeks of her life.

Fourteen

It was a humid, rainy Tuesday morning in Hell's Kitchen and the gloomy weather matched Colby Jackson's mood. His weekend on Fire Island was a bust. It was such a failure that he left an entire day early, in the most unglamorous way; he embarked on an odyssey he hadn't made since his early twenties. Colby took the ferry from Fire Island Pines to the Sayville dock where he boarded a shuttle that deposited him at the Long Island Rail Road which eventually dumped him in the bowels of Penn Station, otherwise known as "the worst place in New York City," according to social media.

Colby and a group of cohorts from their touch football team, Pride Pack, drove out to the large island that runs parallel to the south shore of Long Island on Thursday night to get a jump start on closing out the summer with a bang. Labor Day weekend was always one of Colby's favorite four days on Fire Island or "Chelsea with Sand," as many city-dwellers called it. But this weekend was different. He had an uneasy feeling since Wednesday night when Kenny ditched him at Hole in the Wall Mexican without explanation and then actively avoided him for two days, until she sent the terse message stating that she'd be unreachable for five weeks. It didn't make sense.

Colby couldn't remember a time since that first meeting on the treadmills at the West Sixty-Third Street YMCA that he and Kenny had gone five whole days without some form of communication. Colby had enormous amounts of respect for the dedication and confidentiality she gave to her work assignments, but even when she was embedded in the most restricted environments, she found a way to at least shoot him a text to let him know she was alive. She spent time in a women's prison in Kentucky, two weeks at an inpatient childhood eating disorder center in Colorado, and twenty-eight days at an addiction treatment facility somewhere off of Interstate 81 in Pennsylvania, and always found a way to check in.

He always worried when Kenny was deployed on these "off the record" and "off the grid" trips but he was especially worried about this excursion. Colby *needed* to talk to Kenny. If his boss, Muffin Evans, the Manuscript Eater, got to Kenny with the news that Border Books was not going to publish *Armchair Detective* before Colby could soften the blow, all hell would break loose. When Kenny was given access to these top secret missions, she had to be laser-focused, steadfast. One slip-up at these controlled environments and production teams would get the boot, certainly eliminating any chance of an invitation back and closing the door on opportunities to ask follow-up questions.

Colby assumed she had finally struck a deal with one of her contacts at the Indian reservation, nudist colony, or religious cult compound she had been trying to infiltrate. But regardless of where in the world Kenny was for the next five weeks, no place was going to be a good one to learn that her first novel wasn't going to be sold.

Text to Kenny: Hey Doll! Know you're busy being impor-

*tant and fabulous but can you puh-leez make time for a
check-in? You don't have to tell me what weird, twisted
story you're covering, but I need to hear your voice. You
were SO right about Paolo. Ran into him at The Pines and
he looked like SUCH an old man. LYMIB.*

At least part of the text was true. Colby did need to talk to
Kenny, and he did run into Paolo, his first, much older lover
at a house party on Fire Island. The whole truth was that he
had to tell Kenny that they were both wrong about *Armchair
Detective* being a sure-fire hit. And she was wrong about
Paolo. He did look "older" but was aging like a fine wine that
Colby wanted to guzzle by the magnum.

The combination of running into Paolo and meeting his
new boyfriend, not talking to Kenny in several days, and the
inevitable twinge of dread that comes the morning after the
last holiday weekend of the summer hit Colby like a Mac
truck. He felt like he had a black cloud hanging over his head
and knew it wouldn't blow over until he talked to Kenny.

Fifteen

"Today, I'm most definitely seeing purple," Kenny laughed as she gazed at the lilac and lavender floral wall-papered ceiling.

She felt almost regal tucked beneath the fluffy white comforter, atop the elevated bed frame and extra deep mattress and box spring, surrounded by orchid and violet silk throw pillows of every shape and size. The blinds in the streak-free Pella French Doors were open, allowing the morning sun to stream though. Without moving much, she had a clear view to the pool deck, which meant the women doing water aerobics had a clear view of her Princess and the Pea situation, too.

Note to self: Must shut blinds.

Kenny tumbled out of bed and into her slippers. She had no idea what time it was. Her phone was still on the charger in the kitchen from the night before. After the Instacart delivery, she had scrambled some eggs, took a long, hot shower in the spa-like bathroom, and quite literally fell asleep while she was moisturizing her legs on the folded down sheets. She caught a glimpse of herself in the hallway mirror and the person staring back at her looked like she had either been asleep for a hundred years or hadn't slept for nearly as many.

In this case, Kenny's puffy face and the lines around her eyes were the result of a long, hard, face-in-the-pillow sleep. While her appearance said otherwise, she was refreshed and energized. She plugged in the percolator that was already prepared from the decaf pot she planned to drink after her shower and before bed the night before. She didn't need the caffeine to function today. She just wanted that "first sip of coffee in the morning at the beach" sensation. She pulled a navy blue, oversized whale-shaped coffee mug out of the cabinet, and tidied up around the kitchen while she waited for her beverage to brew.

Kenny opened the sliding door at the far end of the living space and dragged one of the white leather bar stools onto the deck that overlooked the pool since the patio furniture was still on backorder. Cupping her whale mug, she propped her feet up on the banister and sipped her coffee as she scanned the surroundings. It was a little before 7:00 a.m. and Pelican Pointe was awake with activity. This wasn't the "city that never sleeps" kind of activity, where people fired on the same, overextended cylinders whether it was four in the morning or four in the afternoon. This was a quiet, serene, peaceful activity, spearheaded by people leisurely leaning into the day ahead.

Four older gentlemen staked out the pickleball court while women around the same age waded back and forth in the pool, lifting aquatic foam dumbbells up and down over their heads. A dad sat on a wooden bench next to one of the landscaping ponds adjacent to the pool, reading a newspaper while his three kids crouched alongside counting the orange and white koi fish. A mother and two teen girls ate muffins at one of the bistro tables under the pavilion.

Within a half hour, all the neighbors had scattered, and

Kenny took the last gulp of her coffee. She had every intention of going for a run, but since waking up to older women doing their water aerobics, she couldn't stop thinking about jumping in the pool. She hadn't done a lap in years, but she had always been an excellent swimmer. She loved the water, and the sport came easy to her. There weren't too many indoor pools in Manhattan, so her favorite form of exercise fell by the wayside. The one red, racerback Speedo she owned also deteriorated with time, and sagged and stretched out in all the wrong places. But she didn't know anyone at Pelican Pointe, nor did she plan on getting to know anyone, so she slipped into the dry-rotted suit, wrapped herself in a beach towel from the linen closet, and walked down the back steps of the patio to the pool deck.

Kenny bent her left knee and gingerly dragged her right big toe over the surface of the water. The temperature was warm but not hot like she was expecting. She tossed her towel on the chaise lounge closest to the steps of the concrete pool and dipped in one foot, and then the other, holding onto the railing with her right hand and swinging her goggles by the strap in her left. She slowly descended into the pool and acclimated her body—ankles, knees, waist, and bellybutton—with each step. The water sent a quick jolt through her body when it touched certain parts of her overheated skin. She finally hit the bottom of the shallow end of the lap pool and before squatting to submerge her shoulders, she tied her hair up in a ponytail and pulled the goggles over her eyes. She dipped her face to make sure the lenses weren't leaking and then held her breath and slipped under the water. With that one swift movement, she felt like she was nine years old and had just jumped into her uncle's pool for the first time of the season. It was a feeling of pure happiness. She backed up to the to the wall, took a mini head dive with her arms extended in front of her, and pushed off with her feet.

With each circular arm motion, she powered forward through the water, taking a breath after every third stroke. Kenny could hear her childhood swim coach in her partially submerged ears. *One. Two. Three. Breathe. One, Two. Three. Breathe.* It wasn't until this moment that she realized everyone in her life had been telling her to breathe. As she glided through the water, her gaze slightly forward, slightly down, and breathing side to side, she became fully present. She noticed the tiny blue square tiles at the bottom of the pool that designated lap lanes and the bigger tiles on the side of the pool that denoted the changes in depth. She noticed cracks in the concrete walls and weighted diving rings scattered below that were probably dropped in by the kids who were feeding the fish earlier. She noticed acorns that had fallen to the bottom of the pool from the oak trees that hung over it and the dragonflies that were buzzing around the surface.

Her inside heated up and her breathing became heavy. She was putting in a solid workout. There was no method for her swimming, she concocted her own individual medley, jumping from stroke to stroke at random. Not the specific order of butterfly, backstroke, breaststroke, and freestyle that such a race was swam. Out of the corner of her eyes, Kenny saw movement around the pool deck and decided to call it quits for the day. She didn't want to be known as the new tenant in Villa #5 who hogged the pool. And she certainly didn't want anyone watching her swim.

She removed the goggles from her head and pulled the scrunchie from her tangled hair. She bobbed up and down in the shallow end three quick times and on the fourth lingered under water for a little while longer, throwing her head back before coming up for air so her shoulder length hair stayed slick off her face and rested down her back.

She stepped out of the pool and patted her arms and legs

dry. She draped the royal blue and white striped terry cloth towel over her shoulders and twisted and rang her hair out like a soaked sponge. She took the long way around the pool back toward her patio steps to check out the amenities under the pavilion.

The right side of the square structure housed two gas grills separated by a built-in prep station that was stocked with stainless steel BBQ utensils, cleaners, and aluminum foil. The back wall was lined with piles of wood that were protected by yellow caution tape and a sign that read "Construction Area: Wet Bar Coming in Fall." The left side had a built-in counter height ledge with a row of stools facing the pickleball court and a variety of high- and low-top tables, occupying the space in the middle. In the front right corner, there was a marker-stained magnetic white board on a wobbly wooden easel that looked like it had been plucked straight from a kindergarten classroom on the last day of a long school year. *Community News* was sprawled across the top in purple cursive handwriting and one lonely sheet of white computer paper with black Times New Roman font stuck to it.

What: Beach Yoga
Where: Sea Pines Beach Club (Beach Marker #38)
When: Every Tuesday, Thursday, and Sunday @ 9:00 a.m.
Bring a towel, water, and $5!

While the advertisement left much to be desired, beach yoga sounded delightful. Kenny hadn't practiced with Yogi Marah since last Wednesday's meltdown and, mentally and physically, she felt the absence. Her body was still crammed and compact from sitting in the car for so many hours over the weekend, and she was slightly concerned how her unused muscles were going to react to the rigorous swim workout she put them through.

It was already 8:15 a.m. and Kenny's phone told her that the Sea Pines Beach Club was a twenty-minute walk from Pelican Pointe, but she could cut that time almost in half, being the city slicker she was. She could qualify for competitive speedwalking at the Olympic level after so many years of commuting through the streets of Manhattan in stilettos. If she wore sneakers, she'd likely place in the event. She sprinted up the back steps to the villa and started taking down the straps of her bathing suit as she shut the door behind her and charged toward the bedroom.

She slipped into a pair of black leggings; they weren't her fat pair, but the skinny ones were still too tight, and pulled a black sports bra and maroon Rams tank over her head. She tied her wet hair up into a knot with the silk blue scrunchy and quickly dabbed SPF 50 on her face. Although it was already September, Kenny hadn't seen much sun and knew the rays reflecting off the ocean water would be powerful. She filled her water bottle, grabbed a dry towel, and shuffled out the door.

$\mathcal{S}ixteen$

"Welcome! Welcome! My name is Bonnie. Please make yourself at home. I wasn't expecting such a large turnout today, so I'll try to keep my voice up," a soft-spoken middle-aged woman with a sweet southern drawl vowed as she struggled to corral a boisterous group of ladies. "Let's try to form a semicircle. I will set up my mat in the middle so everyone can hear me, and y'all will still have a view of this beautiful ocean behind me."

She continued. "I'm tickled pink to see so many new faces on this sunny Sea Pines morning and am always elated when I get to start the day with my Wine After Nine gals. While we get settled would everyone like to go around and introduce themselves? Tell us what brings you to Hilton Head, and where y'all are visiting from," Bonnie instructed as the gaggle of women floundered around her flapping their towels to the sand.

"I'll start, Miss Bonnie," volunteered a tall, slender woman wearing a tan sleeveless, collared Dri-FIT tank and black skort. "I'm Savannah, and me and my gals are lucky enough to call Sea Pines home. We start our Tuesdays with

Miss Bonnie, have a standing 11:00 a.m. tee time at Liberty Oaks and then hydrate with a liquid lunch at the clubhouse," she bragged on behalf of herself and the rest of her foursome.

"Howdy, I'm Addison!" chirped a perky redhead who wore a cropped white tank with a washed-out American flag on it. "My girlfriends and I are celebrating our forty-fifth birthdays! We missed a fortieth celebration and couldn't wait until we turned fifty for a girls' getaway! We come by way of Austin, Dallas, and Houston."

"Hi, I'm Emma," announced a petite blonde who was decked out in hot pink Lululemon gear from head to toe. "We're from Greenwich, Connecticut and Olivia convinced our Moms Who Tennis Club to come down for a weeklong camp at Smith Stearns," she said pointing to a petite brunette wearing the same spandex ensemble in lime green.

"Good morning, ladies! My name is Suzanne, and I'm here with fellow bookworms from our Roanoke Readers Club. We're open to suggestions for our November Book. We've been on a murder mystery run lately," the gray-haired women advocated from under her Lily Pulitzer visor.

Ironic. If only I had written a crime book that I could suggest Suzanne and her friends read, Kenny thought.

"I'm Bailey, and I'm getting married next month!" squealed a blonde wearing a white sports bra and white boy shorts flanked by five girls in black sports bras and black boy shorts. "We're from Columbus and, no, we didn't drive down in a red minivan!" she giggled, referring to an ongoing island joke popularized by legendary Hilton Head children's entertainer, Greg Russell. "But our Uber driver did pick us up in one from the Bermuda Triangle last night!" she continued from behind her full face of makeup that was likely still intact from the night before.

"Oh, honey, I thought your pretty faces looked familiar," Addison from Austin interjected. "You were the group hanging out with that preppy bachelor party. They were too young and Vineyard Vines for our tastes, but I hope one of you girls got lucky."

Kenny *hated* these round-robin introductions. She had no time for hobbies, going to bachelorette parties, celebrating birthdays, or letting anyone into her life. What could she possibly share with a bunch of strangers?

"Last one, dear," Bonnie smiled at Kenny. "What brings you to Sea Pines?"

"Hi ladies, my name is Kennedy. I'm from Manhattan and"—she stumbled—"and I'm here because I needed a break from life. I haven't unplugged in a long time, and I'm spending a few weeks on Sea Pines, hoping to recharge and get inspired."

"Good for you, Kennedy. You won't have to look too far to find inspiration around here," Bonnie replied. "Many thanks to each of you for sharing and joining our community today. I'm going to ask everyone to take an affirmation card and a chakra stone that we'll keep on our towels during class. The energy these crystals and mantras project will fuel our practice and carry us through the rest of our day. Keep your card face down until the end of class. After Savasana we'll read our affirmations aloud, and I'll tell you the significance of your stone."

Bonnie splayed the deck of light blue affirmation cards in a rainbow shape on her towel. In the middle of the arc was a plush white velvet bag. She invited the group to approach one by one and directed, "Slowly, wave your right hand back and forth over the cards and when you feel a slight pull or force from your index finger, pick up the card your hand is hovering over. Then, without looking in the bag, place your hand inside and pick out the stone that feels like it should be in your palm."

Kenny didn't have time in her overbooked life to balance

her chakras or heal her body through Reiki, she thought it was all yoga voodoo. But she had time today, so she played along and grabbed a card and a stone. She didn't feel any outside force pulling her pointer finger toward a particular card, but she did like the color of the stone she pulled from the velvet bag. It matched the palette of the tranquil bathroom at Pelican Pointe.

Bonnie was no Yogi Marah and beach yoga wasn't a Bikram level workout, but Kenny was challenged by flowing through sequences and holding balancing postures on the sand and towel that shifted and sank with each movement. She aligned herself with the tennis moms and golf club ladies who were taking the class seriously while she tried to tune out the bachelorette and birthday girls and the women of the book club. Kenny thought those parties had mentally moved on to the next activity on their itinerary.

"Warrior one. Open. Warrior two. Reverse your warrior. Warrior two. Flip your palms. Tuck your chin to the left. Windmill your arms. Side angle. Hold," Bonnie instructed.

Beads of sweat trickled down Kenny's forehead as she stood with her body facing the ocean. Her right knee was bent while her left leg was straight. Her left arm stretched to the sky while her right arm reached for the sand. Her gaze was fixed toward the sun. She regretted lathering the sunscreen on her face, her eyes were on fire. The mixture of sweat, sand, and lotion that dripped into them felt like a mad hornet sting. She blinked her lashes open and shut and hoped tears would wash away some of the burn.

Mental note: Buy eyedrops.

Kenny felt like she had been in right side angle pose for an eternity. As Bonnie slowly guided the group out of the hold, a commotion erupted among the class. Before Kenny was vertical or could make sense of what was going on, she felt something brush between her legs. The force knocked at the back of her knees, threw off her balance and brought her face down in the sand swept towel that was crumbled beneath her.

Oh my God. What just happened?

Kenny heard the giggles. The "oohs" and "aahs" all around her.

"I've heard of goat yoga but never dog yoga!" someone hooted.

Kenny struggled onto all fours and when she picked up her head, she was face to face, staring into big blue eyes of a gray and white shaggy-haired, medium-sized dog. Tail wagging, tongue hanging out, panting like *he* had just been in right side angle for the last five minutes.

"Cliff! Come here, buddy. I'm sorry ladies. Please forgive my wingman," a deep, sexy voice bellowed.

Arrogant. Arrogant jackass. Who lets their dog plow through a yoga group? It's not even a cute dog, Kenny thought.

Still on her knees and wrists and shaking the sand out of her hair, Kenny imagined she resembled something akin to an agitated cat pose. Annoyed at being knocked over and now covered in sand, she cringed when she saw the shadow of a body hanging over her.

"Here, let me help you up," the deep, sexy voice offered.

She took a deep breath and stared at her towel, contemplating the best abrupt, stinging remark she could conjure to express she was not amused by the dog or its inept owner, whose help she did not need. But before she spewed out any nasty words, her breath was taken away again. She glanced up and it was him. Bike Boy was standing over her. With a dog securely cradled under one arm and the other extended like an olive branch.

"I'm sorry. Are you okay? Cliff, apologize to this lovely lady," Bike Boy said. "I don't know what's gotten into him. He usually runs away from people. Never to them. Or through them for that matter!" he joked, and the group broke out into a fit of laughter.

"Oh yea, I'm fine," Kenny nonchalantly replied, ignoring his hand, and rising to her feet as she brushed the sand off her shoulders, careful to keep her face down because she knew she was turning a bright shade of red.

"Well, I'll let you girls get back to it. Cliff and I are late for a beach etiquette class. Namaste."

While the rest of the group giggled, waved, and shouted goodbyes to Cliff and his ridiculously attractive handler, the pair strutted away from the no longer serene semicircle. Kenny could only think about laying in corpse pose. Dead. For the second time in as many run-ins with Bike Boy, she thought being dead would have been a better state than the ones he found her in.

"Okay, ladies, we're nearing the hour mark. Let's get back to our Pranayama. And, Kennedy, maybe you'll find some inspiration from that meet-cute?" Bonnie said with a wink as she encouraged the group to inhale and exhale in unison.

The class picked up from the point of Kenny's unfortunate tumble and Bonnie guided the students through the same sequence on the left side.

"This is your last Chaturanga, make it a strong one. Plank pose. Lower halfway. Upward facing. Downward facing," Bonnie guided.

Kenny was still flushed from embarrassment and now that her body was taking the shape of an inverted pyramid, with all the blood rushing to her head, she knew she'd be a deep shade of purple. Peering through her legs, ass in the air, she found herself staring directly at Bike Boy and his dog. Again. This was not a good look for her. She wished she was one of those mole crabs that could burrow in the sand and disappear.

In contrast, Bike Boy and Cliff looked like the photo that

came in a man's best friend picture frame. Bike Boy sat in the sand dunes with his long muscular legs stretched out in front of him. The royal blue shirt he wore showed off his strong arms and paired well with the navy shorts that were just the right length. He gazed out to the Atlantic Ocean from behind his polarized Ray-Ban aviators and Cliff sat human like next to him. Sea oats waved back and forth behind them.

What are they doing? Kenny thought.

She had kicked off her flip-flops and left them with the pile of other footwear at the end of the beach walk when she arrived for yoga. Which meant that she'd be forced to walk right past Bike Boy and Cliff if she ever wanted to leave the beach.

"Lower to your knees, extend your legs and arms out in front of you and slowly recline to Savasana," Bonnie directed.

After two minutes in final resting pose, the yoga leader invited the group to share their affirmation cards and present their chakra crystals. Kenny's face was blazing; she desperately needed to wash it. She would have killed for one of Marah's chilled lavender washcloths. The build-up of lotion, chlorine, and sweat was on the verge of intolerable before the face-plant into her sandy beach towel, and now it was unbearable. Her eyes were agitated and the whites of them had to be fire-engine red.

Embarrassing.

Kenny tried to stay Zen for the last few moments, but her focus waned. Everything around her was distracting, and she needed class to be over. She sensed the golfers, partiers, tennis players, and readers had lost interest, too. They professed their affirmations at rapid speed and most of them even had the same white crystal, although Kenny missed the meaning of the snowy colored rock because she was too busy fumbling for her own. She couldn't find the chakra stone anywhere and discreetly reached under her towel and shoveled her hands through the sand in search of it.

Bonnie explained with a smile that Bailey's pink quartz crystal signified love and happiness. Then she carried her enthusiastic gaze to Kenny.

How fitting, Kenny thought. *The universe continues to bestow love and happiness on the blushing bride through stones of pink quartz while swallowing my stone for breakfast.*

"Today I am grateful. Today my heart is filled with joy. I see positive in everything today," Kenny read aloud from her affirmation card, trying to sound convincing, rather than sarcastic.

"This is one of my favorite affirmations in the deck," Bonnie exclaimed. "How could we be anything but grateful, with hearts full of joy waking up among this beauty today? And let's see your stone, Kennedy."

"Well, this is embarrassing! I can't find my stone," Kenny tried to crack a smile and force a laugh. "It must've gotten buried in the sand when Cliff and I did our little beach dance. I'm sorry I lost your stone. But it was a beautiful shade of seafoam green."

"Oh, Miss Kennedy, a powerful gemstone chose you. Seafoam green is the color of amazonite and is related to your throat and heart chakras. It encourages creative expression, confidence, and self-love. Inspiration abounds around you. And don't worry about the stone. Someone on these sands will eventually stumble across it and reap the benefits of the strong energy the crystal radiates."

"Thank you, Bonnie. I could use all that energy these days," Kenny said with a genuine smile, feeling slightly recentered.

Maybe there's something to this yoga voodoo, she thought.

"Thank you for practicing with me and sharing your energy with one another. The light within me honors and loves the light within you. Together, let's bring our hands to our third eye space, bow our heads, and say 'Namaste.'"

"Namaste," the group replied in unison.

Kenny folded up her beach towel and was relieved that when she looked to the dunes, Bike Boy and Cliff were gone. She walked toward the ocean and dipped her feet in the water. The waves rolled gently over her toes, past her ankles, and then up her shins. The water was calm and warm and almost drowned her with a sense of inner peace.

Her mind started to wander, thinking about what she *should* be doing on this Tuesday morning. It was a little after 10:00 a.m. so she *should* be listening to the Network Editorial Call, the daily meeting of senior and executive producers who discuss story ideas, breaking news, reporter assignments, and predicted rundowns of what shows will broadcast that day. The Tuesdays after long holiday weekends were notoriously busy in the news world. But Kenny stopped herself. She didn't want to think about anything other than being fully present at this moment, feeling her feet sink deeper and deeper in the sand with each current.

Her stomach growled and she took this as her cue to head back to Pelican Pointe. She sauntered up the desolate beach to collect her shoes. The flip-flops were the only pair left from what had been a large pile just a few moments earlier and when she bent over to pick them up, she saw Cliff charging back down the beach walk.

"You have *got* to be kidding me," Kenny accidentally said out loud, her red, itchy eyes growing larger as the tall, dark, handsome vision in blue following the canine got closer.

She was trapped. There was nowhere to go, except into the Atlantic Ocean, to avoid contact with Bike Boy. No vacant beach chair to sit in. No umbrella to hide under. No stranger to strike up conversation with.

"Hey, I'm J.P. I wanted to apologize, again, for what

happened earlier. I really don't know what got into Cliff. And I think this is yours," the vision said, extending his arm and opening his palm to show a sea-foam green stone.

"Yes! That's my chakra crystal. I've been looking for that," Kenny squealed out in a nervous giggle.

"I'm sorry, it's your what?" J.P. questioned with a funny expression.

"Well, it's not technically mine. It's Bonnie the yoga instructor's crystal. She brought a bag of these stones that are supposed to effuse different energies. This one makes you confident and creative," she babbled, taking the stone out of his hand.

J.P. let out a laugh, took the Ray-Ban's off his face, and nodded, trying to pretend he was interested in the talk about the rock.

"Anyway, I'm Kennedy. Or Kenny. A lot of people call me Kenny," she said putting her hands on her hips and shrugging her shoulders.

She could *feel* J.P.'s ocean blue eyes scanning her up and down. Her empty stomach was doing somersaults, and she timidly cast her gaze to the sand waiting for him to say something. She caught a glimpse of her still unpolished toes and quickly buried them underneath the surface.

Of all things to not cross off my to-do list before I stopped making them! she thought.

"Very nice to meet you, Kenny. Gosh, it was bad enough that Cliff knocked you over. Now you tell me he ran off with your confidence stone in his mouth." J.P. laughed at how ridiculous the statement sounded.

"Don't mention it." She giggled, slowly picking up her gaze again to meet his. She was hoping where her eyes went, her confidence would follow.

"I have to ask you, are you staying at Pelican Pointe?"

He remembers me, Kenny thought. *He remembers that*

awkward moment at Fraser's Circle. He must've followed me to see where the new island idiot was living so he could caution the rest of the bikers on the plantation.

"I am staying at Pelican Pointe. I'm going to be there for the next five weeks," she answered.

TMI, Kenny. He doesn't care how long you are there. He's worried about the safety of himself and fellow bikers.

"Wow, good for you. I thought I saw you doing laps in the pool this morning. I recognized that blue thing in your hair." He motioned to the silk scrunchie.

Kenny wanted to die. Freezing at the intersection was embarrassing but she could blame that on exhaustion. Losing balance in yoga was humiliating, but she could blame it on Cliff. But Bike Boy watching her swim in a dry-rotted Speedo with a blue scrunchie in her hair was catastrophic. And she only had herself to blame. That was a situation she would never be able to recover from.

"Guilty, that was me. I haven't done laps in years, but the water looked incredibly inviting this morning. Are you staying at Pelican Pointe?"

It was a loaded question, but Kenny pulled the trigger. She wasn't sure what she wanted the answer to be. Part of her wanted to see J.P. every day for the rest of her life. The other half wanted to never, ever see him again following three unflattering, chance encounters.

"No, no I'm not staying there. I live down at South Beach. By the Salty Dog? I'm not sure if you're familiar with Sea Pines? But my boss owns Pelican Pointe and sometimes I help him out with odds and ends around the complex."

"Oh, you must work for Mr. Cunningham," Kenny interjected like *she* knew Mr. Cunningham.

"I do. How do you know Mr. C?" J.P. looked surprised.

"I don't *know* Mr. Cunningham. Derek, the guard at the

Greenwood Gate, was telling me what a wonderful gentleman he is," Kenny backtracked.

"How do you know Derek?" J.P. shot back, equally surprised that she knew the plantation security guard.

"Well, I don't really know him either. Just from driving onto the plantation yesterday. People seem to talk to me and tell me things, I guess," she admitted, hoping the conversation would end soon. The butterflies were fluttering, and she was terrified about what other ridiculous comments might fly out of her mouth or what rumbles would erupt from her hungry stomach.

"I could see why people would want to talk to you, Kenny. And I am happy that I ran into you. Or rather, that Cliff ran over you." J.P. smirked. "I was at Pelican Pointe this morning dropping off new beach chairs and bikes for the villa guests. You won't miss them. They're bright orange and will be stored under the pavilion. First come, first served, but feel free to use them when they're available."

"Great, thanks. I'll check them out. I better be on my way. Still have some unpacking to do. Nice to meet you, J.P. And you, too, Cliff." She crouched down and rubbed the shaggy mutt behind the ears.

"See you around, Kenny. Let's go, Cliff." J.P. waved and started to walk down the beach.

She pulled her feet out from the hole in the sand she buried them into, relieved that the daddy-dog duo wasn't headed in her direction. She thought she survived a speaking encounter with Bike Boy, relatively unscathed, when he turned back and yelled, "I'm going to send someone over to check out the chlorine levels. Your eyes are *very* red and agitated and I hope it's not from the pool. I wouldn't want anything to keep you from your morning laps."

Sliding her unkempt feet into her flip-flops, Kenny nodded, threw J.P. a double thumbs up and a wink with one very itchy, bloodshot eye. She wondered how many bad impressions she would have to make before possibly giving off a good one.

She topped off her Swell bottle from the dispenser filled with ice water and oranges that was on the bar at the Beach Club and pulled out her phone to plug Pelican Pointe back into GPS.

Text to Hailey: Hi Hailey, I just finished beach yoga at the Sea Pines Beach Club. Is there a place within walking distance I can get a mani/pedi?

Kenny wasn't sure the message had enough time to be transported all the way to West Virginia and the little bubbles were already populating at the bottom of the phone.

Text from Hailey: Sea Pines Center! (Emoji: hand with pink fingers). Dnt kno name, but take (Emoji: person walking) ins

Kenny flagged the message with a heart and interpreted it to mean there was a salon in Sea Pines Center that didn't require appointments. She was grateful to be learning Hailey-bonics, but even more grateful that she passed Sea Pines Center on her walk back to Pelican Pointe. The situation on her toes surpassed vanity. Her feet looked like they would pose alarm to any podiatrist.

Seventeen

From: Muffin Evans
To: Colby Jackson
Subject: Armchair Detective

Have you heard from the Armchair Detective woman since I emailed her last week to inform her that Border isn't going to publish her depressing piece of nonfiction? I'd like you to get in touch with her. I think she was named after a president. Carter or Kennedy? I've been spending time at the St. Regis and Four Seasons pool decks and all these vacationers are carrying around archaic romantic comedies and outdated book club bestsellers. The women's fiction space needs a new, fresh, beach-read author. That girl is a strong writer. Get her to come up with something. I'm boarding the Bora Bora Lagoon cruise, please don't clog my inbox with trivial questions or thoughts.

—M.E.

Colby slunk down in his chair, calmly wheeled himself closer to the workstation, opened the bottom drawer and pulled out the twelve-inch cotton Dammit Doll customized to look like Muffin Evans that his office Secret Santa gifted him when he was M.E.'s assistant. He started whispering the poem that was embroidered on the doll's midsection.

"Whenever things don't go so well and you want to hit the wall and yell, here's a little Dammit Doll that you can't do without. Just grasp it firmly by the legs and find a place to slam it. And as you whack the stuffing out, yell 'Dammit! Dammit! Dammit!"

By the time Colby reached the last line of the rhyme he was in an all-out tirade, shouting other choice words throughout the G-rated poem and pounding the doll so hard against the corner of his cube that the seams on the mini–Muffin Evan's doll burst, and her insides were flying every-where. A small group gathered to witness the meltdown that was grandiose, even for Colby.

"I *thought* the Manuscript Eater was fasting until Friday. I *thought* she didn't have service in her fancy South Pacific bungalow and wasn't going to be able to destroy anyone until she was stateside. It's amazing to me that someone can be halfway around the world and still chew people up and spit them out before lunch. Before breakfast! Bora Bora is five hours behind New York. She probably didn't even have her kale and berry smoothie, yet!" Colby maniacally shouted as he paced back and forth in his cube.

"Colby, take a breath man," said Ed, Colby's cube mate and one of Border Books' longtime contract managers. "How many times do we have to go through this, we're not saving lives. I know we like to project that image, but I promise you, this author M.E. just shot in the foot will be welcomed with open arms when they wobble into one of those boutique self-publishing houses down in The Village."

"No, this time you're wrong, Ed. This time it is life or death," Colby rebutted. "We're not talking about 'some author.' We're talking about Kenny. She didn't know that I had been assigned to lead the review team. I was going to tell her over drinks last Wednesday that Border made the decision to pass on *Armchair Detective*, but she was already down after losing the big Clinton White interview to NBC, so I didn't have the heart to tell her. That *and* M.E. said she was holding rejection letters until this Friday. I thought I had time."

Ed had a major crush on Kenny since the time he first saw a photo of her on Colby's desk and was elated when Kenny eventually agreed to go on a blind date with him a few months after she broke off her engagement to George. Ed knew Kenny enjoyed cycling so he rented two Citi Bikes, and the pair rode along the Hudson River to the Little Red Lighthouse under the George Washington Bridge. On the way back down, they dropped the bikes at the station on West Eighty-Second Street and Riverside Drive and walked down three more blocks to the Boat Basin for a burger and a beer.

Kenny had zero interest in dating, but she did enjoy the afternoon. A large part of her producing career was building relationships with perfect strangers in the hopes that someday, after many meetings, they would sit down and tell their deepest, darkest secrets on national television. She treated this date and countless others like a casual, no strings attached "booking meeting." It was just another afternoon learning all about someone else's life while carefully constructing and concealing the internal wall that protected her own thoughts, feelings, and emotions.

She didn't need or want anything to come out of the afternoon with Ed, other than to get Colby off her back, so she put on a smile and a pair of Hoka's and literally went along for the ride with the book nerd. Ed, on the other hand, said it was the best date he ever had and pined for her since.

The chemistry was undeniable, he told Colby.

"Oh shit, she's going to be crushed," Ed replied, flashing a crooked smile that screamed with sympathy. "You better pick up that phone right now."

"I'm a dead man, Ed. Kenny left the bar when I went to the bathroom last Wednesday and ignored my calls the rest of the night. I thought the day had gotten to her. Then she sent the message that she was deployed on one of those last-minute assignments, and she'd be unreachable. But now it sounds like M.E. emailed her last week! So, she's known. And I haven't heard from her. I'm sure it's all been festering inside her like a time bomb. I really screwed this one up."

"Is *Armchair Detective* completely off the table? Or is M.E. just playing one of those mind games where she rips apart the draft, comes back a week later with a minor edit and then ships it off for publication? Kenny told me the concept of the book and it seemed catchy. Given her background, I'm sure she's a brilliant writer," Ed questioned.

"*Armchair Detective* is dead in the water. M.E. conveyed that in no uncertain terms. But after spending a week's worth of happy hours at the five-star resorts of Bora Bora, she's decided she wants Kenny to be the next breakout beach-read author." Colby laughed with sarcasm. "Maybe it was one too many Mai Tais or M.E. losing her knack for reading an audience, but my best friend is hopeless at love, not a hopeless romantic. Fictitious worlds of happily ever after are not in her wheelhouse. You know! You were planning a proposal after a three-mile bike ride with the girl, and she couldn't even commit to a second date."

"Thanks for the reminder." Ed rolled his eyes.

"Sorry, but you know what I mean. It would never work. Even if I thought that Kenny could put on her best 'fake it 'til you make it' hat and come up with the next book club bestseller, she'd first have to hear me out. Right now, we're about five years away from that."

Colby picked up the polyester innards of the M.E. Dammit Doll that were scattered across the floor and tossed them and the gutted cloth doll body into the trash can under his desk. He shooed away Ed and the two other onlookers that continued to loiter as if to let them know his one-man performance was over.

"I'm going to Starbucks to wallow over a lemon loaf and a Red Eye. I'll be back later," Colby said as he dragged himself down the hall toward the elevator.

Eighteen

Kenny stretched her arms high over her head and her legs long in front of her. The Egyptian cotton sateen sheets felt smooth and cool on her body. It was her fourth day waking up at Pelican Pointe and, if possible, she was more refreshed and rejuvenated than the days before. It also marked a full week since she turned on a TV, read a newspaper, checked her email, and turned on the "out of office reply" message on Outlook.

She was proud of her efforts sticking to The Hiatus of Life Conditions List since she wrote them down and hung them on the refrigerator. The Pelican Pointe groundskeeper showed her how to work the grill, so she stocked the freezer with poultry and meats to prepare salads with protein for lunches and dinner. She developed a workout plan that incorporated running, swimming, biking, and yoga and committed to completing a version of a duathlon every day. Kenny hadn't had a cocktail since she finished the bottle of Clos du Bois and even tried one new thing by choosing to do a gel pedicure in a bright fuchsia color rather than a traditional pedicure with

Essie's Fiji #348 that colored her toes every day for the last five years.

Kenny evaluated her current headspace and was quite comfortable in the distraction-free zone. She decided that checking in on her email or the state of the world could wait another day and poured a coffee, dragged a white bar stool onto the back deck, and enjoyed her new morning ritual of watching the early risers of Pelican Pointe start their days.

Text from Hailey:(Emoji: apple) & (Emoji: carrot) market 2day! Near SP water tower!

I'll take Farmer's Market for $200, Hailey? Kenny laughed to herself as she read the cryptic message.

Kenny assumed SP stood for Sea Pines, but she had no idea the plantation had a water tower. She thought that water towers were strictly a Jersey Shore thing, until Google confirmed that Kenny's travel agent turned friend was correct. A blue water tower stood at the southern tip of Sea Pines, somewhere near Beach Marker #13.

Text to Hailey: Perfect! I need fruits/veggies. Is it by Tower Beach?

Text from Hailey: Yes, ma'am! Must try key-lime pie (Emoji: cookie)

Kenny's legs were on fire from the previous day's four-mile run up Plantation Drive to Lawton Stables and back, so she had already planned to bike as part of Thursday's duathlon; she didn't have a destination in mind. She had a special spot in her heart for farmers markets. They reminded her of vacationing in Stone Harbor and Cape May as a kid. Garden State farmers peddled their famous Jersey tomatoes and other produce under the beach towns' iconic water towers on Sunday afternoons, capitalizing on the foot traffic of local churchgoers, weekend visitors who were leaving town, and out-of-state vacationers checking in for long weeks and frantically stocking rental houses with an overabundance of food for large groups of families and friends.

Kenny threw on a mesh tank top, yoga pants, and baseball hat and dabbled on bubblegum pink lip moisturizer. She wore all black, which is slimming to any physique, but felt more confident in her appearance than she had in months. She pulled out the brown burlap "Shop Local" bag from under the kitchen sink that she made a habit of carrying everywhere after New York banned plastic bags and started charging for paper ones, double checked that the percolator was unplugged and slid out the back door to take her first bike ride of the trip.

She wheeled the bright orange, three-speed beach cruiser out of the pavilion, down the sidewalk next to the pickleball courts, and to the parking lot so she could get adjusted. She placed her reusable grocery bag, cross body bag, and Swell bottle in the oversized basket that hung from the handlebars and jumped on the extra wide, cushioned triangular seat. The saddle was much more comfortable than seats on the bikes at Fly Wheel or Soul Cycle. She'd never achieve the same kind of cardio output on a bike that had foot brakes and a tiny bell to alert other bikers and pedestrians she was coming up on the rear but she was grateful to have the bike at her disposal.

Kenny pulled out of Pelican Pointe and onto Plantation Drive, before making a left onto a long and windy Baynard Cove Road. It was a hot, humid morning, and she welcomed getting sprayed by sprinkler systems that were watering the golf greens and landscaping beds that lined the paved bike paths. The largely shaded lanes were protected by green shrubs and trees of all shapes and sizes, some whose roots grew so big and strong that the pressure they exerted caused cracks in the pavement. The mini speedbumps could be viewed as a thrill or safety hazard depending on the biker riding over them.

She made a right onto South Sea Pines Drive and was awestruck by the sheer size of some of the newer construction homes. All the houses on the plantation were large, but the height and depth of the mansions she passed dwarfed some of the older homes at the northern end of Sea Pines. Many of the single-family homes were bigger than her prewar Manhattan brownstone that housed twenty apartments. The two worlds seemed farther apart than a twelve-hour drive or two-hour flight.

She reached the corner of South Sea Pines Drive and Wren Drive where she saw a giant temporary sandwich board. The hand-painted piece of cardboard was eye-catching for no other reason than it was glaringly out of place and she was surprised the Sea Pines aesthetic police hadn't removed it.

Sea Pines Farmer's Market Every Thursday
8:00 a.m.–12:00 p.m.
BYOT (Bring Your Own Table)
No spaces are reserved. Event is rain or shine.

Kenny hopped off her three-speed and followed the arrow on the sign that led her down a narrow path to a crushed shell lot, adja cent to a large pavilion. The pavilion bustled with vendors and shoppers. She noticed a cluster of bicycles parked around a steel rack and wiggled the front fat tire of the cruiser into an empty slot between an adult raspberry red tricycle and a much sleeker black Cannondale road bike. The bikes were so compact that she didn't even need to put down the kickstand on the flashy orange bike for it to stay vertical.

Kenny grabbed her burlap bag and made her way up the

long ramp to the large octagonal structure. She quickly observed three different groups of people milling from stand to stand. The weekly shoppers who methodically darted from one table to the next with intention, filling their baskets with produce, eggs, and baked goods. The vacationers or first timers, like Kenny, who weaved in and out of the rows of tables to get a sense of what was available before making a purchase. She imagined they made mental inventories of the bushels of berries and ears of sweet corn they passed, before committing to one stand. The final group of marketgoers were either a mix of island retirees and people who didn't have day jobs or paid undercover agents employed by whomever organized the farmers market to push the goods that were for sale. They meandered around singing the praises of the local farmers and craftsmen and initiated conversation with anyone who would listen.

"Kelly's hydrating face mask and Sleep No More undereye serum are going to be featured in *InStyle* next month. Her products are liquid gold!" Kenny overheard a Botox-injected middle-aged woman telling a tired young mother who was pushing a double stroller past the Kelly's Organics table.

Kenny wanted to smell the soy candles at Kelly's Organics, but speed walked past the table for fear of being cornered by the woman whose forehead didn't move and who talked her into buying a cream she didn't need. The Tupperware bin of unused beauty products disguised as self-care supplies under the sink at The Dollhouse was proof that the promise of any age-defying elixir had Kenny reaching for her wallet.

She continued down a long stretch of blackberries, blueberries, apples, and peaches and suddenly craved a giant mixed fruit salad. The vibrant colors and spacious display presented major curb appeal. She barely came to a complete halt when she stopped at the fruit cart on the corner of West

Sixty-Eighth Street every Tuesday morning and grabbed the closest bunch of bananas and bag of grapes she could reach from the top shelf. The method to her fruit purchasing madness was that the produce on the top shelf was less handled. Until the day she wore flats and realized that 99 percent of the Upper West Side's population over the age of twelve was taller than her and eye level with the top shelf . . . therefore, reaching for that exact spot. Then she started haphazardly grabbing whatever fruit looked like it was going to fall off the overcrowded cart and onto the sidewalk. This experience was completely different. She inspected the apples for damaged spots, smelled the peaches for sweetness, and even taste-tested a few berries before she filled her bag.

She made her way through the entire market and circled back around to pick up Vidalia onions and a head of Parris Island Cos. She didn't know that romaine lettuce came in different varieties and imagined the crunchy leaves tasted the same as any other Caesar salad. But she liked the fancy name and the farmer who explained that the heirloom green was developed by Clemson University in the 1950s and had the highest nutritional value of any lettuce, a bonus since healthy eating was high on her Hiatus of Life Conditions List.

If I had friends or knew anyone on this island, I'd invite them over for a pool side lunch and serve marinated grilled chicken breast over a bed of Parris Island Cos, Kenny thought.

The humidity and high temperatures had to be hovering around the yellowish-orange blocks on the National Weather Service's heat index chart. The crowds dispersed, but Kenny stuck around until she was able to find a spot at the salsa and granola stand. The regulars, tourists, meanderers, and even other vendors beelined for the red and white checked tablecloths lined with jars of salsa and bags of granola. All the marketgoers carried around white paper bags sealed with "The Salsa Man" sticker. She wasn't sure if the product was that good or if people made pity purchases after chowing down on The Salsa Man's abundance of free samples, but she wanted to find out.

Kenny began sampling at the table with the granola. She picked up a handful of small plastic spoons and went down the line of seven bowls filled with different combinations of nuts, oats, dried fruits, seeds, and sweeteners. She scooped up tablespoon sized samples and popped them into her mouth, occasionally taking a swig from her Swell bottle to cleanse her palette.

"These are delicious," Kenny said to The Salsa Man, while she shoveled another bite into her mouth. "Next week I'll eat breakfast before I come. I guess this is why they say to never go to the grocery store on an empty stomach." She laughed.

"Don't sweat it, miss. I always have plenty of samples available for people to enjoy. I wish I could give it all away for free, but the wife won't allow it," The Salsa Man said with a wink and smile.

"That's very generous of you. I'll take a bag of Original Oats and Peanut Butter Crunch, please. And I'd like to pay for them," Kenny joked as she dug in her cross-body bag for cash.

"You can't stop there. Salsa Man's rule is if you try all his granola, you have to sample all of his salsas, too," a man chimed from behind Kenny.

"Oh, it's this guy," The Salsa Man huffed. "When are you going to stop scaring away my pretty, young customers?"

"When you stop telling people where you take your golf lessons. It's not good for business," the man replied.

Kenny could tell from the banter and the expression on The Salsa Man's face that the ribbing was cordial and when she turned around to add to the conversation, she forgot her witty one-liner just as quickly as she came up with it.

"J.P.! Hey, how are you?" she attempted to say in a cheerful, but calm, collected, not too over the top way.

"I had a feeling that was you. I noticed a bright orange bike parked near mine and figured I'd bump into someone from Pelican Pointe. There's no flying under the radar on that thing." J.P. laughed, motioning toward the bike racks.

"Yes, I'm sure you can see me coming from a mile away," Kenny smiled and shrugged.

I came down here to fly under the radar and stay to myself. And the only person who I'd potentially want to know thinks I'm an uncoordinated, granola-eating bad driver who falls ass over tin cups when approached by tiny animals and peddles around the plantation on a bright orange clown bike, Kenny thought.

"But I'm lucky to have it," she quickly continued, forcing herself to make conversation so she didn't accidentally blurt out what she was really thinking. "This whole trip was very spur of the moment. I drove down in a one-way rental car and hadn't given much thought to how I would get around the five weeks I was here."

"That's just one of the many great things about Sea Pines. You don't really *need* a car if you don't mind walking and biking. The plantation has a shuttle, and you can always call an Uber if you're in a jam. You might enjoy not having to rely on a car every day," J.P. assured.

"I never mind walking; I love walking. I live in Manhattan, so my feet have been my main source of transportation for the last decade. They've been more reliable than public transportation lately, too," Kenny said, hoping the joke didn't fall flat.

"You're one of those city girls, eh? I don't know how you all do it. I give you credit but think you must be a little crazy to want to live in that chaos. And that subway, forget it. Don't get me started," he shook his head and crossed his arms.

Kenny raised her eyebrows and gave him an inquisitive

look, hoping he'd continue the story. Although she barely knew J.P., she thought the slightly agitated version of him was adorable.

"If I had a dollar for every time I had to hear this story." The Salsa Man laughed and walked away to help another customer.

"I'll give the abbreviated version. My buddies and I met in New York for a night to catch a Yankees-Red Socks game. We splurged on the fancy field level infield seats, we were pumped. We were having a few beers at the Perfect Pint in Midtown before the game and the bartender talked us out of taking a cab to the stadium. He said it was an easy subway ride up to the Bronx. 'Get on the 4 train and follow the crowd,' he said. Easy enough, right? That's what we did. When we got off the subway, we were in freaking Brooklyn!"

"Oh no! I'm guessing the large crowd you followed were all wearing Nets jerseys and *not* Yankee gear?" Kenny poked.

"You know, I've been asked that exact question once or twice over the years and will continue to plead the fifth. *Anyway*, what do you think?" J.P. raised his hands and looked around referring to the farmers market. "Impressive, right. A few years ago, only about five or six vendors set up. I heard there are over forty booths here today."

"It's great. Aside from the produce and, of course, the granola." She nodded to The Salsa Man who had made his way back down the table and started to pack up his samples. "I'm really impressed with all the art. Such beautiful work. I picked up greeting cards from the oil painter. And those basket weavers, I could watch them all day. Such a complicated and tedious craft, I would never have the patience."

"Yea, it's a creative bunch around here," J.P. said proudly. "Why don't you throw a jar of your famous pineapple salsa in Kenny's bag, put it on my tab." He motioned to The Salsa Man.

"Thanks, but you don't have to pay for my salsa." Kenny giggled.

"Think of it as an apology from Cliff. But I warn you, the stuff is more addicting than any of that granola you were loading up on."

Confirmed. He witnessed me shoveling bite-sized samples of seeds into my big mouth. God, I hope I don't have anything in my teeth.

She wasn't sure she ever wanted to eat again but said, "Well, thank you to Cliff! And I'll heed your warning. Where is your little wingman today?"

"Follow me," J.P. motioned to Kenny while waving goodbye to The Salsa Man.

"Catch you later, man! Nice to meet you, Kenny. Hope to see you next week," The Salsa Man smiled.

"Nice to meet you, too," she replied, picking up her, now very heavy, burlap bag and trying to pretend she wasn't bursting on the inside from J.P.'s "follow me" direction.

"Cliff is down here with his old roommates," J.P. said as he led Kenny down the back ramp of the pavilion.

She hadn't noticed the large fenced-in grassy area behind the pavilion where at least a dozen dogs playfully ran in circles.

"About two months ago, the Hilton Head Dog Shelter started showing up on Thursdays. They quickly turned into one of the biggest attractions. Even if the dogs don't get adopted, it's still a win-win. Canine therapy is good for the soul and the shelter workers are happy the dogs get some much-needed attention and exercise for a few hours. I just happen to be one of the suckers who came for produce one day and eventually ended up with a puppy." J.P. grinned, as he took a sip of the iced coffee he purchased from the Island Beans vendor.

"Walks on the beach, playdates at the farmers market. Cliff seems to have hit the jackpot," Kenny exclaimed.

As soon as she let out the words, she instantly regretted them. The last thing she wanted was to sound jealous of a dog. Even if Cliff was living a life better than most humans. Not to mention in a loving relationship with a doting man.

"How did you pick out Cliff from the rest?" Kenny said in a quick pivot hoping that he wouldn't read into the fact that she wished it was she and J.P. taking walks on the beach and trips to the farmers market.

"Cliff really chose me. I had no intention of getting a dog. I work a lot, and it wouldn't have been fair to adopt one of these guys and then never be home. But every Thursday, I'd stop over to play with the pups, and Cliff would always come right to me, like he did to you on the beach," J.P. said in a way as if he just had a breakthrough in thought. "He was the shy one in the bunch, so it always surprised the workers. Anyway, my boss got wind of the story, he's a big animal guy, and sits on the board at the shelter. A few months ago, the morning after a meeting at the shelter, he showed up at the office with Cliff. He said if I was able to care for him, I should keep him; and if he didn't cause a nuisance, I could bring him to work. He's been a staple at the office, since."

"This Mr. Cunningham does sound like quite the guy. And what about the name? Did your boss choose the name, Cliff, too?" Kenny said as she squatted down to pet the homely looking dog that beelined to the fence as soon as it saw J.P.

"They don't make them like Mr. C anymore. He's the brains behind this market. When he found out that a small group of local farmers, who weren't too well off themselves, were donating their crops to needy families, he started paying them for the produce they gave away. Then he bought this plot of land and erected the pavilion so they could gather and sell their goods to the masses. A lot of these little mom and pop vendors would never be able to afford to have brick and mortar stores."

Kenny nodded with intrigue and admiration. She wondered why inspirational stories like Mr. Cunningham's weren't more widely shared in the news.

"As for Cliff, he came with that name." J.P. shrugged. "It wouldn't have been my first choice but I'm not sure he's the brightest bulb and I thought it would've been too confusing for him to learn a new one," he whispered as he put his hands over the dog's ears so he wouldn't hear the insult. "And my niece loved Clifford the Big Red Dog when she was a toddler. She really talked me into keeping the name." J.P laughed, defending the choice.

Of course, he has a niece. She's probably adorable and they clearly adore each other.

"Well, I think it suits him," Kenny said as she stood to her feet and picked up the burlap bag. "I should start making my way back home. I want to get all of this produce out of the sun and into the fridge."

"Cliff and I need to get back to the office, too. We've got a busy afternoon." he said strapping the leash to the dog's collar and picking him up and over the fence.

"It was great bumping into you, J.P. Thanks, again, for the salsa." Kenny flashed a smile before turning and walking away.

The voice in Kenny's heart told her to naively crane her neck and see if he was watching her walk away like the handsome men in Hallmark movies do. The voice in her head told her to stay the course, move on with her day and forget the whole encounter.

Nineteen

Text from Colby: Kenny, please. PLEASE call me. I need to talk to you. I need to apologize. I need to explain what happened. I need to know you're OK. LYMIB.

Kenny stared at her phone and didn't know whether to pick it up to her ear and call Colby or throw it into one of the decorative landscaping ponds that weaved throughout Pelican Pointe. While she contemplated the best course of action for handling the phone, she burst into tears. A lot of tears. Angry tears and sad tears.

She still felt betrayed and indignant, but she was deeply missing her best friend. A full week of not talking to Colby seemed like an eternity. So much had happened in the past seven days that she felt like she was leading a whole new life. But this text message with all the "I's" infuriated her. She knew at some point she'd have to, would want to, talk to Colby again, and she thought it was better to get the first conversation out of the way while she was still partly mad and not completely hurt.

Kenny aggressively punched Colby's number on the screen and before she had time to think about hanging up, he answered.

"Kenny?" Colby asked sheepishly in a tone she had never heard.

She remained silent on the other end.

"Kenny, are you there?" Colby quietly asked again after a few seconds.

Kenny allowed another long pause and replied, "I'm here. Make this fast."

"I am *so* sorry. Please hear me out before you hang up," he pleaded.

"I'm listening. But if this phone call is all about what *you* want and *you* need, I'm not sticking around," she asserted.

"Of course!" Colby interjected. "I never meant to hurt you, Kenny, and I didn't mean to lie to you either. I *was* charged with leading the review team for *Armchair Detective* and *did* know for a few weeks that it wasn't going to be signed by Border, but I was trying to find the right time to tell you. I planned to break the news to you last Wednesday, but you were so upset about the Clinton White interview that I couldn't bring myself to do it. That was selfish of me. You're a big girl, and I know you would've been able to handle it. But I wasn't sure *I* would be able to handle seeing you more upset than you already were. Which shows how immature I am. Then Muffin told me she was going on vacation and holding rejection letters until she got back so I thought I had a few more days. You're always on me about procrastinating. Once again, you were right."

Kenny blew her nose and wiped her eyes as the tears streamed down her face. She knew he wasn't allowed to disclose the names of authors or manuscripts that were under his review until a decision about publication was made and the author was alerted. She also knew it wasn't his sole decision not to publish *Armchair Detective.* He read the manuscript nearly as many times as she had before she submitted it to Border. She wondered if she was being unfair to him. Maybe she exaggerated her anger toward him.

He continued to ramble and apologize on the other end of the line and Kenny could hear him become more hysterical with each second that she remained silent.

"Fine! Colby, stop. I forgive you," she tried to stay stern and not fall to pieces.

"I was heartbroken when I got the rejection email from Muffin. But the most hurtful part of the whole thing was the cavalier attitude you had all last Wednesday. I *know* you can't talk about the projects you are working on, and I *know* you aren't the sole decision maker. But when I was down and out because of the Clinton White interview, you downplayed it and told me I was being dramatic. You should've let me vent. And then you talked me into meeting you for a drink I didn't want and proceeded to list the areas of life where I'm lacking. You should've left me alone. All of this while harboring a secret that you knew was going to *really* upset me! It wasn't fair. None of it was fair," Kenny lashed, feeling weight lifted with each word coming out of her mouth.

"I treated you like a straight man would treat a woman!" he shrieked. "I've tried my whole life to not be one of those guys, and now I've gone and acted just like them to the person who means more to me than anything," he wept.

Her sobs morphed into a fit of uncontrollable laughter.

"Wait, now you're laughing? I can't keep up! The silent treatment, the mixed emotions, and reactions. The anger, the sadness, the underserved forgiveness. It's too much. I am so sorry. Please forgive me for causing you to be this way," Colby dramatically carried on.

"Colby," Kenny caught her breath, "I'm fine. We're fine. Just don't let it happen again."

"Never. Never again, Queen," he said as he regained his composure. "Can you tell me where you are? Are you away for work? Or did you just tell me that, so I'd leave you alone?"

"I really am in South Carolina for the next few weeks," she answered, contemplating how much of the truth she should share, "but I can't get into the details now."

"Of course, I understand. Be careful doing whatever it is that you're doing. And, um, if you get any free time Muffin is interested in you writing a book," Colby cautiously mumbled.

"What? What did you just say!" Kenny cut him off.

"She emailed me from Bora Bora. She thinks you would make a brilliant rom-com writer. The Manuscript Eater decided the women's fiction space needs a fresh author and believes you're capable of churning out best-selling beach reads," he said in his best faux-cheery voice.

"You have *got* to be kidding me! Did she even read *Armchair Detective?* Does she know I won an Emmy for a miniseries about mass shootings and a Peabody for an expose on police brutality? Romance and chick-flicks aren't exactly in my repertoire." She chuckled out of both amusement and offense.

"I know, I know. At least give it some thought. If Muffin Evans wants to publish a new writer in this genre, she will. Why shouldn't it be you?" he rhetorically asked, although he assumed the proposal fell on deaf ears.

"Yea, probably not. I'm hanging up now," Kenny said in a way that relayed to Colby things between them were okay again.

"Thanks for forgiving me, Kenny. Love you, mean it, bi-yee!"

Kenny had a habit of walking around aimlessly while she talked on the phone and when she hung up with Colby, she found herself leaning against the His and Hers sinks in the tranquil bathroom. She turned and looked at herself in the mirror and was surprised by what she saw. She hadn't honestly looked at herself in a long time; and when she did, it was usually only for a quick second to pluck a stray eyebrow or curl her eyelashes.

Although her eyes were still glassy and red from crying, the person staring back at her had a healthy look of relief. The stress Kenny went to great lengths to internalize always crept out on her face, in the forms of lines on her forehand and bags under her eyes. Even the expensive Christian Dior Airflash spray foundation couldn't conceal the anxiety. Today she didn't need that foundation, her complexion had a sun-kissed glow, and the lines and bags weren't visible.

Kenny turned on the spigot, splashed water on her face and massaged a soothing foam wash into her nose, cheeks, forehead, and chin. She worked up more of a sweat than she anticipated while riding her bike and was thoroughly enjoying the few moments of pampering when she was startled by a pound at the back of the house. She patted her skin dry and slowly made her way out of the bedroom. She didn't know anyone on the island and wasn't expecting any deliveries, so presumed the knocker was at the wrong villa and wasn't in a hurry to answer the door.

Thud. Thud. Thud. After the third bang she dropped the towel on the counter and made her way through the bedroom to the door with more urgency.

A short man with olive skin and jet-black hair wearing white painter's pants, work boots, and a blue and white tie-dyed T-shirt stood on the other side of the sliding glass door, holding a duffel bag the size of a toolbox. The man raised his fist and he was about to take another swift rap at the door when he saw Kenny and unclenched his fingers, giving an energetic wave in her direction.

"Hi, how are you?" Kenny asked as she slid open the door.

She never answered the door for unexpected visitors in New York but noticed herself letting her guard down over the last few days, for better or worse. She hoped that if this man did come knocking with the worst of intentions, someone from the pickleball court or pool deck would be able to identify him in a lineup.

"Hello, miss. I'm Jose. I'm with Low Country Hospitality's grounds crew and wanted to let you know that I'll be servicing the pool here at Pelican Pointe. I'll stop by a few times a week for maintenance but if you notice anything needs tending to between visits, let me know," he said slipping her a business card.

She knew her eyes were red and agitated the day she bumped into J.P. and Cliff at beach yoga but didn't think they made an impression that warranted a house call from the property manager's pool boy.

"Nice to meet you, Jose. Thank you for keeping the pool in pristine condition," she smiled, although she found the gesture a bit odd and couldn't help but wonder if the chipper cabana boy knocked on the patio doors of all the guests to hand-deliver his business card.

"It's my pleasure, miss." Jose beamed.

Jose's smile was infectious, and Kenny could tell he genuinely loved his job.

"Oh, I almost forgot," he said as he balanced the duffel bag on a bent knee. "This is for you, enjoy," Jose said as he pulled a small brown lunch bag from the front pocket of the duffel and handed it to Kenny before spinning on his heels and hopping down the steps.

Kenny peered into the brown bag and pulled out a plastic

flip-top sandwich bag that was secured with a blue twist tie. Inside were four perfectly shaped sand-colored cookies topped with drizzled frosting and graham cracker crumbs. The presentation reminded her of a snack she would have bought at a grade school bake sale during Catholic School's Week twenty years ago.

There was also a handwritten note, another thing Kenny hadn't seen much of since her grade school days. The writer in her admired the perfect penmanship that was complimented by dark black ink from an expensive ballpoint pen.

Kenny,

These are Miss Luana's famous Key Lime Pie cookies, an island delicacy. I got her last bag at the market today and thought I should share them with the new girl in town.

J.P.

She almost burst. This island hottie sending her cookies by way of an unsuspecting pool boy was almost too much for her jaded heart to handle. She hadn't felt this level of giddiness because of a boy since third grade when Greg Loftus taped a heart-shaped Reese's cup to the back of a cardboard *Space Jam* valentine when he gave the rest of the class bags of Skittles.

She fumbled with the twisty tie and took a small bite out of the zesty, airy cake-like cookie. It tasted like heaven and the gesture made her feel like she was walking on a cloud. She closed her eyes and finished the cookie, savoring each delicate bite.

*Text to Hailey: These key lime cookies might be the best
thing I've ever tasted (Emoji: smiley face with heart eyes)
Thx for the recco!*

The cookie was delicious, but the emoji was more reflective of how Kenny was feeling about the cookie sender.

Text from Hailey: Yippee!!! (Emoji smiley face: licking lips)

Twenty

Cliff darted up the wide brick staircase and ran back and forth until he found the rolled-up copy of *The Wall Street Journal* that was underneath a teak Adirondack chair on the wrap around porch at the Liberty Oaks Clubhouse. He scooped it up between his teeth and stood at attention at the front door while he waited for J.P. to park his bike and drop off the golf bag at the cart garage.

"Good boy," J.P. exclaimed like he was cheering on a toddler who went to the bathroom on a training potty for the first time.

J.P. pushed down on the brass lever handle and before the door was cracked the slightest, Cliff barreled through and ran down the long hallway, slid on the hardwood floor as he rounded the corner at the end of the corridor, and dropped the paper at Mr. Cunningham's feet.

"You really outdid yourself with training this mutt, kid," the jolly old man yelled to J.P. who popped his head in the doorway in time to catch Mr. Cunningham slip Cliff treats that he swore he never gave until after lunchtime.

"Busted! I knew you were sneaking him morning treats," J.P. accused.

"Cool your horses, he's a growing boy. Who could afford to put on a few pounds, I might add," Mr. Cunningham said as he took the newspaper out of the plastic sleeve.

"He doesn't eat lunch on the days he has morning treats. I know this from experience. When my grandfather would sneak me midmorning Tastykakes, I wouldn't eat lunch either. He and I denied our secret to his grave. At his funeral, my mom pulled me aside and said she knew we lied to her all those years. She suspected the days I wasn't hungry for lunch were the days he filled me with junk food. You can't bullshit a bullshitter, Mr. C." J.P. laughed.

"Let me ask you this, Jonathan," Mr. Cunningham asked, trying to sound serious. "If your mother called out your grandfather, the way you just called me out, would he have stopped giving you Tastykakes?"

"Absolutely not, that was our thing," J.P. conceded knowing where the conversation was headed.

Mr. Cunningham *always* had the last word. But the baffling, albeit frustrating, thing was that he usually deserved it.

"That's what I thought. I didn't have the privilege of knowing your grandfather, but my instincts tell me he was a wise man." Mr. Cunningham winked and dropped another Milk-Bone biscuit to the ground. "I bet you were a tall, lanky kid. You probably needed the extra weight, too."

Cliff was curled up on the overstuffed deep blue velvet couch next to Mr. Cunningham who motioned for J.P. to sit in one of the wingback chairs on the other side of the coffee table.

"Have a seat, you've got time before your first clinic. How are things looking at Pelican Pointe? I had a meeting with the contractor yesterday. Villas #10 and #11, the ten-sleepers, should be ready for occupancy in the next two weeks. That's a whole month ahead of schedule," Mr. Cunningham said.

"That's great. Did you loop in marketing and reservations? They should start advertising and really talk up the renovated kitchens and new appliances. I read in *Conde Naste Traveler* that vacation rentals for the holidays are on the uptick. Thanksgiving is right around the corner."

"I'm impressed, Jonathan. Looks like there might be a hotelier underneath all of that after all," Mr. Cunningham said waving his index finger up and down pointing to J.P.'s tailored charcoal gray golf pants and white heathered polo.

"Let's not push it, Mr. C. I was reading *Traveler* because the floating green at Coeur d'Alene was the cover story. Imagine how many balls those divers fish out of the water each season?" J.P. laughed, trying to change the course of the conversation, regretting that he let it slip he read the magazine and paid attention to industry trends.

Over the past seven years, J.P. worked as the head golf pro at Liberty Oaks Golf Course. He was the sought-after instructor at the acclaimed course for beginners, seasoned golfers, and every level of player in between. His many years on the PGA tour circuit helped elevate the course's popularity among professionals, amateurs and talented youth who had potential to grow and maybe one day compete in the ambitious sport. His congenial personality set a tone of camaraderie that was evident in the clubhouse and on the greens. J.P. effortlessly ran the course with little direction or distraction; and Mr. Cunningham often, and not so subtly, suggested that his managerial skills and style would easily transfer to bigger business models.

"Just like this golf course, Low Country Hospitality and my philanthropies aren't going to run themselves when I die. Or worse, retire." Mr. Cunningham laughed at his own joke.

"Since I don't see either of those two scenarios happening

any time soon, I think all of your business ventures are just fine with you at the helm." J.P. nervously took a swig from the water bottle he was holding.

J.P. always got uncomfortable when Mr. Cunningham nonchalantly talked about death, retirement, or J.P. taking on a larger role in his mentor's operations. J.P. considered himself an expert at golf and people. In his mind, the two went hand in hand and were the reason why the golf course enjoyed such success under his direction. He enjoyed the latitude and freedom Mr. Cunningham afforded him in running the prized greens, but the thought of taking on a larger role in Mr. Cunningham's vast organizations terrified him. J.P. had Mr. Cunningham on a pedestal and didn't imagine anyone was capable of climbing the podium he stood atop.

"Anyway, Pelican Pointe looked great when I stopped by to drop off the bikes and beach chairs. The exterior of all the units has been powered washed, the grill area is being kept clean, and the landscaping is under control. Do we need to post Alligator Safety signage around the koi ponds?" J.P. asked.

"I'll place the order today. They should've been up. We don't need the South Carolina Department of Natural Resources hassling us. Two enough?"

"That should be fine," J.P. agreed. "Also, I asked Jose to keep an extra eye on the chlorine levels in the pool. I noticed one of the renters may have been having a reaction," he continued.

"Trade magazines and paying attention to visitors. How about that?" Mr. Cunningham nodded and smiled.

"I wouldn't say I was paying *attention* to any visitors. It was a mere observation. I mean," J.P. stuttered not realizing he was smiling like a goof and uncontrollably tapping his right foot.

"Looks like I struck a nerve! Who is she?" Mr. Cunningham let out a belly laugh.

"Who's who?" J.P. coolly questioned, making a conscience effort to still his foot and make a serious face.

"The girl. I've seen it before Jonathan. Some woman has gotten into that usually cool, calm, and collected head of yours. I may be elderly but I'm not an idiot." The older gentleman pulled his glasses down to the brim of his nose and peered over the lenses like he was staring through J.P.'s soul.

"You don't know what you're talking about, Old Man." J.P. rolled his eyes. "Remind me why I open myself up to this harassment every morning."

"Because I cut your checks," Mr. Cunningham said matter-of-factly and slid his glasses back up to his eyes.

Last word, J.P thought.

"Let's go, Cliff. This man is looking to stir trouble for us," J.P. joked as he sprung to his feet and made his way to the door.

"Don't forget I'm driving down to Georgia tonight to check out that chain of family-owned resorts on Jekyll Island. I think I'll spend a few days exploring the area and assess if it's worth the investment. Why don't you and Cliff stay at the house? I'm having work done in the master suite on the first floor and hate to have workers coming and going when I'm out of state," Mr. Cunningham said.

J.P. saluted with his right hand. "You got it, boss."

Twenty-One

Kenny's head was partially underwater and the rest of her body mid flip-turn when she heard wind chimes ringing from her phone indicating the forty-five-minute workout was over. Today was the first day since she started swimming that she was still powering through the water when her alarm went off. It was also the first time in fifteen years that she book-ended her laps with the half-somersault tumble to change directions.

She waded to the side of the pool where her phone and Swell bottle lay on a towel. She dried off her hands, took a long swig of water, and picked up the device to swipe off the alarm.

Text from Hailey: TGIF! Wi-Fi 2day @ noon. Need ½ hr.

Kenny hadn't gone nearly two weeks without a reliable internet connection since her eleventh birthday when her parents surprised her with an AOL TV keyboard that hooked up to the box television set in the family room. What surprised her most about the past twelve days without the luxury was that she barely missed it at all.

Text to Hailey: Great! Do I need to be at the villa?

Text from Hailey: Nope!

Kenny was relieved. The temperatures were expected to hover in the low nineties complimented by a sky filled with sunshine, so she planned to spend the afternoon on the beach. She hadn't slept much the night before and was looking forward to taking a long nap on the sand. The insomnia was a combination of trying to squash the new crush jitters that intensified with each unintentional run-in with J.P.—which further intensified with the pool boy's delivery of Miss Luana's key lime pie cookies—and Muffin Evans's proposition that she author a light-hearted, romance novel.

Kenny knew she was equipped to handle the consuming and dizzying heart-skips-a-beat, head-in-the-clouds, can't-stop-smiling phenomenon that overcame her when she saw or thought about J.P. The solution was simple. Ignore it. Ignore him. Ignore the feelings. She was fluent in ignoring the impractical. The brief hiatus of life would quickly culminate and any further meetings with Bike Boy and his dog would end just as abruptly as they started.

The same wasn't true for Muffin Evans. The Manuscript Eater would always be a reality in Kenny's life if she maintained any aspiration of becoming a published author. Kenny knew nothing about writing women's fiction, nor did she care to learn, but thought it might behoove her to entertain the suggestion. Colby casually reminded Kenny during their make-up phone call that Mary Kay Andrews was a serious journalist at the *Atlanta Journal Constitution* before writing thirty feel-good bestsellers. Ina Garten worked in nuclear energy policy and budgeting for the Carter and Ford administrations prior to authoring over a dozen cookbooks. Kenny appreciated these women's career pivots; although she was certain they did so on their own accord and not because some egotistical book dictator predetermined their fate and contributions to the literary world.

Kenny hung her damp towel over the side of the back patio wall and poured herself another cup of coffee while she debated whether she should shower before heading to the beach to bake in the South Carolina sun for the rest of the day. She pulled out the ingredients to assemble a yogurt parfait for breakfast with the granola and fruit she got at the farmers market, but then reached for the bag of key lime pie cookies instead of a mixing bowl. The indulgence didn't exactly meet the early morning nutritional requirements Kenny tried to consume but the sooner she got rid of the cookies, the easier it would be to forget that J.P. sent them. She'd shove the hand-written note somewhere in her overstuffed planner and maybe stumble across it in five years when she decided to house clean drawers.

Problem solved.

To avoid the possible embarrassment of being called out by a stranger she may encounter on the beach for another potential bout of irritated eye syndrome, Kenny showered off the sweat and chlorine from her morning swim. She went a step further and broke out a new razor to shave her legs for her solo Friday afternoon outing. As she lathered her legs with lavender-scented foam, she was briefly thrown back to the idyllic Gillette Venus commercials. The silky-smooth calves of long-legged women flashing one succinct knee pop after another across the television screen like the Radio City Rockettes laying across color coordinated beach towels on milky white sands against a cloudless button blue sky. If one close shave could have those women feeling, looking, and thinking like goddesses, maybe it could work for her, too.

Text to Hailey: Great! Then I'm heading to beach (Emoji: smiley face with sunglasses)

Text from Hailey: Jelly! (Emoji: pink bikini) (Emoji: palm tree)

Twenty-Two

"Cliff! Cliff, get over here. Now." J.P. said in a stern whisper.

The defiant dog stared his owner straight in the face, eyes wide and teeth clutching a bright yellow tennis ball. His grin reminiscent of a cheshire cat.

J.P. squatted a few feet from the corner of the bright pink square beach blanket where Cliff had plopped down. He impatiently tapped the long-handled ball launcher toy on the sand in front of him, hoping the puppy would return the ball so he could lob it down the beach and the two would be on their way before the unsuspecting beach-napper was abruptly awoken from her slumber. He couldn't help but think that maybe Mr. Cunningham was correct about bribing and rewarding Cliff with treats. He wished he had a pocket full of them now.

While J.P. quietly attempted to reel in his intrusive pet, he understood why the dog chose that exact spot on the vast beach to settle. The sleeping sunbather that Cliff was lying next to looked content, at peace, in a happy place. She appeared to be in a bubble of calmness. The slightest smile of her lower lip, the only part of her face peeking out from underneath a strategically placed wide-brimmed straw hat protecting her from the sun, would make any passerby wonder what she was dreaming about. Her legs were stretched in front of her with feet splayed to the sides. Her arms rested on her hip bones and the bright Barbie pink nail polish on her fingers drew attention to a sunburned stomach that probably should've been covered like her face.

The waves crept closer and closer to the beach blanket with each current and J.P. assumed the woman had been in a deep sleep for a considerable amount of time. Surrounding beach goers had already moved their coolers, chairs, and sand toys closer to the dunes in anticipation of the 3:47 p.m. high tide.

J.P. was about to strike the ball launcher on the sand again when a large wave made it all the way to his ankles, startling him and causing him to instinctively jump to his feet. When J.P. leapt, Cliff dropped the ball from his mouth and let out an alarmed howl. The sunbather sprung from her torso like a jack in the box and the straw hat slid to her knees which she instinctively pulled up and into her chest.

"Kenny!" J.P. blurted out in a voice that wasn't as suave as usual. "I didn't realize that was you. I'm so sorry to startle you. Again," he stammered, looking bewildered.

He sensed her insecurity as she jumped to her feet and pulled a light blue Salty Dog racer back tank over her head, covering up her half-naked body. He hoped his clumsiness wasn't the cause of her unease.

"Hi, J.P.," she sheepishly smiled, still in a sleepy haze. "And hello there, Cliff," she said directing her gaze toward the dog.

J.P. couldn't help but notice that Kenny's eyes were smiling as much as her mouth.

"We rescued you from high tide just in time," he smirked as he regained his composure and grabbed a corner of the beach mat. "Let's move this back. It'd take hours to dry if it got crushed by waves."

"Thanks," Kenny beamed as she picked up the opposite corner and tugged the beach mat closer to the dunes. "What time is it? I must've been sleeping longer than I thought," she giggled.

"It's almost four o'clock, Sleeping Beauty," J.P. answered.

"Oh, here we go," Kenny exaggerated an eye roll. "And I guess your role in this is the knight in shining armor who saves the damsel in distress from the aggressive late afternoon whitecaps, just before they swallow her whole." She sarcastically motioned to the gently rolling waves lapping on the sand.

"You're welcome," J.P. grinned ear to ear.

He sensed the sarcasm was an attempt to mask anything she might say to come out as blatantly flirty.

"I really don't know how you'd survive these few weeks down here without me," J.P. said while he slipped out of his REEF sandals and sat down on the mat. "Mind if I sit for a minute?" an already reclined J.P. asked in a way that didn't warrant a response.

"Of course, have a seat," Kenny said as she unzipped her insulated Bogg bag and pulled out two sparkling waters. "Why are you in those long, dark pants? It must be ninety degrees," she exclaimed as she sat down next to J.P. and handed him a Pellegrino.

"Tell me about it. The big guy won't budge when it comes to the dress code. Even in the middle of July, he's a stickler." J.P. rolled his eyes as he pulled up the bottom of his pant legs. "Cheers!" He lifted the bottle, twisted off the cap and took a gulp.

"The big guy being Mr. Cunningham?" Kenny asked, assuming she already knew the answer.

"Yeah. Mr. C doesn't have too many quirks, but he insists

on long pants. He thinks they bring a level of 'profession-alism and old-fashioned class that shorts don't,'" J.P. said using air quotes and deepening his voice as if to mimic the old man.

"Respectable. I mean you look great; it just seems like an odd uniform choice for someone who's running around in the heat all day."

J.P. caught Kenny's eye just as she accidentally doled out an innocent compliment and suddenly felt vulnerable himself.

"I should do more running. Or at least walking and lifting. I've been relying too much on carts these days. I need to keep this in check." He straightened his back and tapped the midsection of his polo shirt.

J.P. instantly regretted that one swift move. He hoped Kenny didn't perceive him as a meathead or a guy whose main concern was six pack abs and a tight ass.

"Carts? What kind of carts?"

"Golf carts. What kind of cart did you think I meant." J.P. laughed. "What other kind of carts are there?"

"I wasn't sure what you meant. There are utility carts, hand carts, valet carts," Kenny rattled off while striking her fingers.

J.P. cracked a smile, realizing that Kenny had no idea who he was. Although J.P. preferred to keep a low profile, he was a local celebrity around Hilton Head. He was considered the best golf instructor in the southeast region and could've chosen to instruct at any course in the country after retiring from his professional golf career. If people inside the golf community didn't recognize his face, they knew his name. If people outside of the golf community didn't know his name, they recognized his face because of his picture on the Liberty Oaks Golf Course ads that were everywhere from church bulletins and weekly coupon circulars to real estate brochures and flyers in *The Sea Pines Sentinel.*

To Kenny, he was nothing more than a billionaire's gopher. And J.P. was fine with that.

"Yes, golf carts are my preferred cart. When I'm not delivering beach chairs and bicycles to Mr. Cunningham's rental properties, I give golf lessons at Liberty Oaks," J.P. said, downplaying his position at the esteemed course that was on par with Augusta and Pebble Beach.

"Why do you know so much about carts? What is it that you do?" He playfully nudged Kenny's left arm with his right elbow. "Are you an heir to Home Depot?"

"I'm a news producer at WBS." She laughed, returning the slightest nudge. "Which means I know a little bit about a lot of things. Some of which are ridiculous, like my unusual knowledge of carts."

"I bet that's an awesome job. Maybe not whatever story you did about different methods of transporting objects, but it sounds like most days wouldn't be boring. Do you have a certain beat?"

"It's a pretty cool job. *Most* days. It's never boring, although some days I wish it were. I've reported on everything from presidential campaigns to potty training but have covered the world of true crime and murder mysteries for a while now." She repeated the generic canned answer she'd given countless times before when people asked about her career. "I know so much about carts thanks to my camera and sound crews who lug enormous amounts of audio and visual equipment wherever they go and are always looking for the fastest, quickest, and easiest ways to move the gear. We, the producers, ask them to film and shoot interviews in impossible locations—like on top of the New Years Eve ball in Times Square or on a tightrope over the Grand Canyon." Kenny laughed. "Sometimes watching these guys wrangle their equipment to wherever we want them to be is more impressive than the story we're filming."

"That's very cool. I geek out when shows share behind the scenes footage of that kind of stuff. And I must admit *Inside Edition* is a guilty pleasure of mine, so I'm pretty tuned into the true crime zeitgeist."

"*Inside Edition*?" Kenny flailed her arms in the air. "I didn't see that coming. You strike me as the type of person whose television only turns to ESPN. Why *Inside Edition*? You don't fit the infotainment demographic."

"Comical. Embarrassing. I know." J.P. laughed, uneasy that he let this stranger in on such a ridiculous indulgence.

"A few summers ago, I had a rather well-off, high maintenance client. She and her husband had their yacht parked at Harbour Town for the summer. The husband decided his housewife needed a hobby, to get her off the houseboat, and 'gifted' her hours of golf lessons almost every day for three months. She, however, had no desire to learn golf and preferred to spend our lesson time talking about her husband's illicit affairs and what was broadcast on *Inside Edition* the previous night. They eventually sailed back down to Palm Beach, but I kept watching. The content is good fodder for small talk during lessons when there's an awkward silence."

"Look at that. *Inside Editon* impacting the lives of one frustrated golf instructor and scorned lover at a time, with their hard-hitting journalism," Kenny joked.

"Exactly. Speaking of scorned lovers, how about the Dr. Love saga? I'm sure you know all about that one. He seems like a real nut!" J.P.'s face lit up like he was personally invested in the story.

"Unfortunately, I do. I know Clinton White and his saga all too well." Kenny's face dropped.

J.P. unintentionally hit a nerve. He never fully comprehended idioms in English class. But they suddenly made sense. He wished he could eat his words.

"Oh no. You're not the producer, are you? If you are, I'm so sorry. I never would have brought him up," J.P. said apologetically, looking alarmed.

"What producer?" Kenny asked. "I'm the producer assigned to the story for WBS?" she questioned him, confused.

"The network producer Dr. Love tried to seduce?" J.P. asked with hesitation in his voice.

"Oh God, no!" Kenny clarified. "I've been in his company and he's very charismatic, a real charmer, but I never misconstrued that for him coming onto me. In fact, most men and women accused of murdering their spouses are very bewitching toward the media. Is that the storyline *Inside Edition* has been leading with this week?" Kenny continued nonchalantly.

"Whew! I would have felt like a real jackass. The identity of the producer hasn't been revealed so I got nervous for a second. But, yes, *Inside Edition* broke the story last night," J.P. replied.

"I haven't watched the news or checked my email since I've been down here." She paused. "I didn't really have a choice because the internet and cable weren't hooked up in the villa, but it's been surprisingly refreshing. The whole reason for me ending up here in the first place was a long-overdue, dire need to disconnect and recharge. Clinton White and a bottle of wine forced me to pull the trigger," she lamented.

J.P.'s eyes widened, and he looked at her like he was waiting for her to continue the thought.

"Wait!" she shouted, throwing her hands in the air again. "That came out all wrong. First 'pull the trigger' was a poor choice of words given that Ada White is assumed dead." She retracted. "In a nutshell, my network WBS and I were supposed to be getting the first interview with Clinton White. Then we got scooped by NBC. I drowned my sorrows in a bottle of wine, came across a pop-up ad for Pelican Pointe while drunkenly surfing the internet, and emailed the reservations department with my credit card information. Apparently, I requested an immediate check-in date," she shook her head.

J.P. sensed undertones of failure mixed with embarrassment in Kenny's otherwise optimistic, nonchalant delivery of how and why she ended up on Sea Pines. He surprised himself by how well he thought he was understanding this woman he just met.

"I'm happy you're here but that's extreme for an interview that never aired! I can't imagine where you'd be right now if the interview *was* broadcast," J.P said. "Probably in Bora Bora. Or one of those places you hear about but don't think exist."

"What are you talking about? It aired last Wednesday. It was a big primetime event that the network—and every other media outlet under the sun—teased for a week. NBC pulled out all the stops for the shebang. I'm sure they'll get an Emmy nod for the interview," Kenny argued.

"You really are out of the loop! NBC didn't air the interview. It was all over the headlines. I'm not exactly sure what happened. There was talk of violated gag orders and cease and desist letters, angry attorneys, and an irate judge. There was a lot of legal jargon in the reports that was over my head. But, whatever happened, NBC aired two hours of *Law and Order* reruns last Wednesday rather than the much-anticipated Clinton White interview."

Kenny leapt to her feet, threw back her neck with her hands on her head, took a deep breath, and then put her hands on her knees and hovered over J.P. who was staring up at her with a look of bewilderment.

"Do you know what this means? This means my life and career isn't over! I want to kiss you right now!"

J.P.'s bewilderment turned to amusement. He couldn't wait to hear what was going to come out of Kenny's mouth next. He didn't know her well, but he was thoroughly entertained by the show unfolding in front of him.

"Oh my God," Kenny blurted. "Did I say that out loud? I don't *really* want to kiss you right now. It's just an expression, you know? I don't even *know* you. It would be like kissing a stranger. And, well, who goes around kissing strangers? People do, but not people like me. Don't worry, I don't do that."

"I'm just going to sit right here and let you have your moment," J.P. said with a wink and provoking smile. "It seems you have a lot of thoughts flying through that pretty little head, so I'll give you time to talk through them."

J.P. watched as Kenny ungracefully plopped back down on the mat next to him, extended her legs long in front of her, crossed her ankles and stared quietly out into the ocean.

J.P. knew he was spot-on with his internal assessment. Thoughts flew through Kenny's head like cars on the autobahn, at a fast and furious pace. But she grew comfortable driving through the chaos and loud noise of life at rapid speeds. That's how J.P. operated, too.

He hoped that, even just for this moment, she would find peace in the sound of crashing waves, the intoxicating smell of salt air, the warmth from the sun and gentle breeze. And maybe silence.

"I'm sorry about that." Kenny clenched her teeth and shook her head. "In case it wasn't abundantly clear, the Clinton White story has been a source of tension in my life lately. I'll save you the details but losing that interview took a hit on my ego and career. So much so that I abruptly left town for five weeks to recharge. This trip is, by far, the most spontaneous thing I've ever done. I don't even cross Central Park from the West Side to the East Side of Manhattan after 7:00 p.m. without weighing the pros and cons."

"No need to apologize, Kenny," J.P. said in a sympathetic tone. "You found yourself in the right place if you needed to get away from it all. Thinking and reflecting and processing life while sitting on this beach has worked wonders for me over the years," he continued as he picked up the green tennis ball, tossed it and directed Cliff to go fetch it.

"Thanks, J.P." Kenny smiled and lifted her oversized tortoise shell sunglasses to her face.

"As for the kiss, the ladies on *Sex and the City* went around hooking up with strangers all the time. If that's how you New Yorkers deal with things, don't let a good ole' Southern boy like me stop you." J.P. tried to change the trajectory of the conversation from serious and personal back to flirty and casual.

"Something tells me you're not as good and naïve as you pretend you are, Casanova. *And* you don't sound like you're from the South." Kenny laughed and playfully tapped her foot against his leg.

"Look at you go all investigative reporter on me. I might have been born and raised in Ohio, but I picked up this Southern charm years ago."

"I can't disagree with that. It was very thoughtful of you to have Jose hand-deliver the key lime pie cookies to my door yesterday when he came to check on the pool. I'm not sure I ever tasted anything like those."

"I wasn't sure they were going to make it to you." J.P. smirked insinuating Jose might've eaten them mid-delivery. "Those cookies are like crack and Miss Luana is the only dealer on the island with the recipe."

"I try to stay away from sweets, but I had no control when it came to those. I finished them for breakfast this morning."

"They have that effect on people. Miss Luana is the head of housekeeping for Low Country Hospitality and when she took them to a company potluck picnic a few summers ago, people nearly lost their minds. She refuses to share the family recipe so people can only get their fix on Thursdays when she bakes for the farmers market. Occasionally, she'll make a few dozen for a coworker's birthday or a holiday."

"Mr. Cunningham ought to take a play out of the Double-Tree's playbook and offer Miss Luana's cookies at check-in."

"You know about those warm front-desk chocolate chip cookies?" J.P. asked with a smile.

"I'm on the road so much for work that I keep a packed suitcase under my desk. I know the pros and cons of all the hotel chains, airlines, and car rental companies." Kenny laughed. "The complimentary cookies score the Hilton chain a few points in my travel log. *But* they have nothing on those key lime pie cookies."

"You might be onto something. Mr. C. is always looking for ways to enhance the customer experience," J.P. said in a serious tone. "He'll be gone by the time I get back to the office tonight, but I'll remember to bring that up with him next week."

"I can't believe it's already after four, I should really get going," Kenny abruptly announced while she strapped her Apple Watch back on her wrist. "I've been out here since this morning," she said and took a big gulp from her green bottle.

"It looks like you put in a full day," J.P. smirked motioning to the burn lines on her legs. "When you were sleeping, I noticed your stomach got a bit pink, too. The hot water in your shower is going to sting tonight." J.P. laughed all while doubting himself.

Again.

Had he gone too far? At what tee, on what course had he lost his confidence in witty banter?

"I guess I missed a few spots," she tapped her shins as she stood up.

J.P. felt the burn. He knew the skin was crunching around her fire engine red kneecaps. All golfers have suffered that unintentional burn when a match goes to a shootout and your sunscreen is still in the locker room.

Kenny started to gather her belongings while J.P. sat quietly, contemplating his next move. He wasn't sure if her cheeks were pink from the sun or flushed with embarrassment.

"One last thought about customer satisfaction. Mr. Cunningham is playing with the idea of supplying water toys —kayaks, paddle boards, that kind of thing—to the rental properties," J.P. said, methodically thinking about every word and trying to sound business-like. "He ordered in a few kayaks to test durability and quality. See if they'd be safe for renters to use on their own or if they'd be a liability. We debate the same issues with gas grills and outdoor electric heaters. Anyway, I was going to check them out tomorrow. Since you seem to be a career hotel-hopper, maybe you'd want to join me and share guest feedback?"

"You want me to be a water toy product tester?" Kenny clarified. "How would that work? Are you going to send me out into the ocean on a kayak and see if I get swept out by the current? Don't forget you're talking to a true crime producer. This sounds like it has all the elements of a perfect murder," she said matter-of-factly.

"I almost forgot you're a trained skeptical overthinker." J.P. laughed, half relieved that Kenny's first thought didn't jump to the invitation being interpreted as a date, though it easily could have been. Maybe some part of him wanted her to perceive it that way. "I appreciate the reminder. The next time I conjure up a murder mystery plot, my target victim will not be a jilted news producer." J.P. laughed.

"You're welcome." Kenny coyly smiled.

"Don't forget I've seen you swim. So, in this plotline you would be the heroine tasked with saving both of us if something were to go wrong while we're out there." He tipped his chin to the ocean.

"I feel like I'm being taken advantage of because of my aquatic abilities but I'll try to look past it," Kenny joked. "When and where should I meet you?"

"How about 10:00 a.m.? Down the beach a bit," he said, pointing to the left with his ball launcher. "There's a discreet, narrow walkway off the bike path between Whistling Swan and Oyster Catcher. You'll see a small sign that says, 'Private Access.' Follow the sign and take that path, I'll meet you at the end on the beach."

"Sounds great, I'll be there." Kenny flashed a smile as she finished folding up her beach mat and walked towards the dunes.

"See you tomorrow, Kenny." J.P. beamed as he walked in the opposite direction and launched the tennis ball that Cliff darted after.

Twenty-Three

No one was in the pool at Pelican Pointe when Kenny got back to the villa, and she realized she hadn't taken a dip for the sake of relaxation since her arrival. For a split second, she debated grabbing her goggles and getting in a quick swim workout but instead decided to soak up the peace and stillness of the surroundings. It was a different kind of happy hour than the one she would be having if she was in New York at this time on a Friday night.

The direct sunlight that the pool received all day made the water feel like a warmly drawn bath, but Kenny still felt a rush of refreshment when she immersed herself under the surface. When she came up for air, she kicked her legs up, spread her arms out into a *T* shape, arched her back slightly, and laid her head back on the top of the water like it was resting on a pillow. Kenny loved to float. She found it freeing. As a kid, she would float for hours basking in the feeling of weightlessness and staring at the sky, mesmerized by the movement and formation of the clouds. She would be fascinated when the puffs of white took the shape of animals or letters or some other geometric object.

Thirty years later, she still relished the feeling of weightlessness, especially when she often felt weighted down from the stress she carried around on her petite shoulders. But instead of looking up and imagining stories about the shapes of the clouds, she would close her eyes and get lost in her own thoughts, which could sometimes be dangerous. The thoughts were usually self-reflective and reminiscent of the recurring dreams about where she was in her life, where she wanted to be in her life, and how she was going to get there. Today she didn't want to wander to that place. She was happy with where she was for the moment and was trying to live by the *Vienna* lyrics that brought her to this paradise. She was giving herself permission to slow down and not race through life. At least for the next few weeks. Kenney opened her eyes just in time to see a cloud that was shaped like a butterfly blow by.

She floated a little longer and started to make her way to the pool steps when tiny droplets of water started sprinkling from the sky. The drizzles collided with the pool's calm surface creating a perfectly choreographed water show. The circular ripples started slow, delicate and sporadic, and increased in speed, intensity, and amount as the rain crashed down harder. Kenny felt like she was watching the musical fountains at the Bellagio Hotel in Las Vegas, minus the music. By the time she gathered her belongings and reached the back steps of Villa #5, sections of the coastal concrete walkway were flooded, and the palm trees whipped furiously back and forth against a darkened gray sky. She got to the interior side of the sliding deck door just in time to hear an angry crack of thunder and see the outdoors illuminate from a bolt of lightning.

Wrapped in her wet towel and hair still dripping from her swift evacuation from the pool deck, Kenny stood in the glass door staring outside in amazement. The intense, brief pop-up thunderstorms that blew out as quickly as they blew in captivated her. Her appreciation for meteorology started and ended in her clothes closet every morning as she decided how she should appropriately dress based on the weather person's predicted forecast. But these regular rain occurrences made her feel small, materialistic, and, frankly, embarrassed to realize how often she took for granted the beauty and perplexity of what was going on around her.

By the time Kenny showered and lathered aloe over her unevenly tanned and burned skin, the storm clouds had given way to a clear sky. She stepped onto the back porch and hung her beach mat over the railing. The air still smelled of rain and wet pine, and the mulch was a darker shade of brown than usual; but most surfaces had dried up and the standing water on the sidewalks had begun to absorb and recede. She noticed that the small community of vacationers was ready for Friday night. A large family with several boxes of pizza and cases of soda staked out a corner of the pool deck. Two men sipped bottles of beer as they flipped burgers and turned steaks at the grills under the pavilion. Three women who looked like they were dressed for dinner walked around the landscaping ponds holding plastic wine glasses. The pickleball courts were fully occupied and a young couple that appeared to have gotten stuck in the rainstorm rounded the corner with two of the bright orange beach cruisers.

Text from Hailey: Hooked up? (Emoji: laptop) Plz let me kno.

Kenny had been so wrapped up in being present during the day she forgot that the service company was scheduled to install the internet and cable in Villa #5. She walked back into the kitchen and found a laminated piece of paper and two television remotes, labeled Remote A and Remote B, on the counter that indicated the unit was connected.

> *Thank you for using Island Cable Services.*
> *Wi-Fi Network: Pelican Pointe*
> *Wi-Fi Password: Villa-5*
> *Use Remote A to power television "On/Off."*
> *Use Remote B to change channels.*
> *To report outages, contact Low Country Hospitality.*

Kenny imagined herself the axis in a universe of information overload and incessant communication that constantly spun around her, and she was surprised by how quickly she adapted to being unplugged for a few weeks. In the beginning of her hiatus, she was nervous she would be filled with guilt and anxiety. How she imagined a soldier who had gone AWOL felt after leaving camp. She feared she would need to go through a methodical and closely monitored digital detox. But the freedom from it all over the last six days was liberating. If Hailey hadn't asked for confirmation that all the systems were working, Kenny would have gone at least another week before reconnecting to the outside world.

She reluctantly picked up Remote A and powered on the large television that hung on the wall. The local NBC channel popped up and *Jeopardy!* was on the screen. Kenny loved *Jeopardy!* and one of her favorite assignments was crisscrossing Canada to produce a documentary about Alex Trebek's death. To people outside the news industry, filming obituaries before an ageing and ailing celebrity or notable figure *actually* passed away was perceived as morbid and offensive. To those inside the circle, the jumpstart in production was viewed as a necessary evil so networks could immediately air an entertaining and informative documentary that a nation mourning the rich or famous deceased would be longing for.

She picked up Remote B with her left hand and flipped through the channels to ensure both remotes were working. She clicked on the local ABC station that was previewing the upcoming episode of *20/20*. It was the story of an oil broker from Texas who "accidentally" killed his philandering son-in-law while the pair were on a big game hunting trip in Wyoming.

She was somewhat familiar with the story, but WBS passed on covering the drama noting there weren't enough twists and turns to the hold viewer's attention for the duration of a show. Kenny had no plans to tune in and determine if the executives' assessment was correct. She powered down the television. Having confirmed that both remotes and the cable were working, she placed the clickers back on the counter next to the laminated instruction leaflet.

Kenny lifted the lid of the ottoman where she stored her laptop bag and pulled out the computer. She fired it up, connected it to the Pelican Pointe network and typed out V-i-l-l-a-5 in the password box. She was about to instinctively double click on Outlook when something in her gut stopped her. The mouse cursor hovered over the icon for several seconds while she contemplated what she was about to do. Opening Outlook for the first time after several days would be akin to opening Pandora's box. Thousands of emails would need to be read, processed, and responded to, and she wasn't prepared to do that. While part of her yearned to know every detail—real and rumored—surrounding what prevented NBC from airing the Clinton White interview, Kenny knew that reading just one article would be like eating a piece of forbidden fruit that could change the course of the rest of her trip. She was further confident that one brief reply to *any* email would escalate to an exchange of dialogue that would morph into text messages, phone calls, and ultimately result in her disabling the sacred "Out of Office" feature.

There was no turning back from either scenario if she gnawed on the carrot that dangled in front of her.

Kenny took her hand off the mouse, closed her eyes, and breathed like Marah taught her. *Breathe in, two, three, four. Hold two, three, four. Out two, three, four. Breathe in, two, three, four. Hold two, three, four. Out two, three, four.* She opened her eyes, put her hand back on the mouse, double clicked on Chrome, and typed www.weather.com into the toolbar rather than opening her email. She searched "Hilton Head Island" and the five vertical boxes boasting graphics of bright yellow suns and double-digit numbers that started with sevens and eights quickly populated her screen. The balmy forecast reinforced there would be no time for phone calls, text messages, or email exchanges over the next few days.

Text to Hailey: Cable works & Internet fast (Emoji: thumbs up)

Text from Hailey: Gr8! Wknd plns?

The last text from Hailey made Kenny smile. Even though she didn't know or appear to have anything in common with the sorority sister from West Virginia, she felt like she had a new friend. She wondered if she and Hailey would have hit it off if they were the same age and met in school; or if Kenny would have had no patience for and envied the assumed carefree blonde from afar, while she was busy being overly serious and focused on the future and post-college plans.

Text to Hailey: Yes! Kayaking on the ocean in the a.m.

Text from Hailey: Love it! (Emoji: dolphin)

As hard as Kenny tried to not think about the morning

kayak excursion, it consumed almost every other thought in her head. And as much as she didn't want to tell Colby about it, because she was still slightly annoyed with him *and* wasn't prepared to be totally truthful about the solo vacation, for fear he would find a cheap flight and crash for a few days—he was spontaneous in every way that Kenny wasn't—she knew she should let someone aside from Hailey know she was going to be paddling on the Atlantic in a plastic boat. Since it was pushing 8:00 p.m. on a Friday, Kenny predicted Colby would be a few cocktails deep, and she'd be able to keep the conversation short. She scrolled through her recent calls log and tapped on Colby's name.

"We were just talking about you, darling." Colby enthusiastically picked up on the first ring. "I'm here with Ed! Say 'hi,' Ed!" Colby's voice was muffled as he pulled the phone away from his mouth so his friend could send a forced salutation. "A new biergarten opened around the corner from the office and Eddy-boy dragged me here!"

Kenny rolled her eyes and heard the commotion of clinking glasses and accordion music in the background. Colby could drink vodka sodas "until the cows came home," a phrase he'd overuse when he had too many of the mixed drinks and started reverting to his midwestern roots, but he could not handle a night of Oktoberfest beers.

"Hey, Colby! Hi, Ed! Sounds like you guys are having a time for yourselves. I was just calling to say 'Hi!' and see what I was missing up there on a Friday night." She tried to make it sound like either of those two statements were true. "I won't keep you!"

"I'll call you tomorrow morning, love! It's loud in here," Colby screeched into the phone.

"I'm going kayaking in the morning, so I'll call you when I get back from the beach. Don't do anything dumb tonight!" Kenny said, relieved the conversation was kept short and she was able to relay her plans in case something went wrong. Even if Colby didn't remember, Ed would.

"Kayaking! In the ocean? You're terrified of the ocean! I'm impressed you're facing that fear. And Ed wants to know when the two of you are going on your second date. But he's standing right here so I better hang up before I say anything else that'll piss him off. Love you, mean it, bi-yeee!"

Kenny dropped the phone on the couch next to her, smiled, and slunk into the cushions. She was happy she had forgiven Colby, and that their relationship was on the mend. She couldn't remember a time that Colby didn't answer when she called him. No matter how monumental or trivial the topic, or how long or short the conversation was, she *usually* felt better after talking to him.

No one knew Kenny like Colby and that was both comforting and annoying. Few people knew Kenny was terrified of the ocean, but Colby did, and he was proud of her for facing the fear. He'd be doubly proud if he knew a handsome man was at the root of her facing it, but that fact was irrelevant. For Kenny, this pending exercise fell under the "try something new" category on the Condition List. She also knew Colby was correct about her personal life even if she was resistant to admitting it. For a fleeting moment she thought maybe she should give Ed a second chance when she got back to New York.

Twenty-Four

J.P. put his bag of take-out food on the oversized, custom-made, live-edge, walnut and blue epoxy dining table that was designed to replicate the real-life ocean scene that was visible on the other side of the glass floor to ceiling windows that spanned the length of the back of the three-story coastal-style beach home. He opened the French doors in the center of the perfectly Windexed wall and Cliff ran out onto the second-tier deck that overlooked the pool and was high enough to see over the dunes, creating a picturesque, unobstructed view of the Atlantic. J.P. visited Mr. Cunningham's home hundreds of times over the years but was always struck by its grandeur. It may have been one of the largest homes on Sea Pines, but the comfort and familiarity gave J.P. the same sense of nostalgia and security as the two-bedroom condo on the other side of the plantation his parents rented for annual summer vacations when he and his sister were kids.

J.P. left Cliff to occupy himself on the deck while he went inside to change out of his golf clothes and into a bathing suit. When J.P. house-sat for his boss, he always stayed in the guest bedroom on the second floor. It was considered the least desirable room to some because it shared a wall with the main entertaining area and the exterior wall was a sliding door that opened to the deck that sprawled the length of the back of the house, offering little privacy and a lot of sunlight if you forgot to shut the blinds, but it was J.P.'s favorite room. He liked sleeping with the blinds open and being woken up by the light streaming through the glass, with a front row seat to the sunrise over the ocean without leaving the bed. He liked being able to sit in the hot tub outside the sliding door and stare at the stars and moon reflecting over the water until late in the night and have access to his bedroom without traipsing through other parts of the house. Most importantly, he liked the memories. For three summers during his college years, he stayed in this bedroom while he worked toward his dream of touring in the PGA. If it weren't for the opportunities J.P. had been given over the course of those summers, he never would have enjoyed the accomplished golf career he went on to have, nor would he be in the current position he found himself in to create a prosperous and successful future.

J.P. hung his polo shirts and golf pants in the walk-in closet. Along with Mr. Cunningham's "no shorts rule" while an employee was on the clock or on the course, he had a strict "no wrinkle rule." J.P. wasn't sure if it was a generational thing or if it went back to Mr. Cunningham's days as a cadet at the Air Force Academy, but he was a stickler for pressed cotton. He kept an ironing board and an industrial steamer in the men's and women's locker rooms at the Liberty Oaks Clubhouse and once got into a heated conversation with Miss Luana about the viability of her housekeeping teams starching and pressing the bedsheets when they turned over a room. From cowardly observing that debate, J.P. learned there was one person aside from Mr. Cunningham who was capable, and deserving, of having the last word—a woman of Gullah descent who was fiercely protective of her staff. And family recipes, it was later learned when she unveiled her famous key lime pie cookies at the company potluck.

J.P. unpacked his toiletry bag in the bathroom that was connected to the bedroom and pulled out two towels from the linen closet. He hung one on the towel bar inside the shower and draped one around his neck for when he got out of the hot tub. If there was one thing J.P. didn't miss about being on the tournament circuit, it was living like a vagabond. The lifestyle required him to check in and out of hotels for weeks at a time, for the better part of a year. He made a practice early in his career to always unpack his belongings in the closets and drawers of wherever he was staying. He also never hung the *Do Not Disturb* sign on the door like many business travelers. He welcomed housekeeping entering the room every day to freshen the towel supply and neatly make up his bed. It was these little routines that helped J.P. keep a clear mind and forget he was a visitor away from the comfort of his surroundings.

Satisfied that his belongings were put away and organized, J.P. grabbed a Heineken from the refrigerator and the lobster roll he ordered from the restaurant at the clubhouse and opened the French door to the deck where Cliff was patiently waiting for him.

"Buddy, it's time to wind down," J.P. said to the dog who started at him like he was ready for an intense game of tug of war.

He placed his sandwich and the bottle on the plastic tray that was affixed to the side of the tub and then hoisted himself up and over the side, slowly lowering his legs and torso down into the bubbling, hot water. J.P. scooted his way around the perimeter and found his favorite spot where the jets hit his shoulders, lower back and calves at all the right pressure points and rested his head back.

"Tell me Cliff, why do you gravitate toward Kenny? Over

two million people visit this island every year and you don't bother with any of them. Most of them make a fuss over you, some even beg for your attention. And you ignore them. I've noticed sometimes you're even rude," J.P. questioned and chastised his four-legged friend as he stared up at the stars.

As if to defend himself, Cliff sprung up on his hind legs and rested both paws on the side of the hot tub. His tongue hung out of his mouth and his tail wagged.

J.P. sensed the dog's head next to his own and cast his gaze to the right, looking into his eyes. "You don't know, do you? That's all right, boy. Me either," he said, giving Cliff a sympathetic grin and patting him on the head.

Twenty~Five

Kenny woke up earlier than usual and lay in the cocoon of purple pillows while she stared at the purple garden on the ceiling, hoping she would fall back to sleep for at least another hour. She had three hours to spare until she had to meet J.P. for their kayaking excursion, which meant she had roughly two hours and forty minutes to talk herself out of going. Kenny planned to ride one of the beach cruisers down Lighthouse Road to North Sea Pines Drive, which would take her straight to the entrance of the beach path between Whistling Swan and Oyster Catcher. She predicted the ride would take fifteen to twenty minutes at a leisurely pedal cadence and didn't want to arrive sweaty, late, or early, so determined her departure time should be promptly at 9:40 a.m.

Filled with anticipation and anxiety about the adventure, she gave up on the notion of getting additional rest and stumbled into the kitchen to plug in the coffee pot. While she waited for the beverage to percolate, she stepped out onto the back porch where she could see the early risers begin to stir. The water aerobics women, foam weights in tow, congregated at the pool steps where they recapped their dinner experiences from the previous night before beginning their synchronized aquatic routine. The older gentlemen, presumably the husbands of the water aerobics squad, began to inadvertently convene by the pickleball courts, like most mornings, because there were two plastic, coin-operated newspaper boxes to the left of the playing area that offered *The New York Times* and *The Sea Pines Sentinel*. She imagined they talked about their tee times and exchanged fishing tales. Young mothers stealthily sneaked out the back sliding doors so they could enjoy a quiet cup of coffee before their children woke up and their husbands returned from their sunrise jogs.

Kenny took a big inhale and could feel her lungs expand as she breathed in the scents of pine and cedar. She wished she could bottle up the earthy scent and take it back to Manhattan. It was a smell she couldn't get enough of. She picked up the damp cloth she kept on the railing of the porch and wiped off the dew and fallen copper-colored tree needles from the surface, so she had a dry place to set her phone and mug.

It had been almost two weeks since Kenny arrived on Sea Pines, and she still couldn't believe this was her reality, even if it was temporary. She was enamored with the vitality that Mother Nature had on full display. She was no horticulturist, but it seemed to her the palm and oak trees grew taller and sturdier every night and the mossy greens turned lusher and more vibrant each morning. The flecks of yellow from the sun, bursts of blue from the sky, and pops of purples, pinks, and oranges from the flowering shrubs perfectly accented the predominantly green canvas. Kenny closed her eyes and thought about Marilyn the therapist's morning homework assignment which she had forgone since she started her vacation from reality. While gratitude was an easy feeling to identify, there was no way she could choose to focus on just one of the full of life colors she would see when she opened her eyes again. The sight was enchanting. A vision that no photograph or watercolor, lens or paintbrush, could ever capture.

Kenny went inside, poured a cup of coffee, and rifled through her overstuffed computer bag to find the *Meditations from the Mat* book. She hadn't flipped to a daily reflection since the morning after the night she played drunken travel agent and booked the extended stay at Pelican Pointe to escape life, but she was in a contemplative mood. She sat down on the ottoman and opened to page 317.

"Day 275. 'One must be able to let things happen,' by C.G. Jung."

Kenny reread the line a few times, both silently and aloud. It amazed her that these short mantras always spoke directly to her, whether it was a quote from the Dalai Lama, Deepak Chopra, or C.G. Jung, whom she'd never heard of until now. She imagined "letting things happen" somehow equated to letting go of the past, not controlling the present nor attempting to predict the future. These seemed to be common themes among the intellectuals Marilyn worked hard to introduce Kenny to. And, maybe not so ironically, all hot button issues for her.

She allowed herself to fall down the meditation and meaning rabbit hole to learn more about the author and the quote. She thought if she was going to heed the life advice, she should know it was coming from a credible source and have some understanding of it. She Googled C.G. Jung and learned he was a famous Swiss psychiatrist by the name of Carl Gustav who was regarded as one of the most influential psychologists in history. She found scholarly articles equating his esteemed words to the Buddhist practice of "action in nonaction," a phrase Kenny heard tossed around in yoga classes but never really understood. She read Mommy Bloggers who wrote philosophical posts about the internal struggles of going after what you want versus letting things come to you. And saw the quote written in a variety of fonts with various images attached on countless Pinterest boards. But the explanation Kenny liked best was an easy, straightforward one. The idea was to simply bring awareness to any situation, without fear or control, and just *experience* it.

She made a pact with herself that she would approach the pending kayak trip with this effortless awareness. She was going to focus on the act of being in a small boat and paddling on the ocean rather than thinking about the frenzy of sharks that would be swimming in circles a few feet below. She was going to enjoy J.P.'s company and conversation without expectation or reading into any possible chemistry between them. She was going to take Jung's advice to let things happen. Shark attacks or kisses, so be it!

Underlying it all, she remembered that the excursion was purely a business venture to determine if kayaks would be a safe amenity to provide to guests at Mr. Cunningham's properties—and nothing more. She would *never* agree to a first date that required her to wear a bathing suit. She was fitting comfortably back into to her skinny leggings and her face was noticeably less full, so she was hopeful the twelve IVF pounds from the egg preservation ordeal had finally disappeared; but she could never justify not being fully clothed for a first date.

Kenny rummaged through her bathing suit drawer and was relieved she packed the black Roxy surf shirt she bought for an interview she produced at an indoor water park in the Poconos about the lifeguard industry. She pulled the surf top over a modest and practical black one-piece suit and slipped up a pair of bright yellow running shorts. After inspecting herself in the mirror and satisfied with the ensemble, she closed the dresser drawer only to immediately open it back up and fish out the same pair of running shorts in black.

Although she wasn't superstitious and decided she wasn't going to dwell on sharks, she had flashbacks to a Steven Spielberg interview where he talked about his use of the bright color to signify danger throughout *Jaws*, and thought wearing yellow shorts would be like playing with fire.

There was never more than a whisper of a breeze on the beaches of Hilton Head, but Kenny thought the wind might be a little gustier on the water that could result in disastrous matted knots in her hair. She pulled up a "French Braid for Beginners" YouTube video and after thirty minutes of trying to overlap multiple strands of hair into an artful twist on the crown of her head with only two hands, she gave up. Despite the blue scrunchie keeping Kenny's hair secure when she was active, that was simply not an option for the non-date. She dug through the travel bag where she kept all her hair accessories and found a wide, black athletic headband that would hold her hair back and prevent sweat from dripping into her eyes.

I should've been wearing this during my first beach run-in with J.P., Kenny thought. But then maybe my eyes wouldn't have been so irritated. And Jose wouldn't have been sent to Pelican Pointe to tend to the pool water and deliver the key lime pie cookies. And J.P. and I wouldn't have had anything to talk about on the beach yesterday and he never would have asked me to go kayaking.

Kenny started playing what Marilyn called the "What If, Should Have" game. The therapist said the game was more dangerous than playing ice hockey without pads or a stick, and if Kenny found herself out of the box and on the ice, she should immediately call a time out.

"Time out, Kenny! You're overthinking, and we're not doing that today," she said as she pulled the stretch wrap to her forehead, brushed her hair back into a high ponytail, and secured it with a black elastic tie.

She gently rubbed sunscreen onto her sun-kissed face and

when she bent over to lather her legs and feet, noticed the lobster-red burn from the previous day's beach nap had begun to fade. When she realized this was the first time that she was leaving the villa with the intention of running into J.P., she brushed a small swipe of waterproof mascara on her lashes and dabbled her lips with pink gloss.

Text from Colby: I had the craziest dream: You told me you're going kayaking with sharks? Tell me it's not true! LYMIB!

Text to Colby: I'm wearing my favorite yellow bathing suit (Emoji: shark)

Text from Colby: Nice try. I knew you were lying . . . you don't own a yellow bathing suit. Call me later. LYMIB!

Twenty-Six

J.P. opened the door of the garage that, from the outside, looked like a smaller version of Mr. Cunningham's beach front monstrosity on Marlin Manor. Mr. Cunningham didn't drive expensive cars, own a yacht, or take lavish international holidays but he spared no expense when it came to his "coastal cottage." Outsiders or the envious labeled the compound as pretentious and wondered who would need a home of such luxury and extravagance. But those who knew Mr. Cunningham and his lifestyle admired and viewed the estate as they did him—a pillar of the community.

Mr. Cunningham was the wealthiest man on Hilton Head, possibly in all the Lowcountry, and the only thing bigger than his bank account and business smarts was his heart. He donated more money than he could spend and was hands-on in all his philanthropic endeavors. Several weeks of the year he invited visitors to stay at his home for a much-deserved vacation. He would host veterans who recently returned from deployment; single mothers who worked full time while also going to school to earn a degree, along with their children and a team to provide childcare; nuns from the Order of the

Immaculate Heart of Mary who served in the Diocese of Savannah and foster children who struggled to survive in an overcrowded system.

Mr. Cunningham was well-traveled and well-educated and used his inherited privilege and wealth to better the lives of the less fortunate. He had doormats at every entrance, of which there were many, inscribed with the words *Is E Mo Theach Do Theach* meaning *My House is Your House* in Gaelic. The only price to pay for lodging was to commit to doing something kind for another, every day without fanfare.

With Cliff on his heels, J.P. rolled the two-wheeled kayak trolley to the center of the garage and lifted two blue, sit-on-top kayaks from the storage rack that hung on the wall. He wondered if Kenny had ever seen *this* kind of cart before. He strapped the first kayak to the trolley and secured an oar under two bungee cords that were fastened to the front and the back ends of the boat. He scooped up two purple and green zip up life jackets from a large plastic storage bin with his right forearm and pulled the trolley out of the garage, over the crushed oyster shell and concrete driveway, and down the private beach walk.

Cliff darted for the water as soon as his paws hit the sand. It was a rare day when J.P. didn't have to be at the clubhouse for an early morning lesson or tee time and today was one of those days. Which meant he took advantage and slept in, leaving Cliff with more pent-up energy than usual for this time of day. He ran in and out of the water with abandon and only stopped for quick breaks to scratch his back. J.P. didn't always encourage Cliff to jump the waves and roll around in the sand——he loved Cliff, not the smell of ocean wet dog— but didn't mind when they were staying at or passing by the compound. Mr. Cunningham didn't have a dog of his own but installed a stainless steel dog grooming tub next to the outdoor shower for humans. At first glance, it could be mistaken for an industrial sized Weber grill-smoker combo. Upon closer inspection, there was no denying it was the equivalent of a car wash for pets.

J.P. had time to spare before Kenny arrived, so he dropped the trolley and life jackets a few feet from the water's edge, took off his shirt, and walked into the ocean until the waves reached his knees. The temperatures hovered in the eighties. He didn't remember September waters being so warm; but then he didn't remember the last time he took a few hours to enjoy the ocean. He took Cliff for walks on the beach almost daily, but he rarely took time to enjoy the water. J.P. continued to walk until his waist was submerged and, without thinking, dove headfirst into the waves. He bobbed up and down for a few minutes and when he turned around to face the shore, he saw Cliff pacing back and forth at the water's edge, frantically barking in J.P.'s direction.

This dog J.P. laughed to himself.

"I'm coming, Buddy! Look, I'm fine!" J.P. yelled, waving his hands in the air as he waded in the water and closer to shore to appease his panicked pup.

J.P. had a hard time admitting it to himself or anyone else, but his life while he was on the tournament circuit had been a lonely one. There was a fellowship among competitors, an inherent appreciation and respect that everyone shared a similar existence—eat, sleep, golf, repeat—with the common goal of becoming the next Tiger Woods or Phil Michelson. The golfers bonded over the free breakfast buffets and talked about *Sports Center* which seemed to always be on the television during prime workout time in the hotel gyms. They'd share nightcaps in the lobby lounges to commiserate about poor performances and occasionally grab a meal at one of the restaurants recommended by the locals in whatever city they were competing. But the lifestyle made it hard to maintain meaningful relationships. Tournaments lasted days at a time and often ran consecutive weeks, making the dating scene difficult.

Most women J.P. was attracted to wanted something more than on-again, off-again flings when he happened to be available. Even when he was physically present, he wasn't always mentally. He knew that his drive to succeed ruined a few potentially good romantic relationships, but it was a price he was willing to pay for his dream career. He missed holidays with family and reunions with friends during the years he dedicated to the Korn Ferry Tour to earn his PGA Tour card. And since giving up on his aspiration of qualifying for The Masters, he was content living the bachelor life on Sea Pines. After parting ways with his swing coach, mental coach, and trainer, J.P.'s relationship with Cliff was the most time-consuming and accountable one he had in years.

Cliff sprung up J.P.'s hips on his hind legs like a pogo stick when the trusty owner emerged from the water. J.P. laughed and enjoyed the attention and affection he didn't realize he was missing.

"Come on, Cliff. Let's get you up to the house before Kenny gets here. Your little heart wouldn't be able to handle seeing both of us in the water," J.P. said as he removed the kayak from the trolley and pulled it back up the beach to collect the second one.

Twenty-Seven

Kenny was unusually calm as she peddled down Lighthouse Road and rounded Fraser's Circle. Oncoming traffic forced her to stop at the exact spot on the bike path where she first laid eyes on J.P. the morning she arrived on Sea Pines and froze behind the wheel of the rental car. The driver of the landscaping truck that she found herself head-to-head with waved her on much quicker than she waved on J.P. and Cliff. She laughed at the irony of the circumstances and mouthed "thank you" to the friendly man behind the wheel as she cycled across the street. She passed The Plantation Golf Club and admired the manicured greens and charming clubhouse that made her want to sit on its porch with a good book and glass of lemonade. Well-dressed golfers whose black SUVs hailed from Alabama, Florida, Mississippi, Georgia, and the Carolinas zipped around in green golf carts. A few hundred yards ahead, a steady stream of cars pulled into the Sea Pines Beach Club and her quiet mind began to chatter. She knew that she was getting close to the north end of the plantation and would be arriving at the beach access path soon.

She slowed down her strokes and hoped the thoughts in

her mind would follow suit. She recently read a study that hypothesized a person has an average of 60,000 thoughts per day; she was confident, without taking any test or filling out any survey, the number of thoughts that passed through her head daily drove up that statistic. If she were going to stay true to the morning's meditation, she would have to leave the surplus of swirling thoughts on the bike path that ran parallel to North Sea Pines Drive. Kenny finished up her inner pep talk just in time to see the small, nondescript *Private Access* sign that was mostly covered by a dwarf palmetto tree.

She hopped off the beach cruiser and saw a person at the far end of the path pulling something behind him. Her heart fluttered for a second, but she quickly realized it couldn't have been J.P. The man's exposed tanned shoulders looked broader than J.P.'s and his dark hair looked like it had been slicked back. Granted, Kenny had never seen J.P. without a shirt or a baseball hat, but he didn't seem like the kind of guy who spent hours gelling his locks. And there was neither sight nor sound of Cliff, who would surely be a third wheel on this voyage.

She continued down the path, struck by the size of the homes that were on either side of it. Along most walkways of this length that Kenny wandered down to admire the southern architecture, there typically were six or seven homes on each side dotting the pathway that dead ended in the dunes. But there were only five homes all together flanking this private walk: two on one side and three on the other. She assumed less houses meant less beachgoers, which made it less likely for a kayaker to collide with a swimmer; and probably the reason why J.P. chose this spot on the beach to meet.

As Kenny got closer to the beach, she noticed the sleek black Cannondale that she squeezed her beach cruiser next to at the farmers market and a red golf bag with the initials JLP embroidered on the pocket, in the driveway of a home that looked like it would occupy one of the small, city blocks in lower Manhattan.

Strange, Kenny whispered. But she stopped herself from overthinking why J.P.'s belongings were in the driveway of this mansion. She knew he lived on the other side of the plantation by the Salty Dog.

She pushed the clunky, orange bike up the wooden ramp, over the dunes, and paused for a moment when she got to the top, looking around for J.P. The beach was desolate except for the shirtless man she had seen from a distance on the beach walk. He kneeled between kayaks near the water's edge.

Oh. My. God. That is J.P. Why isn't he wearing a shirt?

Kenny's first instinct was to quickly look away, like she was caught staring at something she shouldn't be. She felt like a kid who was caught with her hand in the cookie jar. But, if she couldn't look at J.P., who she was planning to spend the morning with, where was she supposed to look.

"You made it! It's fine to leave the bike up there, no one will bother it," J.P. shouted as he walked up the beach to greet Kenny.

"Hey there! I'm here," she managed to reply while she waved and pushed down the bike's kickstand with her foot.

"I should've given you my number in case you had a hard time finding me. I know that walkway is a little off the beaten path, for lack of better words." J.P. laughed.

He's here. He's shirtless. He's talking about exchanging numbers.

"It's all good," she said enthusiastically. "I figured if I made it all the way to Oyster Catcher without noticing the sign, I would've taken one of the other paths and walked down the beach until I found you."

Idiot! Don't make it sound like you don't want him to have your number.

"Smart girl. It's surprising how many people probably

wouldn't think about that alternative route. Between what I overhear at the golf course and questions I hear asked of the hotel group, it's astonishing to learn of the naiveté—or lack of common sense—of some vacationers," he said like he was letting Kenny in on a secret only the island locals were privy to.

She could see that the stupidity of some people fired up J.P. in the same way that thinking of the New York City subway system and failed attempt to make it to Yankees stadium did. She found the reaction strangely adorable and giggled at how animated the sheer thought of certain things made him. It also diverted her attention from his chiseled abdomen and muscular chest that made her weak at the knees; so, she thought it was in both of their best interests to keep the silly, even if juvenile, conversation going.

"Oh, yea? What's the craziest question or assumption you've heard?" Kenny asked as she grabbed the beach bag out of the basket on the bike handlebars and the two walked down the sand toward the kayaks.

"Alligators. In my opinion, any question or statement regarding an alligator is dumb. 'Can we feed the alligators?'" J.P. asked in a mocking way. "No, Sea Pines is not a petting zoo," he answered himself. "Alligators only prey on small mammals, right? No! They'll prey on you, after you fall in *their* pond while trying to feed them," he continued. "But my favorite question is when golfers ask me what I do with gators when I find them along the course. 'Nothing! I don't do anything. Do I look like a relative of Jack Hanna's?'"

"No wonder people come to you with gator safety questions, you seem to be quite the expert." Kenny laughed. "Here's a question that I don't think is dumb. I, of course, would never approach an alligator *but* if one ran after me for whatever reason, I'm supposed to run in zigzags away from it, right?"

She tried to maintain eye contact with him as he pulled his arms through the life jacket and zipped it up. She could get lost in his perfectly round, bright blue eyes that had navy rings around them with visible golden specks when the sun hit them. But her curious mind was at high risk for directing her eyes to gawk at his torso and shoulders, which she didn't necessarily want to do, or get caught doing. It was bittersweet knowing he was covering it all up with the feminine-looking Kelly green and purple life preserver.

"I should've assumed the reporter would have a question." J.P. smirked and put his hands on his hips. "It's not a terrible one, though. That myth has been around for years. But no, you should not waste your time or breath running in zig zags if you're being chased by an alligator. Just run. Run straight, fast, and far. The only thing running in zigzags will do is slow you down and make you dizzy."

"Luckily the only place I've seen an alligator is in the World of Reptiles exhibit at the Bronx Zoo. And I'd like to keep it that way. I imagine I'd freeze in place out of panic and fear and forget to run in any direction if I came face to face with a gator," she admitted.

"Like you did that day at the intersection of Fraser Circle when you wouldn't let Cliff and me cross the street?" he asked with a satisfactory grin. He had been waiting for the perfect opportunity to bring up the encounter and Kenny had just opened the door wide open.

"You recognized me?" she blurted out. "I'm slightly horrified. I never thought I'd see you again! And I certainly never thought you'd put two and two together if you did," she said, shaking her head in disbelief.

"We're not in New York City anymore. You're not one in eight million down here, Kenny." He winked. "Honestly, I never would've remembered the encounter, those little stand-offs happen all the time. But Cliff started barking at your car, and he *never* barks, so I took notice of the situation. And you."

"Aside from my poor driving etiquette, I hope you didn't take notice of too much else. I was still fresh into my unplanned, third-of-life crisis and running on little sleep. I was also very confused by all those traffic circles. I think I went around four roundabouts in a span of twenty minutes."

"It's probably for the best you don't have a car down here. Hopefully you're better behind the paddle of a kayak." J.P. grinned as he handed Kenny the other life jacket. "Let's see how that fits. We may need to tighten the straps. It needs to be secure in case you go overboard. I waxed down these bad boys with Eelsnot, so we'll be flying through the water." His face lit up with the excitement of a nine-year-old boy whose parents finally let him retire the boogie board and buy a skim board.

His loaded statement had Kenny's mind firing on all cylinders and she wasn't sure which cylinder to focus on first: J.P. getting close enough to her to snuggly fit the life preserver to her body; the indication that kayakers *can* fall off the boat; or the reference to Eelsnot? *What the hell is Eelsnot?*

She zipped up the vest and buckled the three straps that laid over it.

"Feels secure to me." She looked up for J.P.'s approval. "Correct me if I'm wrong but isn't the point of kayaking to stay above the water?"

"It is. And the point of yoga is to stay vertical for the entire length of a standing pose." He smiled and raised an eyebrow. "Things don't always go as we plan, though, do they?"

"You're like a one-man comedy show today, aren't you?" Kenny rolled her eyes and tried not to smile. "And did you say something about Eelsnot? What on earth is that?"

"Terrible name, isn't it?" J.P. replied like he was hoping to get a rise out of Kenny. "It's just a protective coating that people use on their boats and boards to safeguard the watercraft from the elements. It usually makes the ride smoother and faster, too." He pulled out a small black tub that looked like a chewing tobacco container from his pocket.

"I'm getting quite the education this morning. So many things to worry about on this island that don't come up in regular conversation on my sheltered oasis of Manhattan." She loosened a paddle from under the bungees of one of the kayaks, indicating she was ready to go.

"When was the last time you kayaked?" He asked as he picked up the other paddle and stood it tall in front of him.

"Over the summer I rented a paddle boat at the Lake in Central Park. Does that count?" She attempted to sound convincing while wondering if she was in over her head.

"Not even close to counting."

Kenny shrugged her shoulders. "Okay. Then never."

"Maybe we should be down closer to the Beach Club in view of the lifeguards?" He half-joked but immediately stood down when he caught a glimpse of her exaggerated eye roll. "Or not! Here, hold out your paddle out in front of you like this." J.P. lifted his arms straight in front of him, his palms facing down, and wrapped around the shaft with the long sides of the blades pointing toward the sky.

Kenny extended her arms horizontally and mimicked him with her paddle, the long side of the blade facing up and the curved back of the blade closest to her body.

"Great. Now lift your arms and rest the paddle on your head. Move your arms so they are at a ninety-degree angle. This is the spacing for where your hands should be on the paddle, so your arms don't get too tired, too quickly," he instructed.

Kenny followed suit and stood proud as a peacock at the water's edge with a seven-foot oar resting on her head, hanging on every word J.P. said. Staring out at the ocean, in this awkward position, there was no place in the world she would rather be.

"You can bring that down, Hulk." He laughed and nodded to her lifted arms. "You're going to want to keep your grip loose. Don't white-knuckle it, your joints will get sore. Then you're going to stroke side to side, submerging the blade into the waves to push the water back and propel yourself forward." He paddled from side to side in thin air.

She took a few faux strokes and burst out laughing. "I think I'm ready for the water. Put me in, Coach. I'm ready to play!"

"If you say so!" He handed Kenny his paddle, grabbed the two kayaks by the bows, and pulled them closer to the shoreline. "The water is ridiculously warm today. I took a dip right before you got here. Hence, the Guido hair." He motioned to his wet, slick-backed hair that started to dry into something that resembled a pompadour.

Although she was mostly distracted by everything that was happening below his chin, she was relieved to learn that the slicked-up, voluminous mop on top of his head wasn't his go-to style when he was sans baseball cap. The look reminded her of a ribbed wife-beater, chain-wearing bro from Staten Island rather than the athlete in preppy, Dri-FIT golf attire he usually donned.

"When do we actually get *on* the kayaks?" she asked as she slowly trudged through the water, the waves now breaking just below her knees.

J.P. stopped dead in his tracks and turned to face Kenny. "Are you afraid of the ocean?"

"I'm not afraid of the *ocean*. I might be afraid of sharks *in* the ocean." She nervously giggled as she scanned the top of the water for fins.

"You have better odds of having an up-close encounter

with an alligator in the ponds that run through Pelican Pointe than an encounter with a shark while kayaking but, here, hop up." J.P. laughed and steadied one of the kayaks with both of his hands so Kenny could climb on top.

"You and these alligators. You're so funny," she mumbled as she struggled to lift herself onto the boat, pulling up her torso by pushing down with her forearms. "Do I look as ungraceful as I feel?" she asked as she swung her right leg onto the boat and shimmied the rest of her body to the center of the kayak, where she propped herself up to a seated position.

"Don't they teach you in journalism school to not ask questions you don't want the answers to?" J.P. smiled and tapped her knee. "And clearly you haven't read the "Alligator Caution" signs that are all over this plantation. 'Assume every body of water contains an alligator,'" he said as he effortlessly hoisted himself onto the other kayak in one swift motion.

"At least now I know I don't have to run in zigzags in case I do spot one on my walk from my back door to the pool deck," she sarcastically said while she thought about the absurdity of an alligator taking up residence in a foot deep decorative landscaping pond filled with koi fish.

"I've said it before, and I'll say it again. I don't know how you would manage down here if you hadn't run into me. Race you to the next house down, let's see what you've got!" J.P. put his oar in the water and started swiftly paddling through the current, parallel to the beach.

"I don't even get a head start!" Kenny called after him as he left her in his wake.

She thought there must be some validity to scrubbing down the kayaks with the Eelsnot because paddling came easier than she expected and found herself cruising through the waves with little effort. The mist that brushed her face and arms from the blades cutting through the water was warm but refreshing. The sun cast beams of light onto the water the way stage lights shine through a theater, anticipating the star of the show to appear. She felt small, free, and energized by her surroundings. She wasn't far behind J.P. and certainly wasn't taking the race as seriously as he was. She also knew that if she put her mind to it, she'd be able to keep his pace. But she was too consumed with the beauty around her to focus all her energy on paddling at a quick clip. She was also distracted by the ocean view of the monstrous house she passed on the beach path.

"You're not even out of breath!" a winded J.P. said to Kenny who coasted her kayak alongside his.

"And you probably shouldn't be, I wasn't even trying to race you! You do need to start walking the golf course and not relying on those carts," she needled. "Hey, where's Cliff today?" she pivoted, hoping she didn't offend or embarrass him with her observation.

"I left him up at the house." He nodded to the mansion behind the dunes. "He went bonkers when I was out here earlier. He'd lose his mind if he saw both of us this far from shore."

"*That* house? Is it really a single-family home? It's larger than most boutique hotels I've stayed in over the years." She stared at the house that stretched so long it still seemed to be in front of her.

"Yep. That is one house, for one guy." J.P. laughed as he and Kenny started to leisurely paddle again.

She looked at him confused.

That couldn't possibly be his house. Or could it?

"I know what you're thinking. I am *not* that one guy," J.P. assured. "My place down by South Beach would fit in the guest garage. It's Mr. Cunningham's place. Cliff and I are house-sitting for him while he's away on business this week."

"Wow! That isn't too shabby." She wasn't sure what else to say without the words potentially coming out wrong or offensive.

The house was so opulent it appeared out of place on the island that was notably unpretentious and unassuming, despite the wealth and elegance among some who lived and others who vacationed there.

"Some think it's a little . . . over the top? Which I guess I can understand. But that's not what I see when I look at it. I see it as a symbol of all the old man's best intention; the good fortunes and opportunity he's brought to so many people," J.P. said in a serious tone.

"You seem to have a lot of respect for Mr. Cunningham. And the feelings must be mutual if he asks you to crash there while he's out of town," Kenny replied.

"I've known Mr. C for more than twenty years and I still remember the first time I met him. Like all stereotypical Ohioans, my family came down here every summer for vacation. The year I turned fourteen, my big gift was a round of golf with my dad at Liberty Oaks. Golf wasn't big in our small town outside Columbus, so I didn't play much. I was a three-sport athlete, but golf wasn't one of them. Anyway, after our eighteen holes we were sitting in the clubhouse having lunch when this guy came over to my dad and introduced himself. His name was Mike Cunningham. He told my dad he saw me on the course and thought I had real potential for a kid my age. They chatted while I chowed down on my burger and when we were leaving Mike gave my dad a piece of paper with his number on it and told him to call the next time we were in town." He smiled at the memory.

"Huh? I guess your dad called him the following summer?" Kenny asked, genuinely interested in what transpired over the course of two decades that forged the strong bond between an inexperienced teen golfer from the Midwest and a billionaire from the Lowcountry.

"On the way back to Urbana, we got a call on my dad's big black bag car phone that I got a starting position on the varsity soccer team at my new high school, as a freshman. That same year I got pulled up to the varsity teams for basketball and baseball, too, so we both forgot about Mike. Fast forward, my dad arranged for us to play the course for my fifteenth birthday and Mike was the first guy we saw when we got to the clubhouse. That's when we learned he owned Liberty Oaks and several other properties and businesses around the area. My dad and I played our game and then Mike crashed our lunch again. That time, though, he was more focused on me than my dad. My interests, hobbies, school grades, friends, what I wanted to be when I grew up."

J.P. took a deep breath and another deliberate stroke of his paddle to keep the current and conversation moving. He hoped Kenny wouldn't sense his trepidation. He wasn't sure if he was more hesitant to share details of his past or the fact that he noticed a fin grazing the surface of the water had been closely following the kayaks.

"At the time, I had never been to a job interview, but I imagined that's what it felt like. I didn't have answers to many of his questions, and he told me that I should by the age of fifteen. That kind of resonated with me. I liked this guy. I liked the way he interacted with people and how people responded to him. I realized I liked everything he had and that I really liked golf. On the drive home that year, I called my coaches and quit soccer, basketball, and baseball."

"You put a lot of stock into a stranger you randomly met in South Carolina. What did your parents make of all of it? Were they okay with you quitting? I'd imagine they sunk a lot of time and money into you and those sports over the years?" Kenny questioned.

"They were skeptical at first," J.P. continued. "Especially since my school didn't have a golf team, and my athletic director guaranteed them I'd graduate with some type of athletic scholarship if I stuck with soccer or baseball; but we found a club program that I joined, and I got more serious about my studies than I had ever been. I was eventually accepted into the Professional Golf Management program at Penn State which was a double-edged sword for my parents who were die-hard Buckeyes fans and alum. They got over it after my first home match at State College. Then over the summers I'd stay down here with Mr. C, free of room and board and out of trouble, interning at various courses and perfecting my game."

"Let me get this straight, you spent the summers of your late teens and early twenties *there*? Playing golf by day and unwinding on those decks at night. Life was tough for a young adult J.P! Did Mr. Cunningham have a wife or children at home?" Kenny wanted to know so much more about this man—or family—who opened their home up to a teen from outside Columbus they knew little about other than he had a good swing and SAT scores.

"No. It's a tragic story." J.P. turned somber. "After Mr. C graduated from the Air Force Academy and served his time, he returned to his native New York. He reconnected with his childhood sweetheart, and they quickly got married, eager to start a big family. They planned to have a few biological children and eventually expand their family through adoption. Mr. C worked as a hedge fund manager on Wall Street and his wife was a schoolteacher at a public school in Washington Heights. They were active in the city's social and philanthropy circles but were close to retreating to a quieter life somewhere around Hilton Head and running a bed and breakfast." J.P. nodded toward the mansion on the beach. "But when Mrs. C was seven months pregnant with their first child, she was killed in a car accident on her way to Brookyln to meet Mr. C at a fundraiser for the Boys and Girls Club."

"Oh my God. That's heartbreaking. I'm not a parent and I don't have a spouse, but I can't imagine how anyone would ever get over that," Kenny sympathized. Like so many of the stories she covered, she couldn't help but question why terrible things happen to good people.

"Me either. I didn't know Mr. C before the accident, and he's only shared snippets of his past over the years, but people have told me he's never been the same. The accident that stole the perfect life he had at his fingertips is the reason he does a lot of what he does today. Like that house, it's not a bed and breakfast but he opens it up to people year-round. You never know who's going to walk through the door." He laughed trying to lighten the moment.

"From the little bit that I've heard from you and Derek at the guard house, it seems like he is an extraordinary man who is important to a lot of people." Kenny smiled. "But let's get back to you! With your education you may be more than a glorified handy man who occasionally teaches a golf lesson?"

"I wear a few different hats down at the course. I manage the teams who work in and around the clubhouse."

"Is that a cryptic way of saying you run the whole show?" she asked.

"Something like that," he replied. "You can grill me more about it later, reporter woman. There's a more interesting story unfolding behind you that I'd hate for you to miss." J.P. grabbed the side of Kenny's kayak so both boats stopped and started floating with the current.

She turned her head and out of the corner of her eye saw a fin grazing the surface of the water. It was so close she could touch it. She gasped but nothing came out. She could feel her hands loosen the grip of her paddle. J.P. grabbed it before she completely let go and dropped it into the ocean.

"Breathe, Kenny. It's a dolphin! Actually, it's a pod of dolphins! Four of them have been trailing us for a while now. Let me turn us around." He dragged the blade of his paddle in the water and spun around the kayaks.

She hadn't opened her eyes or closed her mouth since the initial shock of seeing the tip of the dorsal fin at the rear of her boat. Her focus was squarely on trying to not shake so violently that she tumbled overboard into what she determined to be shark infested waters or throw up from the instant wave of nausea that overcame her when she saw her life flash before her eyes.

Breath in, two, three, four. Hold two, three, four. Out two, three, four. Breath in, two, three, four. Hold two, three, four. Out two, three, four.

When her heart rate tempered and she was confident that the organ wasn't going to beat out of her chest and through her life jacket, she slowly opened her eyes.

"Oh my God," Kenny shrieked. "J.P., look at them!"

Two dolphins bobbed up and down like buoys on either side of the kayaks, clicking and squealing with excitement. Their curved rostrums were wide open which made the friendly pair look like they were displaying the widest, happiest, toothiest smiles Kenny had ever seen. She couldn't help but smile back.

"Look at those two over there," J.P. said with a grin as big as the dolphins. "They look like they're waving to us." He nodded to another duo a few feet away that were upright and spinning in circles, flipping their flappers faster than Kenny's heart was beating a few seconds earlier.

"I think they're dancing, putting on a show for us." She looked in awe as the set that bobbed next to her disappeared below the water. "Where do you think those two are headed?"

"I'm not sure exactly, but not too far. About 400 of these

bottlenose dolphins call Hilton Head home. Most groups migrate every year, like retired snowbirds, but these Lowcountry dolphins stick around."

"Why is that?"

"Because they are smart. Next to humans, they have the second largest brain of all mammals." J.P. laughed, thinking Kenny would have some snarky comment about him possessing a useless wealth of knowledge. "Would you ever want to leave if you didn't have to?" he followed up when she didn't immediately have a quick-witted response.

"No," Kenny replied, thinking J.P.'s simple, yet loaded question was deeper than he intended.

Despite being on vacation and away from the stressors and problems of everyday life, she couldn't help but wonder if there was a life outside the one that she was living. Maybe even a version entirely different than the desired life she was seeing in those nagging dreams. In her mind, there was no world outside her fast-paced, deadline-driven, adrenaline-fueled life in New York, squeezing in an occasional yoga class as a thinly veiled attempt to balance her equilibrium. But the peace and calm of the last two weeks made her question that notion. And maybe even her priorities.

J.P. handed Kenny the paddle she almost dropped, and they began kayaking back in the direction they came from.

"Me either. I guess in many ways I haven't." He shook his head almost in disbelief that he made the decision years ago to never leave. "When I was still playing golf, I had the opportunity to travel the world and visit some of the most magnificent places in America but when it came time to make a decision about laying roots—well professional roots, I haven't gotten around to the personal roots." J.P. paused, trying to reel in an accidental tangent. "Anyway, I never had a second thought about coming to Sea Pines."

"Do you mean you golfed professionally? Or did you

happen to find someone to fund your expensive hobby?" Kenny asked, half joking, half serious.

She didn't know much about golf, but she did know there was a not so thin line between a golfer who could make a career out of the sport and a golfer who won leagues at their municipal courses or hit a once in a lifetime hole in one at their fancy country club.

"I guess you could say a little bit of both." He smiled. "I played well my four years at Penn State and knew my game was at a level that would be competitive in the professional realm, but no matter how talented a player is, it's a very expensive endeavor—the coaches, the tournament fees, the travel. I started applying for jobs at courses in Ohio and when someone from a club in Cleveland called Mr. C for a reference, he hung up on them and called me to say he wanted me to consider going pro. He offered to back me until I landed some bigger sponsorships. I stayed pro for eight years before hanging up my cleats and joining the crew at Liberty Oaks."

"All this time you led me to believe you're a glorified maintenance man who has a penchant for *Inside Edition* when really you're a retired professional athlete who runs one of the most prestigious golf courses in the country?" She shook her head, thoroughly impressed with her own exceptional taste. "I'd love to hear more about your adventures some time. Good chance we've crossed paths at airports in the past and didn't even know it."

She took a minute to realize how much she enjoyed the process of getting to know him. Every encounter she learned something new, something different, something that made him more attractive than the day before. In the spirit of Carl Gustav, she was letting things happen. Two weeks ago, Kenny would have employed the stealth stalking skills of Colby and the research department at WBS to cull every detail and fact about J.P. that was public record. There would be no mystery, learning, or peeling back layers. This was refreshing.

"You know, I think I've told you more about me during this time on the water than I've shared with anyone in a really long time," J.P. said. "What about you? Why are you *really* here? It doesn't seem like one messed up interview would be enough to rattle someone like you so much that you leave home and basically take a sabbatical. Journalists usually have thick skin."

"It's not for the faint of heart," Kenny admitted. "Clinton White wasn't the only catalyst. The same day news of the interview broke, I found out that the manuscript for a book I wrote was turned down by a big publishing company. *And* I got into an epic, let's say, situation with my best friend. 'Fight' sounds so juvenile, doesn't it? It was a perfect storm of events that led to me being here," she said, surprising herself she wasn't embarrassed to admit these failures to J.P.

"You're a hotshot network news producer *and* an author? Looks like someone else hasn't been totally forthcoming."

"First, there's nothing 'hotshot' about the producer gig." She laughed. "Second, I'm *not* an author. I poured my heart and soul into this piece of important, compelling work of investigative nonfiction and the only cover it'll ever see is the white, plastic binder I stole from the WBS supply room where I keep edited versions."

"Why don't you shop it around to other publishers? I'm sure there's more than one out there?" he asked with an expression that she interpreted as *why didn't you think of that.*

"Unfortunately, it's not that simple. The woman who turned down the manuscript is the GOAT of the publishing world. No one will give it a second thought if they know that Muffin Evans passed on it. To add salt to the wound, she's asked me to write a romantic comedy! I've been called a lot of things over the years, but a hopeful romantic is not one of them." Kenny laughed.

J.P. scratched his head. "Who names their kid Muffin?"

"I know. Don't let the name fool you, there's nothing sweet or savory about her. She's known in the industry as the Manuscript Eater."

"Then it's even more flattering that this Manuscript Eater has the confidence that you can go outside of your comfort zone and be successful. I think you should give it a shot," J.P. said with a wink. "That is sacred advice from a fifteen-year-old J.P. who used to wear a soccer uniform. See what happens."

"Well thank you for the vote of confidence," Kenny managed to say before being surprised by a giant wave that sneaked up behind them, causing the two kayaks to collide together and crash to shore.

They braced tightly but barely stayed atop the boats on the unexpected, bumpy ride that whisked them back to land. They ended up with mouthfuls of ocean water and appeared as if they had gone white water rafting through angry rapids but looked at each other with amusement and bewildered relief once the kayaks halted to a hard stop, front ends grounded into the sand, and they regained their composure.

"I guess that's a wrap." J.P. climbed out of his kayak and swept his wet hair back and out of his face with one hand while reaching to assist Kenny up with the other.

"That's a wrap." She smiled and gladly gripped J.P.'s strong forearm, allowing him to pull her to her feet. "That was the most fun I've had in a long time," she said with sincerity. "One thing, J.P. How did you know that first fin you saw wasn't a shark?"

"Honest answer?" He hesitated. "I didn't."

Twenty-Eight

Text to Hailey: Kayaking was AMAZING! Saw (Emoji: dolphin) up close!

Kenny contemplated a witty message to send to Colby to prove that she faced her fears and went kayaking in a body of water inhabited by sharks. For a hot minute she debated taking a selfie before leaving the beach but didn't want J.P. to think she was one of those girls who needed to document her whereabouts and activities to justify her existence or prove some point. Although, in this case, that's exactly what she was guilty of doing.

Text from Hailey: So fun! (Emoji: clapping hands)

After drafting and quickly deleting three texts to Colby, Kenny's phone vibrated.

"Hello?" she answered confused. She was so taken up in trying to find the right words to send to Colby that she thought she hit the wrong button and accidentally called him.

"Queen, *what* is going on? Those three little dots have

been dancing around the bottom of my screen for an eternity. I thought I'd call so you could verbalize whatever narrative you're typing, and save you a serious bout of carpal tunnel," Colby announced.

"Oh, oops! Well, now that I have your undivided attention, *unlike* last night," Kenny said sharply, "you should know that you might be right about the yellow bathing suit, but you are wrong about me! *I* kayaked for two hours *on* the ocean this morning and a giant fin knocked the side of my boat with such force that I almost tipped over and ended up *in* the water." She dramatically described the encounter.

"That sounds horrific!" Colby gasped. "Are you, okay? It's time to come home, sweetie. City girls like you aren't cut out for things people down there confuse for fun."

"You're wrong, Colby. It was the most fun I've had in a long time, and I think I *am* cut out for the things they do down here." She closed her eyes and couldn't get J.P.'s piercing blue ones out of her mind. "And it was a dolphin, not a shark. There were four of them. Dancing, waving, and singing all around us," she excitedly continued.

"Who is 'us?' And why do you sound giddy?" Colby asked suspiciously. "Remember when you were hanging out with that guy from Long Island, and he took you fishing? You caught a baby duck on your hook."

"That was a fluke," she said defensively. "After that I reeled in an impressive Cod that made enough fish and chips to feed half of the share house for dinner that night."

"Whatever. You're still far from being the face of REI," Colby rebuked. "I know you can't share details of the story but tell me there's at least some hunky piece of meat associated with this one. A brawny investigator? A strapping attorney? A rugged boat captain or whoever led this kayaking expedition."

"Colby! Is your mind always in the gutter?" Kenny

quipped. "I'm only saying this to shut you up and prove that I haven't totally shut my eyes to the male race, but there is a rather attractive man down here. He's totally off limits to me other than being a tour guide and providing the occasional few hours of good company. But it's nice having someone around."

"Off limits? *Yass*, Queen, you naughty girl. Tell me more. Is he married? A Catholic priest? A bank robber? What's the scandal?"

"What?" she yelled into the phone. "There's nothing more to tell. There's no scandal and he's none of those things. He's a golfer from Ohio who's never been married."

"You are so vanilla, Kennedy Sloane. But you do you. I guess I should simply be happy that the lights are on, and somebody is home," Colby said with undeniable disappointment that she didn't share some salacious, Harlequinesque anecdote.

"Most importantly, you should be happy I'm speaking to you again *and* sharing this detail."

"I concede," Colby whispered. "With any luck this GQ guy will be enough inspiration to entice you to dabble in some pull at your heartstrings, love-at-first-sight, can't-live-without-you prose."

"Muffin's proposition is under consideration. Nothing more, nothing less right now. I don't want to hear another word about it or allusion to me writing a piece of women's fiction until I bring it up. The ball is in my court now. Understand?"

"Yes, ma'am!"

"Good. I'll talk to you later, Colby," Kenny announced, feeling confident she was ending the conversation with the upper hand.

"One last thing. Since you're now coming out of your man-draught, maybe you'll consider giving Ed another shot when you get back? He *really* likes you," Colby blurted out before she hung up.

"Colby!"

"Sorry, too soon. I had to try. Love you, mean it, bi-yee!"

Kenny rolled her eyes and pulled up Giuseppi's Pizza on her phone so she could scroll through the menu. She was still riding on such a high from the morning and afternoon she spent with J.P. that she couldn't bring herself to be annoyed with Colby's pestering about Ed. She reached for the refrigerator to pull out the Brita and bowl of sliced lemons when she caught a glimpse of her Conditions List. The list remained in the same spot since the day she hung it on the freezer door but rarely took the time to reread the rules she established for herself. Even though she hadn't been romantically involved with anyone since the actor/model/trainer guy, whose name slipped her mind, she was proud of herself for having the foresight to add "No new male relationships" to the list. If she hadn't enacted this simple rule, Kenny knew she'd be at severe risk of overthinking or over-complicating her acquaintanceship with J.P.

"Eat healthy, every day," also popped off the page.

Kenny put down her phone and pulled out what was left of the head of Parris Island Cos romaine hearts and strips of flank steak she grilled the night before.

Twenty-Nine

J.P. stood over the electric burner of the commercial-size copper stove that spanned half a wall in the spacious kitchen of Mr. Cunningham's house on Marlin Manor. He scrambled eggs and simultaneously opened the oven to check the crispiness of the bacon. There was a giant overhead copper range hood affixed to the ceiling that he assumed had something to do with smoke, but he was still terrified of setting off the fire alarm during his culinary expedition. Cliff eagerly ran in and out of the sliding door to the patio, from the table to the stove in anticipation of J.P. dropping a piece of bacon for him to eat.

"Cliff, I was nervous, Buddy. I know they say you can tell a dolphin from a shark because dolphins' dorsal fins are more rounded than sharks', but you still get this uneasy feeling when you're out there, totally exposed. The fin *looked* rounded, but I wasn't wearing my contacts and had no plan B if it turned out to be a shark. Hell, I didn't even have a plan A," J.P. recounted the previous day's kayak encounter.

By the time he finished his dissertation about the anatomy of marine life, Cliff was back in the kitchen, prostrate and whimpering next to his empty water bowl.

"Shit! How long has that been empty? Did I forget to fill it yesterday or have you been extra thirsty?" J.P. rushed to fill the bowl while the dog gazed at it like he had just stumbled upon a cactus after a long hike across the desert.

He waited while Cliff aggressively and sloppily lapped up the water and then refilled the bowl before removing the tray of bacon from the oven and turning off the burner under the eggs. At home he would eat straight from the pan, but today decided to pull out one of the fancy melamine plates from the cabinet where Mr. Cunningham neatly stored his collection of outdoor serving dishes and place settings. J.P. thought the plates looked like slabs of tree bark that could be found among the pine needles and fallen palms that lined the walkway to the beach but assumed the earthy accent pieces came with a hefty price tag.

He sat at the sectional sofa next to the hot tub on the second-floor balcony and put down his coffee mug and plate on the table that doubled as a fire pit. He was impressed with the feast he had prepared without disrupting the morning of the crew on duty at Fire Station Two. The eggs were light and fluffy, the bacon had just enough crunch, and the mixed berry fruit salad looked like it should be on the cover of *Eating Well* magazine. He even took the time to boil water and grind coffee beans so he could use Mr. Cunningham's French press.

Sunday mornings were usually quiet on Sea Pines. Most locals went to church services off the plantation and visitors were still settling into their vacation properties, making trips to the Piggly Wiggly or waiting for weekly bicycle rentals to be delivered. But the beach was already bustling with activity this morning. Power walkers and joggers paraded along the water's edge on the hard, compact sand that was conducive to aerobic paces. Crews from the beach patrol scurried up and down the dunes erecting blue umbrellas and oak beach chairs with footrests for vacationers who opted to pay for the convenience of not having to set up and break down their own beach gear.

In the distance, workers at the Beach Club arranged symmetrical rows of white, fold-up resin chairs with salmon-colored sashes and constructed a white resin trellis that was wrapped in salmon-colored flowers. J.P. never understood the fuss around weddings, especially after hearing horror stories from his buddies whose fiancés mysteriously transformed from bragged about girlfriends of the year to unrecognizable bridezillas during the engagement period. But he silently stood in solidarity with the ladies who convinced their poor schmucks to tie the knot on the beach.

He sipped his coffee and stared out at the ocean and then down to his plate. He glanced back and forth a few times, reluctantly taking small bites and feeling guilty he was the only one enjoying the view and the breakfast. J.P. had a brief notion that perhaps he was confusing guilt with loneliness but quicky popped that thought bubble. He wasn't alone, he was single. He was a single guy who was with people all day, every day. Sometimes he wished people would give him space and leave him alone. He concluded that most men—single or attached—would pay money for this quiet time on a Sunday morning.

"Here, Cliff. Want to share my bacon?" J.P. dropped a paper towel with crumbled bacons bits on it to the floor as the dog charged out of the house. "Enjoy it. After I clean up here, we're both going for a run."

Thirty

Kenny changed out of the cotton pants and tank she slept in into another set of cotton pants and tank that some post-COVID retail marketing genius dubbed loungewear versus sleepwear, thereby making it appropriate to be seen in public in such attire, and poured a cup of coffee from the percolator. She slid on her flip-flops and decided to take a walk around the grounds of Pelican Pointe. She was struck by the quiet and stillness of the complex. The water aerobics women didn't occupy the pool, the pickleball courts were free of picklers, and there were no children teetering on the edge of the koi fish and carp ponds that Kenny was now all too aware may or may not be infested with alligators. If she hadn't done a clean sweep of the property, she would have thought she missed the memo for an enticing welcome brunch that many resorts host as a thank you to guests, all while really trying to hook them into a tour and four-hour spiel about the latest timeshare opportunities.

Kenny rolled up her pant legs and walked down two steps in the pool. Part of her wished she was wearing a bathing suit so she could completely submerge and spring into laps or lazily float, while the other part of her was completely content where she was. She sat down on the pool's edge, extended her legs straight in front of her so they were resting on the water's surface, and laid back on her forearms, gazing up at the sun. It was against her Conditions List, but she longed for a Post-it and pen. She had a whole day ahead of her with no plans or obligations; a clean slate, and she wasn't sure what to make of it. She trained her brain to lean on Post-its to prioritize her life, to keep her on point and in focus, weigh pros and cons of any situation. Her Post-its had Post-its. The square, sticky pads made Kenny's life productive and manageable. But her will was stronger than her reliance on any piece of tangible paper list and she decided to mentally go down the list of possible activities she had saved for such a day.

Mental Post-it/Possible Activities Sunday, September 17

- *Bike ride to the Stoney-Baynard Ruins (Note: the tabby remnants of the Plantation built by Revolutionary War hero Jack Stoney are haunted. You hate horror films and despise Halloween.)*
- *Visit the Sea Pines Shell Ring in the Forest Preserve (Note: the small shell ring built 4,800 years ago by Indian Moundbuilders, around the time of the Great Pyramids of Egypt, is located inside the Forest Preserve. Forests are filled with wildlife, you will be chased and eaten alive by an alligator.)*
- *Take a day trip to Savannah on The Spirit of Harbour Town (Note: The ship departs at 9:00 a.m. and it's already 10:30 a.m.)*
- *Go on a dolphin sightseeing tour (Note: Had that experience during kayak "research" trip.)*

- *Watch the sunset from the top of the Harbour Town Lighthouse (Note: the sun sets at 7:34 p.m. You just ate breakfast.)*
- *Brainstorm plot lines and characters for the next "book club bestseller" (Note: What does book club bestseller mean? Who makes up these genres, anyway?)*

Kenny felt the rays of sun beaming stronger on her skin and knew that if she didn't put on a hat or sunscreen, her face would be sufficiently burned within the hour. She took the last sip of coffee and one by one struck a mental line through everything she jotted down on her cerebral Post-it. The only bullet she didn't have a justifiable reason for crossing out was the last one.

She biked to South Beach Marina, the New England style waterfront village at the southernmost tip of Sea Pines and set up shop at one of the outdoor plastic tables at the Salty Dog Café. When she was deep in the trenches writing *Armchair Detective*, she spent countless hours at the plastic tables with the iconic lime green umbrellas at Pier i on Riverside Boulevard, overlooking the Hudson River on the Upper West Side of Manhattan. The causal vibe, the views of the water, and inspiration that could be drawn from people-watching were much the same. She ordered a lemonade, and the server brought her a basket of popcorn from the vintage popcorn cart on the side of the octagonal bar. She closed her eyes for a moment and briefly felt like she was back in New York, pen in hand and ready to write. Only this time, she had no idea where to start.

Kenny scribbled *Luck is when preparation meets opportunity* on the top of her college-ruled, spiral bound notebook.

She wasn't sure where she first heard the quote, but it was something that stuck with her over the years. It could have been something a sage, edgy Jesuit at Fordham prophesized in passing or it could have been advice of a freelance cameraman from Timbuktu who WBS hired to film an interview in a small, one stop-sign town. Regardless, she thought of the quote often. She detested the idea of applying these wise words to her current literary standoff with Muffin Evans, but deep down knew that half of the equation to her becoming a published author was already completed. Muffin had given her the opportunity. It was up to Kenny to rely on her decade of writing experience to round out the rest of the equation.

She sat for nearly an hour with a serious case of writer's block. She watched two small, shark-fishing charter boats leave port and saw the sixty-three-foot Salty Dog catamaran afternoon happy hour cruise sail in. She observed the line at the ice cream shop start to wrap around the deck and watched as parents clenched their breaths and children's hands while climbing the metal spiral staircase next to Land's End Tavern to reach the Salty Dog T-Shirt Factory. She heard the repeated, clipped "Hello" and "Goodbye" of the throaty-voiced, rainbow colored macaw and Amazon parrots that happily resided in the oak trees of the marina's open aviary and took pleasure in surprising the unsuspecting passerby with their presence. She got occasional wafts of fish and salt-water that blew in from the marina, but it was mostly masked by the smell of the platters of fried hushpuppies and gator bites that were delivered to midafternoon snackers at neighboring tables.

She knew she should be able to draw inspiration from any of these people or scenes, but she couldn't quite put her finger on any of it. She had *The Canterbury Tales* of the Deep South at her fingertips and there had to be more than one protagonist and antagonist among them. All the people who descended upon the South Beach Marina at the same time on a sunny, Sunday afternoon had stories, backgrounds, and secrets.

Kenny had questions, and possibly assumptions, about most of them but quickly realized that the storytelling of a news producer was starkly different than that of a fiction writer.

"Can I refill your basket of popcorn, Miss?" a young, freckle-faced girl with auburn hair and large, round circular glasses asked Kenny with a smile.

"Sure, that'd be great. And can you please bring me a menu?"

Kenny was satisfied with the popcorn but thought that she should order something of more substance if she was going to be occupying the server's table. She also wanted to ward off the table stalkers who lingered around the seating area, ready to pounce as soon as they saw take-out containers, or a check delivered to a party who was nearing the end of a meal. Kenny knew the type well as she was a seasoned table stalker who practiced her craft often during warm weather months at the Central Park Boathouse and outdoor bar at Tavern on the Green. Before she lifted her gaze to assess how many people had already observed her sitting alone at an empty table and were prepared for a standoff with other hungry diners for the coveted spot out of the way of foot traffic and unobstructed views of the water, the young girl was back with the menu and basket of popcorn,

"Here ya go, ma'am. It's a picture-perfect day out here, isn't it?" The girl looked admiringly toward the boats on the water.

"It sure is," Kenny replied. "You must love coming to work with this view."

"I do. I'm from Kansas, and we don't have anything like this where I grew up."

"Are you here seasonally?" Kenny asked the young lady who didn't look like she was more than seventeen years old.

"Yep. I'm doing an internship at one of the resorts during the week and pick up a few hours here on the weekends. My boyfriend has the same internship and helps the captains on some of the deep-sea fishing charter boats to pick up extra cash. We squeeze in a few hours each week to sit on the beach or go sight-seeing." She beamed and nodded to the lines of boats adorned with nets and fishing poles at the end of the dock.

This girl should be writing the next beach read, Kenny thought. Young and in love at the beach; getting college credits to entertain already-happy vacationers; making money at a seemingly stress-free job with tips that presumably grow higher with each round of beer buckets and frozen drinks; and spending any free time exploring paradise. Kenny pondered using this girl's life as a catalyst for a storyline of her book.

"*Wow*. What an awesome experience. I regret that I never took a summer or semester to work in a beach town." Kenny wondered if she had taken that chance, where the path would have led.

"It's the chance of a lifetime! I go back to the intern apartment every night and journal about my day and the people I meet. I don't want to forget any of it. Maybe someday I'll even write a book about this summer," the excitable server announced. "Are you ready to order? The kitchen is getting backed up, and I don't want you waiting all day for lunch!"

Ironic. I guess that plotline is off the table.

"I'll have the Ceasar salad and a side of the Bow Wow shrimp," Kenny said, although she wasn't particularly hungry for either and was certainly in no rush.

"Coming right up. Enjoy this table, it's the best one in the house." The girl winked and spun on her heels to greet the table behind Kenny and take drink orders.

For years, Marilyn encouraged Kenny to journal or write letters to herself—or others—about what she was experiencing; but Kenny chalked up the practice to busy work and shelved the idea on the same mental rack as self-care, over-rated and unnecessary. She also equated the dozens of filled notebooks in the drawers of her workspace at the office to some version of journaling. In her mind, those overly detailed reporter's notebooks were a precise account of her daily life. Practically, a diary. The notes were primarily work-related, but work was primarily her life, so to keep a separate journal would be redundant and time consuming in a life that was already strapped for time.

However, Kenny was intrigued by what she heard directly and indirectly from the summer intern. If a college student from Kansas could pull enough fodder from three months of her life to write a book, then Kenny suddenly became confi-dent that she could cull something from her decades-long career in the news business that would satisfy Muffin Evans and the easy-read audience that she was plotting to comman-deer. It was time to put the Clinton White debacle and *Armchair Detective* rejection in the rearview mirror.

Kenny picked up the black ballpoint, bold tip pen and began writing. What started off as an exercise in making bulleted lists turned into structured sentences that morphed into short paragraphs and resulted in a mini story of her experiences.

Before I Got Scooped

I've met presidents, politicians, celebrities, movie stars, profes-sional athletes, and had high tea with a dame. I've interviewed killers, criminals, convicts, men on death row . . . and the wrong-fully accused and convicted. Survivors, victims, those who felt they had no voice—and their loved ones—confided in me, sharing deeply personal, emotional, tragic, and resilient stories. I've spoken to medical heroes, scientific heroes, law enforcement heroes, religious heroes, and everyday heroes. I've filmed in sugar cane fields, gun ranges, and morgues; at crime scenes, movie premieres, and water parks; on red carpets, horse farms, fashion shows, urban superhero conventions, under Niagara Falls (over Niagara Falls), and in feet of snow on Alex Trebek's college campus; in houses of worship, prisons, police stations, theaters, airports, and hospitals.

I've reported on the biggest courtroom dramas of the decade, spending more time in courthouses than many trial attorneys. I've covered mass shootings, terror attacks, natural disasters, plane crashes, inaugurations, elections, and a once-in-a-lifetime pandemic. I've logged more air miles, checked into more hotels, and driven more rental cars than I could ever count. I've landed the big interviews, lost the big interviews, and cried over both. I've scooped stories, my stories have been scooped, and I'm learning that life goes on.

Kenny put the pen behind her ear and leaned back in the plastic chair to read what she wrote and noticed two arms reaching over her table.

"Look at that! You like writing, too? My creativity runs wild down here," the server said and set down the salad and appetizer plates on the table away from Kenny's notebook. "Enjoy! I'll be back in a few minutes to see if you need anything."

Thirty-One

Before J.P. could get to the end of the long hallway to open the door to Mr. Cunningham's office, he heard a loud *Thud!* and then a soft whimper from Cliff whom he assumed ran head-on into the locked door in an attempt to deliver *The Wall Street Journal* he retrieved from under the Adirondack chair on the wrap-around front porch of the clubhouse in exchange for a morning Milk-Bone from Mr. Cunningham, who was still in Georgia on business.

"Cliff, you clumsy pup. We need to work on pumping those brakes," he said to the dog who he found lying on his belly, defeated with the rolled-up newspaper still clenched in his mouth.

J.P. unlocked the door and Cliff slowly and dizzily stood on his paws, walked to the large mahogany pedestal desk, and dropped the paper next to the bottom right drawer where he knew the treats were stashed.

"You're not as simple as you sometimes act, are you?" He nodded and raided the drawer, breaking his own rule of no snacks before lunchtime.

He sat down in the mahogany and leather swivel executive chair and waited for Mr. Cunningham to call his office line. J.P. anticipated the discussion would entail big news as such conversations always did when the esteemed businessman was away scouting new investments. When Mr. C asked that J.P. be in his office and in view of the oversized desk calendar for the conference, he knew the old man had something up his sleeve.

Precisely on cue, the landline rang as the digital clock turned to 9:15 a.m.

"Good morning! How are things on Jekyll Island?" J.P. asked, slightly nervous to hear the predicted enormity of whatever his boss was about to tell him.

"Peachy, Jonathan. Just peachy," Mr. Cunningham said with a hefty laugh.

"You're getting funny in your old age," J.P. indulged the older gentleman, knowing he had likely waited all weekend to deliver the kitschy joke.

"I'm happy you appreciate the humor," Mr. Cunningham replied.

"Let's cut to the chase, Mr. C. What's going on down there? The only time you want me in your office for phone calls is when you have big news to share."

"You're nothing if not intuitive, Jonathan. The resorts I came down to tour are beautiful. The properties are pristine and lucrative. They need some updating but are centrally located and family friendly. They're owned by two brothers who are ready to sell, with the caveat that much of the business remains the same. They want to keep the name along with their employees, vendors, and service providers. I've looked at the books and spoken to several of the staff and I'm fine with most of that. The place runs like a well-oiled machine," Mr. Cunningham explained.

"What's the catch? And what's your plan?"

His mentor always had multiple plans in place to secure what he wanted.

"There's that inquisitive and self-starting mind churning. The catch is Mariott and a family squabble. Marriott is interested and, of course, dangling an offer significantly over asking price. The younger brother is only seeing the dollar signs. The older brother is enticed by the proposition but recognizes the hierarchy at the international chain may be paying the family lip service regarding keeping the name and employees, among other things, to secure the deal. He's more realistic and understands their quaint, familiar lodges could be transformed into cookie-cutter Courtyards or Fairfield Inns faster than ink dries on the dotted lines of a contract," Mr. Cunningham continued.

"Between the Marriott's portfolio and acquisitions that I read about on *PRNewswire*, I can only imagine what they are offering if they want the properties badly enough. I can't believe we're still in the running. Low Country Hospitality would never be able to compete with the Mariott?" J.P. rhetorically asked, though he was largely in the dark, about the revenue that Low Country Hospitality generated annually and how much Mr. Cunningham, himself, was worth.

"Don't sell us short, Jonathan. We can compete with customer experience and satisfaction. The brothers are big fish in a little pond, and I sense they prefer to remain that way, without having to work. Their grandfather and then father took pride in building this mini empire and, while I do believe the fortune has gone to the heads of the 'new money' generation, the brothers want to keep the name alive and prominent in the community. They also want to have the luxury of stopping in the resorts and being recognized when they're not busy blowing through their bank accounts and inheritance. All that goes out the window if they strike a deal with a major chain."

"Fair assessment," J.P. said. "Though I'm still not following how you strike the deal if they're money hungry."

"I suggested they come to Sea Pines for a few days. Stay around our properties and observe how we manage and operate. I'll set up meetings with the brothers and other family-owned chains Low County Hospitality has acquired and they can hear and see firsthand how and why our transactions and transitions succeed. I also advised them to sit with their financial advisors, who *will* reassure them they won't end up in the poorhouse if they accept the offer from Low Country Hospitality," Mr. Cunningham stated matter-of-factly.

"I'm sure they didn't take offense to that," J.P. said sarcastically. "I think you're the only person on this planet who can get off saying such things to people."

"Part of business is meeting people at their level, Jonathan. You'll learn," Mr. Cunningham responded. "They're going to make the trip in a few weeks, after they meet with their investment bankers."

"Of course, they are. What do we need to do to prepare so that the team seals the deal with these yahoos? Secure tee times, reservations at the spa, replenish the wine cellar and cigar room. What else? I can outsource one or two people from the clubhouse to help plan and execute an itinerary."

"First, let's do one of those impromptu Employee Appreciation Weekends. Get the staff reenergized after the busy, albeit successful summer. I looked at the clubhouse and hospitality reservations' calendars and we have a slow weekend ahead. On Saturday, I'll host an open house at Marlin Manor for cocktails and a seafood boil. Why don't you call Hudson's to see if they can cater lunch and dinner, that way employees can come around their shifts. On Sunday, all meals at the clubhouse for employees and their families will be comped. Any available tee times over the weekend will be offered to employees on a first come, first served basis. Let's allow them to use that simulator, too. If our remote employees can make the trip, they can charge airfare to their respective managers' corporate cards, and they can stay at the new ten-sleeper units at Pelican Pointe. Sound good?"

"That sounds more than good. I'll call over to Hudson's now. They should be pulling in grouper and seabass this week. Anything else?"

"I don't think so. Just leave my house the way you and Cliff found it when you move out tonight. Did I tell you I'll be home tonight? And don't encourage those youngins' who can't hold their alcohol to get too out of control this weekend."

"Yes, sir. Copy all that," J.P. obliged.

"And what about those kayaks? Did you test them? Should I buy more and stock the properties?" Mr. Cunningham asked.

"We did a 'dry' run this weekend and kayaks are great. We had a blast!" J.P. laughed at his own joke. "But they're too much of a liability to offer guests. Kenny almost dropped the paddle in the water when we thought we saw a shark. Then we both nearly capsized when a giant wave came out of nowhere and almost took us out. We averted catastrophe twice," J.P. enthusiastically recounted.

"Guess you had to be there," Mr. Cunningham responded, clearly not as amused as J.P. about what happened on the water. "Who's Kenny? The new caddie you hired down at the clubhouse?"

"Oh no, ugh." J.P. bit his tongue, wishing he hadn't mentioned her name. "Kenny is one of the renters staying at Pelican Pointe. I thought maybe she could offer a guest perspective about the kayaks. She travels often for work so has a lot of experience with hotel amenities."

"Jonathan, please tell me you're kidding," Mr. Cunningham chided from the other end of the phone.

J.P. didn't know what to read into the comment or how to interpret the tone. Until now, he didn't think through the ramifications if something were to go terribly wrong when he took a guest onto the water under the guise of a company sponsored activity. He was playing with fire.

"Let me get this straight. You had free reign of my beautiful home with amenities that are on par with a five-star hotel, you are the controller of one of the most prestigious golf courses on the eastern seaboard and you choose to woo the only woman you've shown an ounce of interest in since you retired to this island by throwing her atop a plastic boat and pushing her out to sea?" Mr. Cunningham questioned.

"Let me set *you* straight, Mr. C. I'm not trying to 'woo' anyone," J.P. replied attempting to convince himself and his boss this was true. "Don't get me wrong, Kenny is a great girl, and I enjoy her company. But her life is in New York, and she'll be going back there soon. She's also married to her career and her work assignments take her to prisons and courtrooms, not Pelican Pointe or Calibogue Sound."

"Let me think. Where have I heard that one before?" Mr. Cunningham asked in a way that J.P. could visualize the older gentleman sitting back in his chair, right leg folded over his left knee, with his thumb under his chin and tapping his temple with his index finger.

"Heard what before?" J.P. sheepishly responded to the question with a question.

"The tried and true 'focused on your career' story. The same one that you tell me when I point out an attractive woman at the clubhouse or suggest you find female companionship? Personally, Jonathan, I think all that gibberish is code that smart people, like yourself and this Kenny girl, use when you're afraid of letting your guard down and getting hurt.

But what do I know? I'm just an old man who fell in love with his soulmate at the Washington Square Park playground when he was nine years old," Mr. Cunningham said like he was delivering a sermon.

"I wish I was around for this prehistoric era you speak of," J.P. defended, "but things *are* different these days. Even if they weren't, it would be completely impractical to try and make things work with a woman who lives seven states away."

"Love isn't practical. Business is practical, law is practical, finances are practical. You can agree or disagree."

"Point taken, Mr. C."

"You know what else is practical? Eating dinner. Why don't you take her to Charlie's for a nice meal? Practical people eat dinner seven nights a week."

"You missed your calling, Counselor," J.P. said. "You've made your argument, and I'll *think* about it. Now if you'll excuse me, I need to check out of your estate and brace myself for the influx of overzealous golfers that will flood the clubhouse when you send out the email about the Employee Appreciation Weekend."

Thirty-Two

Kenny skipped her morning laps in the pool and biked to the Beach Club to practice Tuesday morning beach yoga with yogi Bonnie. Bonnie enthusiastically greeted the mixed bag of students and directed them to lay their towels in a semicircle around her own, facing the ocean. Savannah and the Wine after Nine foursome had already staked their territory and were carefully selecting their affirmation cards and chakra stones.

She could always use a good stretch but that wasn't the root of today's mindful motivation. Every part of her considered—maybe hoped—that she may run into J.P. and Cliff on their morning walk. It was exactly one week since the infamous meet cute on the beach and she couldn't believe how much more confident she felt, mentally and physically, since she commenced her hiatus of life. She wore her favorite pair of yellow running shorts that she deemed safe to wear on the sand, just not in the ocean, and a white racer back tank. The night before she spent hours on the computer attempting to master the French braid, so her hair was swept off her face in some version of a decent twist.

She hadn't seen J.P. in four days, and she wouldn't have minded if their paths happened to cross today. In the back of her mind, she had been longing to run into him since Sunday afternoon at the Salty Dog when, after snacking on popcorn and a shrimp appetizer, she had an epiphany about the book club bestseller she was ready to write.

Kenny unfolded her towel between the golfers and a group of tweens who wore short sleeved fitted T-shirts with Nutmeg Ballet Conservatory Summer '24 scrawled across the front and black bike shorts that were so tiny they looked like they would fit an American Girl doll. She conscientiously chose an affirmation card and chakra stone and laid down on the towel, eyes closed and face to the sun, while she waited for Bonnie to open class with the round robin introductions that, surprisingly, Kenny wasn't entirely dreading.

"I heard that he's the grandson of Charles Fraser, you know, the guy who founded Hilton Head," one of the Wine after Nine girls declared to her friends.

"Really? I heard he's the great-grandson of Ely Callaway, the company that manufactures all the golf equipment. Which would make more sense than being the descendant of a real estate developer. But it must be on his mother's side because I don't think his last name is Callaway," another friend chimed in.

"It's Long," another voice said. "The media had a field day with the play on words. *It's Never a Long-Shot for Long, One Long-Drive Tops the Leaderboard.*"

"He's so dreamy. And mysterious. How can he be considered the most eligible bachelor on the island, yet so little is known about him? He's been around for eight years now and the most aggressive circles of women on the prowl haven't been able to crack him. Even his name is mysterious. J.P. must stand for something. But what?"

Kenny shot up like she was being ejected from an airplane

and quicky faked a coughing jag, so it didn't look like her sudden movement was in reaction to the conversation she was guilty of eavesdropping on.

"There's something so attractive about the unattainable, ladies," Savannah, presumably the leader of the pack, said to her girlfriends. "We should invite him to join us for liquid lunch one of these Tuesdays. We'll knock down that guard." She giggled mischievously, and the rest of her posse clapped in unison.

"It's time to get started. Let's calm our bodies and quiet our minds. Begin to rid yourself of any distraction. It's a beautiful day to practice in this paradise we call Sea Pines," Bonnie said as she attempted to reel the rowdy class back to silence and stillness.

Bonnie led the class through a series of planks, wide legged forward folds, high and low lunges, and warrior poses before she guided the group to their towels and finished class with a few Bikram postures. The pace was faster than the first beach yoga class Kenny took with Bonnie, and she couldn't believe how quickly the sixty minutes passed. The sun and air were warm, but the humidity wasn't as high as it had been since she arrived a week ago, and a light breeze blew off the ocean.

Bonnie invited the class to wiggle their fingers and toes and pulled them out of their final, two-minute Savasana. Still in a trance-like state, the group slowly sat up to their sit bones or knees. They shared their affirmation cards and Bonnie explained the meaning behind the color of their stones. Kenny partially listened while she intently stared out to the ocean, but the sound of the waves crashing ashore and the cicadas buzzing in the dunes drowned out most of what the other women were saying.

"Last but not least, we have our friend from Manhattan. Kenny, would you like to share?" Bonnie prompted.

"Of course!" Kenny jolted her mind back to the group. "Today I am glowing. Today I have huge amounts of energy and focus to take on any challenge," she read from her card. "And I have this pretty, deep red crystal. It looks to have a bit of black in there, too," she said, picking up the gemstone and inspecting it closer.

"That is a beautiful stone and one that has restorative powers," Bonnie excitedly shared. "Red garnet revitalizes feelings of love, passion, creativity, and determination. Last week, you mentioned you were hoping to find inspiration. If you haven't already found it, you are well on your way with the energy you will receive from this stone." The yoga instructor stared Kenny dead in the eyes and smiled.

Bonnie delivered a closing thought about gratitude, folded her hands, and bowed her head.

"Namaste," the class replied in unison and quickly rolled up their towels and returned their cards and stones to the bag on Bonnie's blanket.

Kenny took her time walking back to the Beach Club and tried to decide how she could distract herself from being envious of the Wine to Nine ladies who were on their way to Liberty Oaks for tee-off. She knew she had no right to be jealous. There was no chance that anything could ever develop between her and J.P., especially now knowing he was deemed the most eligible bachelor not just on Sea Pines, but on all of Hilton Head Island. Regardless, a part of her was irked that these women with their perfect tans, physiques and lives were on a mission to win J.P. over, like he was the biggest prize at the toughest game at the county fair. She unzipped the pocket of her cross-body bag to pull out her phone and noticed a text from Hailey.

*Text from Hailey: Will b in SP this wknd! (Emoji: palm tree)
Wud (Emoji: pink heart) 2 meet u!*

Text to Hailey: That's awesome! Would be great to meet you in person! When will you be in town?

Text from Hailey: (Emoji: plane) in Sat ayem. U free Mon (Emoji: moon)? (Emoji: champagne glasses)

Kenny interpreted this to mean that Hailey was flying into Hilton Head on Saturday morning and was proposing drinks on Monday evening.

Text to Hailey: Monday evening sounds perfect!

Text from Hailey: Yay! C u then (Emoji: smiley with star eyes)

Kenny doubted that she and Hailey would have much in common, but she looked forward to a night with her new girlfriend and chatting over a fruity cocktail. She threw her phone back in her bag, tossed the bag in the basket on her bike and took off for Pelican Pointe.

She couldn't believe it was already time for lunch. Her morning duathlon turned into something of a sprint triathlon. Following the bike ride back to the villa after yoga, she felt so rejuvenated that she decided to go for a jog to Lawton Stables and back. She wasn't an equestrian, but she always thought horses were beautiful animals and the horse farm made a good destination when she tried to get in a decent jog. She credited the burst of energy to a combination of the powers of the red garnet chakra stone and vanity. She was satisfied with how she looked in the yellow running shorts and white tank and wanted to keep the shape she worked hard to reclaim.

Kenny was unlacing her sneakers when her phone vibrated.

*Text from Colby: I haven't talked to you since Saturday
night. It's Tuesday afternoon. Is this assignment keeping
you away from* The Bachelor? *I CANNOT believe I didn't
hear from you last night! Call me. LYMIB.*

Colby was part of the culture that was obsessed with *The
Bachelor.* He became more invested with each season and
even made a hobby out of befriending hopeful contestants
who would descend on the Upper West Side for auditions
several times a year. Throngs of women, in all shapes and
sizes, from all corners of the country, would quite literally
campout, rain or shine, on the sidewalks surrounding the
ABC headquarters in full makeup, high heels, and risqué
clothing with remarkable, almost admirable, confidence they
would catch the eye of casting producers, who would catapult them to Hollywood fame.

Kenny rolled her eyes at the text. In her reality, there was
only one bachelor she was consumed with. She reluctantly
dialed Colby.

"*Oh. My. God.* Can you believe he did that to her? My
heart stopped. It literally stopped. Can you imagine what
those producers thought? How did the crews not drop the
cameras and mics out of utter shock!" Colby dramatized
upon answering the phone.

"For the millionth time, I haven't watched *The Bachelor* or
any of its spinoffs since season one. And reality TV is about as
real as the boobs of all those contestants," Kenny said,
deadpan.

"You're just jealous. Did you know that Brazilian butt
implants are on the rise, too?" Colby needled. "In other news,
how's that golfing kayaker? I googled 'hot golfers' and stumbled across a very eye-pleasing article in *Golf Digest.* I was
impressed. It wasn't a bunch of beer-bellied men wearing

visors, saddle shoes and Geoffrey Beene polo shorts from 1980. You might be onto something!"

"There is something seriously wrong with you. I haven't seen him the last few days, which is for the better. He'd probably just become an unnecessary distraction," Kenny lied.

The truth was J.P. had already become a distraction.

While Kenny was out on her run along Greenwood Drive, she realized she had seen J.P. four out of five days the previous week but not once in the three days following their kayaking trip. She could not help but wonder if the island's most eligible bachelor was actively avoiding her. She also pondered if today was the day that J.P. would be roped into drinks with the gaggle of Wine after Nine girls. Much to her chagrin, Kenny assumed they would be a fun bunch, especially after their touted liquid lunch. It was conceivable that a round of group drinks could lead to a second, more intimate drink with him and just one of the ladies in the group; that would inevitably escalate to dinner, dating, and happily ever after.

"When you do 'bump' into him again, or whatever serendipitous encounters the two of you have been having, don't run in the opposite direction. You sounded happy on Saturday, and happy Kenny is my favorite Kenny," Colby said sincerely.

"I was happy," Kenny said with smile.

"Since I can't ask you about the new book project, what else is going on down there? Is the assignment moving as scheduled?"

"Everything is going well, moving in the right direction. But I gotta run. I have something at a lighthouse tonight," she abruptly said, thinking back to her mental to-do list from Sunday. "I'll send you pictures of the sunset."

She was both looking for an excuse to get off the phone and give herself something to look forward to. She knew nothing productive could come of sitting alone for the rest of the day planning J.P.'s wedding to a woman he likely hadn't even met, yet.

"Pictures of the sunset from the top of a lighthouse? Maybe you *are* turning into a romantic. Love you, mean it, bi-yee!" Colby chimed before hanging up.

Thirty-Three

J.P. took one last look around the second-floor deck, kitchen, and guest bedroom with the attached bathroom of Marlin Manor and locked all the doors behind him. He put his golf bag, garment bag and duffel in the back of his red Wrangler and Cliff hopped up and into the passenger seat.

"Everything is how we found it. Right, Boy?" J.P. said as he slid down his Ray Bans from the top of his head to his face.

Cliff sat on his hind legs and stared squarely at J.P.

"Good, I thought so, too." He threw the car in reverse, pulling out of the two-car guest garage where Mr. Cunningham kept many of his water toys.

"Maybe I should've asked Kenny for her number." J.P.'s eyes caught a glimpse of the kayak racks right before the door closed them out of sight. "The Old Man is right. Grabbing dinner with her doesn't have to be a big deal. People share meals all the time."

Cliff barked as they pulled down the driveway. J.P. interpreted this timely reaction as Cliff agreeing. Deep down he knew the dog was responding to nothing more than the squirrels scurrying up and down the trees that he wanted to jump out of the moving vehicle to chase.

"What do you say we stop at Harbour Town?" J.P. drove down North Sea Pines Drive and turned on his blinker to indicate he was going to make a right-hand turn on Lighthouse Road. "My legs are too sore for a run tonight, but I'm too stiff to sit around at home and watch TV."

It wasn't often that J.P. opted to drive the Wrangler rather than ride his bike around the plantation and was struck by how different the views were from behind four wheels instead of on top of two. J.P. realized that he was like a character in a scene of a play when he was peddling around on a bicycle. When he drove a vehicle, it was like he was a spectator observing the scene. The island seemed busier from this vantage point; the trails that ran parallel to the roads seemed more congested, the parking lots seemed fuller, and the tennis courts all looked occupied. The shrubbery seemed more abundant, and the ponds appeared smaller.

J.P. did two loops around the parking lot before he pulled the old Jeep into the overflow area near the Harbour Town Bakery and Café. He hadn't realized it was so close to dinnertime and, judging by the parking areas, assumed wait times at The Quarterdeck and The Crazy Crab were peak summer tourist kind of long. J.P. hooked Cliff's leash to his collar and the two walked toward the red brick walkway that lined the perimeter of the famous yacht basin.

J.P. and Cliff walked past the playground, where strollers and bikes with training wheels lined the short wooden fence that kept rambunctious children at bay. Inside of the fortress, older children climbed trees, and younger children were pushed on swings by the parent who drew the short straw that day. The other parent was undoubtedly sipping a cocktail while waiting for the family's name to be called by a maître d', indicating their dinner reservation was ready.

J.P. and Cliff continued down the strip of covered walkway that was home to a toy store, women's luxury pajama store and antique store. The two reached a small deck that was outfitted with the iconic red, wooden rocking chairs that were symbolic of Harbour Town and abundant around the waterfront community.

J.P. took a seat, and Cliff calmly laid down next to him, seemingly oblivious to the activity around him, his gaze fixed toward the water. Subconsciously and slowly, he pumped his feet back and forth, from toes to heels, and back again. It was a sight, an experience, he couldn't get enough of. Growing up, he anxiously paced this deck waiting for Gregg Rusell, the infamous child entertainer who had as much acclaim and notoriety among his young audiences' parents and grandparents as the kids who flocked his stage, to begin his nightly set under the stars and majestic Liberty Oak Tree.

In his teen years, he'd sit on this deck with a Coke while his dad enjoyed a cold beer and the two would make small talk with the other men and their sons who had lost their daughters, wives, and wallets to the boutiques. As an adult, J.P. sat on this deck for hours listening to the live music from the acoustic guitarist singing his best James Taylor at the Harbourside café and admire the yachts and sailboats parked in the basin against the backdrop of the Harbour Town Golf Links course and distinctive red and white peppermint striped lighthouse.

The blue sky gave way to hues of pinks, purples, oranges, and yellows. The combination of the varied palettes and the glare that reflected off the water turned the white cumulus and stratus clouds to puffs of aqua and magenta. Harbour Town was one of the most coveted spots on the island to see a sunset and observers were always guaranteed a spectacular light show. But J.P. could feel that the marina was in for a real treat tonight.

"What do you say, Cliff? It's been a while. Want to go up?" J.P. patted the dog on the head and pointed to the lighthouse.

The dog jumped to his four paws and tugged on his leash before J.P. rocked out of his chair. The two walked down the crushed shell path, along the wall of boats that docked in the circular marina, and he hoped he knew whoever was working the door. Dogs weren't permitted to climb the 114 steps of the historical landmark, but he was confident he could pass off Cliff as a service animal. J.P. wasn't one to pull strings or use his minor notoriety to his advantage, but this was a case where he was willing to bend the rules.

He gingerly opened the door and recognized the teen collecting money from one of the booths at the farmers market.

"Hey man! Service dog." He glanced down at Cliff and slid the young man a twenty-dollar bill, despite the admission being seven dollars. "I don't need change."

"There's hardly anyone up there." The kid grinned wide and gave a reassuring nod toward the steps, to be interpreted as neither party would be in trouble for allowing Cliff to be in the lighthouse.

Despite the warning, J.P. was surprised, but relieved, he didn't pass a single person on his trek up the narrow, steep steps that were marked every eight feet. He ran more miles in the last two days than he logged in the last year and his body was feeling the effects of being out of condition. When he reached the forty-two feet marker, he was ready to turn around. By the time he reached the top of the ninety-three-foot octagonal stucco tower, his legs felt like Jell-O, and he was ready to sit down. He regretted not staying reclined in his rocking chair closer to sea level.

"Remember, you're not supposed to be up here, so behave," J.P. gave Cliff a stern warning before going to the observation deck.

Once he regained steadiness in his feet and caught his breath, he opened the door. His instinct was to walk to the right, but Cliff pulled unexpectedly hard in the opposite direction and J.P. lost the loose grip he had on the leash, and sight of the dog.

"Hi, Cliff! What are you doing, boy?" J.P. heard a female voice say to the mildly disobedient canine.

He paused for a moment. It sounded like Kenny. Deep down he hoped it was.

"Does J.P. know you're up here?" the sweet voice asked.

Confirmed. It's Kenny.

For a split second, he felt nervous. Aside from admiring beach weddings from afar, he didn't consider himself a romantic by any stretch of the imagination. But the thought of being on top of the lighthouse with Kenny during this magnificent sunset intrigued him.

"J.P. does know he's up here," J.P. said as he turned the corner. "He's a service dog tonight." He winked as he bent over and picked up the dog's leash.

"I see the emotional support he provides you. He seems to know what you need," Kenny lightheartedly laughed.

J.P. laughed because he thought it was the appropriate reaction but in the back of his mind found immense irony in what Kenny said. Since she had arrived on the plantation, Cliff led J.P. directly to her whenever the opportunity arose.

"How about this view?" He spread his arms wide, placed his hands on the ledge, and peered out over the water.

"It's breathtaking. I've been wanting to come up here around sunset and can't imagine I could have picked a more perfect night." Kenny situated herself next to J.P. trying to find the right balance between not being too close but not leaving too much space between them. It was no longer just the view creating circumstances for a perfect evening.

"Catching a sunset from up here is one of my favorite

things to do," J.P. said. "There's something so peaceful about it all, especially when it's a sparse crowd," he said, alluding to the fact that they were alone on top of this tower.

"When I'm having a bad or busy day, I try to get to the running path along the Hudson River at dusk. I've seen some beautiful sunsets. But, at the end of it, you're still looking across the water to the chaos and bright lights of northeastern New Jersey. There's something about the tranquility behind this vast view that is overwhelmingly serene."

"It's something else," J.P. replied. "It's not quite the pandemonium of the Garden State but you can get glimpses of life in other parts of the Lowcountry from up here. This body of water is Calibogue Sound." He leaned over the railing and looked down. "Across the Sound is Daufuskie Island. You can only get there by boat and the population is less than a thousand."

"Wow. There aren't many city blocks in Manhattan that house less than one thousand people." Kenny laughed.

"You want to see unique? Check out the chunk of land over here." He led Kenny to the other side of the observation deck. "That's Deer Island. It's a community of tree houses." He excitedly pointed to a group of elevated octagonal structures at the far end of Harbour Town.

"Tree houses?" Kenny questioned, although that's exactly what they looked like from where she stood.

"Technically, they are referred to as Sea Lofts. But they're circular homes built among the trees with panoramic views of Calibogue Sound and nature. I've never been in one, but I've checked them out on VRBO. They are high-end tree houses."

"Huh. Some homes along the Jersey Shore were elevated to stilts following Hurricane Sandy, but they still look like houses, not life-size tree forts." Kenny laughed.

"Down that way is the port at the mouth of the Savannah

River. You wouldn't know it from here, but it's one of the busiest seaports in the country."

"Have you always been such a fact junkie? Every time we run into each other I feel like I'm on some type of island education tour. The reporter in me usually needs to pry this information out of people."

"You've been on this island long enough to know who Gregg Russell is, right? Everyone who has spent more than ten minutes on Hilton Head has heard of him."

Kenny pointed to the other side of the lighthouse. "The child entertainer who plays under that big tree over there during the summer?"

"Yes, that's him. And that's the Liberty Oak Tree." J.P. gave a dorky grin, acknowledging he slipped in another factoid. "Anyway, he's notorious for dropping bits of Sea Pines history into his sets, and I've heard enough of his monologues and taken my niece on enough of his Bubble Gum cruises over the years on the *Vagabond* down there, that I'd be a fierce competitor in a game of Hilton Head trivia." He pointed to a large white ship docked below them, next to another, larger white ship that had *Spirit of Harbour Town* scrawled across the side.

There was a still silence as both of their attentions turned back to the bold, colorful spectrum in front of them. The blazing orange circle at the focal point deliberately slid down the vista.

"This is my favorite part," J.P. said quietly, as if not to disturb the moment.

"Me too," Kenny agreed, as the sun disappeared into the horizon.

They stood in quiet for another few moments, each trying to anticipate what the others' next move was going to be. They turned their bodies inward and when they locked eyes, Cliff barked and broke the silence.

"We should probably get going. I'm sure the lighthouse keeper is waiting to lock up for the night," Kenny said, even though she never wanted this moment to end.

"You're right. And he won't forget we're up here with Cliff barking," he replied, wondering if Kenny could sense the disappointment in his voice.

They made the trek down the dozens of steps, mostly in quiet.

"Cliff and I started running this week, thanks in part to you putting me to shame on those kayaks. These steps nearly killed me tonight. My legs felt like Jello-O before the climb, now I'm not sure I can feel them at all," J.P. confessed as they turned the corner on the last flight.

"Those first few come back runs are the worst. What made you think scaling a lighthouse would be a good idea tonight?"

"I have no idea. I was perfectly content sitting in my red rocking chair outside of Nell's Harbour Shop."

"You're a glutton for punishment; your quads are going to be on fire tomorrow. But I'm happy I wasn't up there alone." Kenny curled the edges of her lips up and smiled.

I am a glutton for punishment, J.P. thought. *I don't fall for anyone and here I am falling for a girl who lives eight hundred miles away.*

They got to the bottom of the steps and walked out the door, past the young lighthouse keeper who was taken up with his phone.

J.P. abruptly turned around and handed Cliff's leash to Kenny. "If you have a half hour to spare, why don't you find two rocking chairs? I'll grab us a beer from the Quarterdeck. They have a few drafts on tap from a new microbrewery down in Savannah that they've been serving. Mr. C has been on my case to check them out. He strives to keep things fresh in the kitchen and behind the bar at the clubhouse."

"Sure, that sounds great," Kenny stumbled for words and took the leash.

She led Cliff down the brick walkway in search of two unoccupied red rocking chairs that were next to each other, and J.P. shuffled inside to the bar. As he stood in line waiting to be served, he wondered why he couldn't have simply asked Kenny if she wanted to grab a drink. Instead, he couched it as a work assignment, like the kayaking excursion. He easily could have tested the beer or kayaks on his own. He wasn't sure which scenario would be perceived as more pathetic, that he didn't want to conduct these easy tasks by himself, or he couldn't ask a girl to spend time together without some elaborate justification.

He was thrown back to the time in high school when he feigned to not understand trigonometry because he had a crush on the peer tutor, who also happened to be captain of the cheerleading squad. Katie George not only understood triangles on paper, but she was always the bubbly, tiny one at the top of the triangle when the team built pyramids. Katie and J.P. went on to date for four years and he eventually admitted that he never, once, had a problem in a math class, but he still felt like that seventeen-year-old boy who couldn't go straight after what he wanted. He always thought there was a fine line between the guys who came off as overly confident and the guys who came off as arrogant. He never wanted to come off as either; as a result, he never mastered how to straddle that line.

He sat down next to Kenny. "Nice find on the rockers! I thought you'd still be looking, or we'd be walking around drinking these."

"See that boat over there?" She pointed to a yacht that took up most of the harbor.

"*Silver Tops* from Mobile, Alabama? That's not a boat. That's a floating city."

"Yes, that one. Two of the older gentlemen who own that 'floating city' were sitting here with a small dog who got all riled up when he saw Cliff. We got to talking and when they found out I was on the hunt for rocking chairs they told me to have a seat because they were heading home for their nightly ritual of Manhattans and Mahjong."

"I couldn't have been gone for more than ten minutes and you scored seats *and* made new friends. Impressive. That yacht shows up for a few weeks every autumn. I've admired it for years. Everyone on the plantation has admired it for years," J.P. clarified and handed Kenny one of the plastic cups filled to the brim with gold colored beer.

"It's a cool story. A group of nine siblings and their spouses pulled their retirement when the men left their decades long careers in the aerospace industry and bought that ship. The crew, nicknamed 'The Silver Tops' by their children, always loved to travel but when they realized how much they spent in hotels and airfare, they decided to invest their money elsewhere," Kenny continued.

"Geez, people really do tell you things." J.P. shook his head. "Well, cheers to The Silver Tops and the possibility of one day having a life of cruises, Manhattans, and Mahjong."

"Cheers." Kenny clinked her plastic cup and took a sip. "So how have you been? Are you still at Marlin Manor? Holding down the fort for Mr. Cunningham?"

"No, we got evicted earlier today," J.P. joked. "Mr. C drove home from Georgia this afternoon. We are back to slumming it, our little life of paupers."

"I don't want to hear your sob story. When I go back to New York, I'll be going back to a Polly Pocket sized two-hundred-square foot concrete rectangle with bars on the windows," Kenny said matter-of-factly.

"Are you going back to Rikers? Are you here on some extended work release program or something?"

Kenny playfully pushed J.P.'s arm. "Shut up!" She surprised herself by instinctively touching him and blamed it on the few sips of beer she had taken. "My studio, I call it The Dollhouse, is quite cozy. Right now, I wouldn't trade it for anything. It's safe and comfortable, and I love my neighborhood."

"The Dollhouse? That's funny. You'd probably adjust just fine at one of those places on Deer Island."

"What about you? What kind of digs does the island's most eligible bachelor live in?" Kenny let slip.

Ugh. Did I just go there? Tell the pale ale to leave the Wine after Nine girls out of this!

"What?" J.P. almost spewed out his beer. "Are you talking about me?"

"Oh yes. You were the talk among a group of golfers at beach yoga this morning. But I shouldn't have said anything. I didn't mean to embarrass you," Kenny quickly retracted.

"Whatever you do, don't get caught up with that crew." J.P. laughed. "The Wine after Nine ladies? They're nothing but trouble. I run as fast as I can when they step off Wisteria Lane and into the clubhouse every Tuesday.

"They seem a bit . . . high maintenance? I guess you should accept their come-ons and attention as flattery." Kenny smiled, though on the inside she kicked herself for bringing up the aggressive golfers and their gossip. Trying to change the subject, she asked, "Is it a busy week at the clubhouse?"

"Yes and no. As far as activity on the course is concerned, it's about the same as this week last year. Numbers, clinics, and tee times are steadily climbing to where they stood pre-COVID. But the workload for anyone employed by Mr. C is abundant. He's constantly growing and expanding his empire," J.P. explained with admiration and a bit of hesitation.

"That's great for job security. It seems that everyone who works for him really enjoys what they do. But you sound a bit apprehensive. Do you think Mr. Cunningham is setting expectations too high?" Kenny inquired.

"No, that's not it, necessarily. Mr. C is the smartest businessman I've ever met; and I met a lot of successful people while I was on tour. Everything he touches turns to gold. He leads by example and people work hard for him. He'd never dabble in something he wasn't confident was going to be prosperous."

"What's the hesitation about then? Are you not satisfied in your role in all of it? You have a job a million guys would kill for." Kenny didn't want to put J.P. on the spot, again, but the journalist in her couldn't help but ask follow-up questions.

"I love my job. If you can call it that. It sounds cliché, but it never seems like work." He laughed before taking a more serious tone. "For a while now, Mr. C has been talking a lot about succession plans and setting up his corporation for a seamless transition in the event he ever walks away, which I never see happening. He wants me to take on a larger role, much larger role in the organization. And I guess that's an overwhelming thought for me," J.P. said while glancing toward the sky.

"Like, second in command type of role?"

J.P. drew his attention back to Kenny. "He hasn't come out and said it in so many words, but yes, that's what he has in mind."

"Congratulations, J.P.! I understand why that's intimidating but what an opportunity. For someone you have so much admiration and respect for, to have such faith in you that he wants you to carry on his legacy, that's huge!"

Kenny hoped these words didn't come out insincere or rehearsed. She believed what she said but wondered if J.P. perceived it that way. The conversations she had with interview subjects were always deep and intimate and she truly cared about their emotions, thoughts, and feelings; but it had been some time since she had a heart to heart with someone who she wasn't going to put on national television. Someone that, whether she wanted to or not, she was developing a personal connection with. There was a line between personal and professional, work and play. But she had lost all sense of how to navigate the line when it came to him.

"It's a funny thing, Kenny. I've thought that. I'm not afraid of the hard work that comes with his success. I was born a competitor. I'm a boot on the ground, all-hands-on-deck kind of guy. The fear is disappointing him. Or failing his legacy," he said somberly. "The guy is like a freaking unicorn. This is all off the record, right? Or whatever the phrase is that people invoke like the Fifth Amendment when they say something to a reporter but instantly regret it?" He laughed as if trying to lighten the mood. "I've never said any of that out loud. And I've *never* called another man a unicorn."

"Your secret is safe with me." She swept her right pointer finger and thumb across her lips and flexed her wrist toward the yacht basin like she was tossing away the key that zipped up J.P.' s secret into the water; that would be washed into Calibogue Sound and eventually make its way into the Atlantic Ocean. "But maybe you should give it a try and see what happens."

Kenny coyly smiled, imparting the same words of wisdom on J.P. that he shared with her when she disclosed her book debacle.

"I see what you just did there. You don't miss much, Kennedy, do you?"

"Did you just call me by my *real* name?"

"It seemed like a good opportunity to call you by your first *and* last name, but I don't know your last name. So, your full first name had to suffice. Anyway, how are things going with your romantic comedy? I don't think I should be the only one on the hot seat tonight."

"I've decided to give it a valiant effort." She straightened her back and firmly planted her feet on the ground.

She imagined she looked like the Speaker of the House sitting behind the president of the opposition party at a State of the Union address, who wanted to believe everything the leader of the free world said but wasn't fully on board.

"Good for you. I admire people who can go outside of their comfort zone," J.P. asserted. "Can you tell me what it's about? Or do authors keep those details private until the swanky launch party?"

"A swanky launch party isn't quite on my radar. I'm not a household name like Carrie Bradshaw," Kenny quipped. "I'm at the stage in my publishing career that I'll be canvassing independent bookstores begging them to stock their shelves with a copy or two."

"Even smart girls like you compare themselves to fictional characters like Carrie Bradshaw? Guys get a bad rap in the commonsense department but at least we aspire to be real men—like Matthew McConaughey or a Manning brother," J.P. shot back.

"Touché. I do have a few thoughts swirling around up here." She lifted her hands to the sides of her head and started making circles. "But I haven't settled on one, yet."

"Let's hear these ideas that are 'swirling around up there.' I was never much of a writer. Term papers were the bane of my existence in school, but books always fascinated me. How people take simple thoughts and create stories about people and places . . . it's pretty cool if you think about it."

"Are you saying that I'm cool and fascinating?" Kenny blurted out, knowing that it was the additional sips of beer that were talking.

"Maybe." J.P. grinned. "I guess it depends on what kind of

people and places you're dreaming up for this romantic comedy that the ladies of Sea Pines are going to be running around the plantation with copies of next summer."

"Fine. Just remember, this is stuff that someone *wants* me to write. The type of books *I* want to write are much deeper, smarter, and more intelligent."

"I get it. You're not the warm and fuzzy, get swept off your feet, fall head over heels, kind of girl." Her rolled his eyes.

She took a pause at hearing those words come out of his mouth. She wondered if she'd be happier being a little more of that kind of girl and a little less the overly cautious and practical one that she always was.

"These are the top three contenders, as of now. An aspiring actress from Toad Suck, Arkansas, works two jobs and saves her earnings for a year so she can make the trip to Park City, Utah, to volunteer at the Sundance Film Festival. She's assigned to help at a bus stop for the shuttle system that transports festival goers from theater to theater. There, she befriends one of the regular passengers, whom she eventually learns is one of the most revered film directors in the industry. He casts her in a film he's directing, she wins an Oscar for her performance, they fall in love and live happily ever after."

"That sounds like it has real possibilities. Park City would be a cool setting. But Toad Suck? Where did you pull that?"

"I never heard of a famous person coming from Toad Suck, so I thought it sounded like a real stretch for this young girl from an obscure place to strike it big at life and love. That's the whole point of these chick flicks, right? For the seemingly impossible to become possible."

"Absolutely, I love it. But you mean to tell me that you didn't make up that name? Toad Suck is a real place?" J.P. asked with his eyes wide in disbelief.

"Oh yes, it's a real place. The story goes that there was a

tavern in Perry County along the Arkansas River where local fisherman would suck down so much beer that they'd swell up like toads. I bet Gregg Russell didn't know that. Reporter nerds acquire a lot of bizarre trivia, too." Kenny laughed.

"That's as obscure as knowing that fly fisherman Brian Vaughn broke a world record in 2018 when he caught a thirty-five-pound crevalle jack in Calibogue Sound. We would dominate at bar trivia," J.P. said, beginning to think that the two would be compatible in more ways than winning at a game that would score them a free basket of chicken wings on a Tuesday night. "What else have you got?"

"How about this? A student who is getting his MFA in photography from RISD—Rhode Island School of Design—is scheduled to go on a class trip to a game reserve in South Africa for a few weeks to work on his wildlife portfolio. But when there is a mix-up with his passport and required travel vaccines, he bitterly ends up backstage at New York's Fashion Week. Things get worse when the Chanel models fly in from Paris and there is a language barrier."

"This guy seems to be in a win-win situation. Surrounded by beautiful women he's forced to get up close and personal with *and* they don't speak English. So, he doesn't have to pretend to listen to them complain about how difficult it is to walk up and down a runway? I see no dilemma." J.P. shook his head.

"You're such a guy." Kenny rolled her eyes. "You didn't let me finish *and* you're missing the point. "Things begin to turn around when the CEO of the fashion company arrives in New York. She's the brains behind the company, who lives in London and speaks English. She's not tall or waif-thin or glamorous in anyway; she doesn't have a sexy accent, but she does tell the photographer that the models have been swooning over him. In an unlikely choice, the photographer falls for the plain Jane CEO, not the beautiful models. And the two live happily ever after."

"I'm sure the CEO was slightly attractive. She might not be a model, but she still works in fashion. It must be some type of requirement?"

"Are guys really that superficial?" She glared. "Don't answer that. The last contender is about a highly decorated former combat pilot who starts flying international flights for United Airlines in and out of Dulles International Airport after he was honorably discharged from the army and falls in love with a TSA agent."

"Let me guess, they live happily ever after."

Kenny shot him daggers that quickly morphed into a smile. "The last one isn't my favorite. At first, I had the TSA agent being a flight attendant but that's too cliché, like a doctor falling for a nurse. It'd all be very predictable."

"Agree. I'm also not a fan of the Washington D.C. airport as a setting. Are they going to get to know each other over an overpriced candy bar from the Hudson News Stand or cold slice of Sbarro's pizza at Gate A22? As a reader, I'd much prefer to be taken to Park City, Utah," J.P. stated.

"What about the second scenario?"

"I'd be more inclined to read it if the photographer ended up on a safari in South Africa. You know my thoughts on New York." J.P. laughed.

She slowly rocked back and forth in her chair and looked up at the clear sky that was brightly lit with stars. "Thanks for hearing me out, J.P. People say the hardest part about writing is letting other people read your work. But it's just as hard to share your ideas." She brought her gaze back down and turned her head to him.

"Anytime. I like to hear what you're thinking. Can I get you another?" He motioned to Kenny's almost empty plastic cup.

"No. Thank you, though. I haven't been drinking much since I've been down here. Another one would go right to my head. I should probably start heading home." She leaned forward in her chair and tapped Cliff on the head, who had fallen asleep and not stirred since they sat down.

"I should probably get going, too. Mr. C will be in his office with guns blazing tomorrow. He's all hyped up about the Jekyll Island opportunity. *And* he called for an impromptu Employee Appreciation Weekend. Like I said, he doesn't do anything small, so it'll be a busy few days of entertaining the staff." J.P. popped to his feet.

"You have fun with that. I'm happy I ran into you . . . again. And thanks for the drink." She started to walk away.

"Kenny, wait." J.P. took a step in her direction.

Alarmed by the sound of her own name, she halted and spun around so her face was almost resting on J.P.'s chest. She took a step back and looked up.

"Can I take you to dinner? How about next Wednesday? There's a great seafood place off the plantation on New Orleans Road. It's called Charlie's. I think you'd really like it." J.P. looked so deeply into Kenny's eyes that she felt like he was staring through them.

"That sounds great, I'd love to go to dinner with you," she softly responded.

"Great it's a date," he confidently said as he leaned in and gave Kenny a kiss on the cheek near the corner of her right lip crease.

Thirty-Four

Kenny saw stars, both literally and figuratively. The moon and constellations were still shining bright when she made it back to Pelican Pointe and her mind fluttered, dizzied with excitement. She sat down on the pool deck, pulled up the skirt of the green maxi dress and dangled her feet in the water.

She relived the night in her mind. It was like a song that makes you either deliriously happy or catastrophically sad and you physically can't stop yourself from hitting the repeat button because you don't want to leave the moment. But as much as she didn't want the unexpected night to end, she wouldn't have changed a thing about how it came to its inevitable conclusion.

Text from Colby: Did the sun not set down there tonight? What happened to my picture?

Kenny stared at her phone for a few seconds and attempted to give considerable and reasonable thought about how she was going to respond to Colby's text but was distracted by the movie of the night that was still a full-blown feature film playing in her mind. She was tired of lying to her best friend but wasn't completely ready to come clean about her current situation.

Screw it.

Kenny picked up the phone and dialed Colby.

"I was getting nervous, doll. I was starting to think you fell over the side of this unnamed lighthouse, trying to get the perfect shot of the sun for me," Colby greeted.

"It sounds quiet, are you actually home and alone at 9:45 p.m. on a Thursday night?" Kenny asked, genuinely surprised.

"Our team had the early touch football game tonight. Pride Pack won. Go us! We're such little engines that could. We qualified for the playoffs! The rest of the hussies are still celebrating at Boxers but the Manuscript Eater called one of her infamous sunrise meetings for tomorrow."

"I'm proud of you, Colby! You never know when to go home." Kenny commended, sarcastically.

"Thanks, Mom," he replied mockingly. "Is this little lecture over? Can I go to bed now?"

"Actually, no. I have something to say, confess really, and I need you to hold all commentary until the end."

"Okay? I think," Colby cautiously questioned.

"I'm not down here for work, there is no assignment. After that day, the day I lost the Clinton White interview and *Armchair Detective* was rejected, *and* you and I had our 'situation,' I needed a break from everything. I needed a break from life. I found a villa for a good price on Hilton Head Island in South Carolina, took five of my unused vacations weeks and cashed in on my National Rental Car points. I drove down here for a solo vacation to reenergize and find myself. I reduced or eliminated all those things that self-help books say can clutter or be a detriment to our minds: men, carbs, booze, social media, a sedentary lifestyle; and I threw in my obnoxious Post-it notes. I've added healthy doses of exercise and sun and I feel amazing. I can't tell you a time I've felt more at peace and refreshed." Kenny stopped to take a breath and collect the rest of her somewhat rehearsed thoughts.

"This is simply fantastic!" Colby interjected. "Can I—"

"Stop. I'm not done. It's true that I did meet a handsome golfer and we went kayaking. His name is J.P. I keep bumping into him around the island and he happened to be at the lighthouse tonight. He bought me a beer, and we chatted for a long time. Before we parted ways, he asked me to go to dinner next week and kissed me on the cheek," Kenny blurted out, her voice taking on a more singsong tone with every word she uttered.

"My heart is screaming! Can I let the screams out of my mouth, yet? Are you done?" Colby didn't attempt to hide his enthusiasm.

"I don't need you to go all Colby on me. This isn't a *real* date. When J.P. walked away, he said 'it's a date.' I'm sure he was just referring to a day on the calendar, since he specifically mentioned next Wednesday. We're going to some seafood joint called Charlie's, it sounds super casual, like picnic tables. And it wasn't a *real* kiss. It was just a little peck, you know. I'm not reading anything into it because there's still the possibility that he falls under one of the dating red flags: freak, gay, married, or serial killer. And if he doesn't have a red flag next to one of those categories, I still live in Manhattan, and he still lives here. So, it's really all a moot point."

"Queen, are you done with your rant, yet?" he asked and continued without giving her time to respond. "A quick search of 'J.P. + Hilton Head + golf' shows a delicious *but* straight man. He's not gay, which is largely unfortunate; he doesn't have crazy eyes, so he's not a serial killer; and there's enough other articles about him on the internet from his time on the PGA tour that it would be public by now if he was married or a freak. We can safely clear all those boxes."

"Oh my God, Colby! Isn't this what I just told you *not* to do?" She sighed. But mostly a sigh of relief that Colby did the quick Google search she was afraid to conduct on her own.

"You did, but you didn't sound like you meant it. Now that I know you'll be safe with this J.P. character, I won't dig any further until you give me the green light."

"Stop, no more. Red light. I don't need or want to know any more. If I decide I *do* want to know more about J.P., I want to learn it from him and not some inaccurate posting on the web," Kenny stopped Colby in his tracks.

"Fine. Then we can move on. You'll thank me for this tidbit. Is it Charlie's on New Orleans Road?" Colby asked.

"Yes," Kenny apprehensively answered.

"I knew it! This *is* a date. J.P. is taking you to Charlie's L'Etoile Verte, an intimate, French-inspired bistro with white linens, white string globe lights, and charming wrought iron tables for two on their cozy and inviting wrap around porch." He breathlessly described the setting like he was writing a review for a restaurant under consideration for a Michelin star.

"You are extreme, Colby Jackson." Kenny giggled. "But that does sound lovely. Maybe I should treat it as a real date? It's been a while since I've had one of those that I genuinely wanted to go on."

"Now that you agree it's a date, treat yourself to something new and fabulous to wear. I'm really excited for you, Kenny. It's been too long since my best friend has sounded this happy," he turned down his theatrics and turned up his sincerity.

"Thanks, Colby. I am happy. And I'm happy that I can share it all with you."

"Me too, Love. Now go get some sleep and call me tomorrow so we can discuss wardrobe. Love you, mean it, bi-yee!"

Thirty-Five

Ding!

The only alarm Kenny set the past week and a half was the one to clock how long she spent swimming morning laps, so she was startled when her phone sounded while she was still lying in bed. Before she rolled out of the covers or reached for the device, she glanced around the room. The sun shining through the French doors casted bright, warm rays on the right side of the mattress where Kenny's body was still comatose. Through the slightly tilted Pella blinds, she could see the water aerobics women gathered around the pool deck but they hadn't yet started their synchronized, aquatic routine. She deduced it couldn't have been later than 7:00 a.m.

Kenny hadn't answered a phone call or replied to an email before the crack of dawn in twelve full days and the *Ding!* of her phone made her realize she wasn't ready to go back to that routine. She stared at the purple wallpapered flowers on the ceiling and thought about the many times that *Ding!* changed the trajectory of her day.

There was the *Ding!* the night that Whitney Houston

unexpectedly died, and Kenny had to abruptly end a first date that, shockingly, didn't lead to a second. There was the *Ding!* about a gunman who killed an entire classroom of elementary school students in Connecticut that came in when Kenny was out for a birthday lunch with her brother. There was the *Ding!* that a man from New Rochelle, who commuted in and out of the Grand Central train station, had contracted COVID-19, and exposed the entire tristate area to the deadly virus. Soon after, the country shut down. Although she didn't physically hear the *Ding!* the day she lost the Clinton White interview, because she was in the hot room at her yoga studio, she swore she could hear after-*Dings!* in her sleep.

Kenny apprehensively reached for her phone and prayed that it was an indecipherable text from Hailey or a snarky message from Colby about his dalliances from the night before. But she knew both were unlikely possibilities since it was daybreak on a Friday morning.

She assumed Haiely would be driving to the Pittsburgh International Airport to catch her flight into Savannah, since she was terrified to board the delicate puddle jumper that departed from Morgantown. Kenny had been on that exact aircraft when she covered the story of Jack and Diane, the teen killers who plotted to murder their parents, and couldn't blame Hailey for not wanting to get on the plane that resembled a model figurine. And while Colby would normally be sleeping off Thirsty Thursday, she remembered that the Manuscript Eater had called one of her infamous sunrise meetings. Which meant Colby was making a mad dash across the wide avenues of Midtown Manhattan, barking orders to whomever was on the other side of his Apple air pods and bulldozing over any unsuspecting pedestrians in his path, while trying not to spill an ounce of his Trenta Starbucks latte that would hold him over until lunch.

Kenny took a deep breath and looked at her phone.

Text from Lonnie Locke: Luke and I both emailed you and received your out of office reply. Can you spare a few minutes? We have intel you'll be interested in. You might call it a "scoop." Call either one of us.

"*Ugh!*" Kenny yelled into one of the overstuffed down pillows and threw the phone on top of the pile of purple decorative ones that were stacked on the floor next to her. "Why can't you people leave me alone?" she screamed and angrily kicked the tops of her feet against the mattress from under the covers, knocking the throw pillows that remained next to her on the bed, to the floor.

After the mini exaggerated tantrum, she grabbed the phone with her left hand that dangled over the side of the bed, sat to her knees which remained under the sheets, and peered out the French doors. She wished she was lifting foam dumbbells up and down over her head with the women in the pool who were forty years her senior.

Breathe in, two, three, four. Hold two, three, four. Out two, three, four. Breathe in, two, three, four. Hold two, three, four. Out two, three, four.

She contemplated ignoring the text, or at least putting off her usual immediate reply, but knew that was simply delaying the inevitable. The result would be having this "thing" hang over her head until she decided to deal with it. She was also unnerved by the term "scoop." Until the day she lost the Clinton White interview, Kenny had been the one doing all the "scooping" in this story and didn't realize what an ugly word it was until the shoe was on the other foot. If she wanted to regain her scoop streak, she had to hear out the Locke brothers.

She remained slightly annoyed with the elder brother, Luke, for calling her "Dear" in the email he sent her trying to explain away the debacle with their rogue client, so she dialed Lonnie's number.

"Kennedy, I'm happy you called. I wanted to touch base before I head into court in a few minutes and the weekend gets ahead of me," Lonnie answered on the first ring.

"Good morning, Lonnie. What's going on? What can I do for you today?" Kenny tried to sound chipper and not disgusted that she felt forced into an unwanted conversation.

"You can't do anything right now; this is all off the record. But things, *big* things, are happening behind the scenes. Of course, you're my first call," Lonnie said, breathlessly.

She rolled her eyes at the last few words of that statement and could tell the robust attorney was walking the stairwell at the courthouse and not riding the elevator.

"Remember when Luke and I told you there was a second set of footprints found at the White home?"

"Sure, I remember that. I also remember you saying that it's not the job of the criminal defense team to identify or solve *who* killed Ada White. It's solely the job of the defense to convince the jury that *your client*, Clinton White, *isn't* responsible for the murder," Kenny parroted.

"Correct. That is still all true. But get this," Lonnie gave a pronounced pause, indicating to Kenny he had reached the landing of the fourth-floor stairwell of the Stamford Court-house. "Around the time Ada White was killed, a woman from Idaho went missing while she was out for a jog. Pressure and eyes have been fixed on the husband but there hasn't been enough evidence to make an arrest. A few weeks ago, the missing jogger's husband made a call to Phil Flora, my friend who's the attorney from Boise, to retain him as counsel. I intro-duced you to Phil last summer at the National Association of Criminal Defense Attorneys conference in Palm Beach."

"You did. Phil is great. You brought him over to the WBS

exhibit booth between your sessions. We hit it off because his daughter is interested in going to my alma mater."

"Well, this is going to blow your mind," Lonnie continued. "The husband—Phil's new client—was Clinton White's roommate during undergrad *and* medical school! He steadfastly maintains his innocence and told authorities that in the weeks leading up to his wife's disappearance, he found suspicious footprints on and around his property. He alleges on the day his wife went out for the jog she never returned from that he confronted her about having an affair."

"What? That's wild! Do you think the two are connected? In any way?"

"I don't know. Luke and I are still skating on thin ice with Dr. Love. It's going to take a while before we believe anything he says. But I told Phil Flora to call you as soon as there are any developments with his new client. I hope you don't mind. It's going to be a media frenzy when something breaks, and I assured Phil that he can trust you with fair and accurate reporting."

"Thanks, Lonnie. That means a lot," Kenny said.

"You're welcome. Your out-of-office reply says you're gone until the second week of October? We'll make plans to have dinner when you're back in the city. I'm sure you know the NBC interview never aired, what a shitshow that whole situation was. Judge O'Toole is still furious, and he hasn't scheduled the next court appearance on the docket."

"Got it. I look forward to connecting when I'm back. Send your brother my best and I'll see you both in October. Thanks for reaching out, Lonnie," Kenny said before hanging up.

As much as she didn't want to think about life outside of Sea Pines, or life after Wednesday's date with J.P. at Charlie's, the conversation with Lonnie Locke left her reassured and relieved. She never bought into the saying *When one door closes, another one opens*. She perceived the notion as a weak excuse people fall back on when things don't go the intended way and self-proclaimed victims are incapable of handling the truth. But, in this case, she felt like a window had cracked ajar, due to a door slamming in her face. The professionalism and work ethic she displayed while working on the Clinton White case, gave her one foot inside the next big story that was about to break in the true crime world. When this hiatus of life came to its unavoidable end, Kenny would be positioned to hit the ground running. In the meantime, she intended to float through the remaining three weeks on a euphoric cloud.

Thirty-Six

Mr. Cunningham sat behind his stately mahogany pedestal desk reading the newspaper and sipping coffee out of a red poly-paper cup when J.P. and Cliff appeared in the doorway.

"Come in, fellas. Have a seat," the jolly man invited. "I beat you to it today, Cliff, but come here, Mr. C still has a treat for you." He motioned to the copy of *The Wall Street Journal* spread open on his desk, while he bent over and pulled out the bag of doggie treats from his side drawer.

"Welcome back, Mr. C," J.P. said enthusiastically. "You and those cups. I can't believe you refuse to drink out of that Yeti I got you a few years ago; or even an old-fashioned ceramic mug, for that matter"

"It's important to remember your roots, Jonathan. Growing up in Manhattan, I bought a black coffee from the corner bodega or the bagel cart at Washington Square Park every morning."

"Yes, I know. Those cups were blue, white, and gold and had *We Are Happy to Serve You* imprinted on them. A cup company made them to appeal to Greek food vendors who pushed their love of coffee on unsuspecting New Yorkers.

You've shared this tale many times, Mr. C," J.P. took over the storytelling, regretting he had pointed out the cup.

"That *cup*, Jonathan, has been described as the most successful cup in history by *The New York Times*. If Solo started manufacturing the original version, I'd be sipping out of one of those; but this is the best I have." He tapped his paper cup. "I don't need any fancy mug or thermos."

"You never cease to amaze me, Mr. C. For how progressive and 'fancy' you are in some regards, you're quite archaic in others."

"Archaic? I prefer to call it 'old-fashioned,'" Mr. Cunningham defended.

"It took me twenty minutes to brew a cup of coffee at Marlin Manor on Sunday morning. I had to crush beans; I had to boil water. You do that every morning to dump the beverage into a cup that retains no heat and will get soggy and leak if you don't drink it fast enough? I don't understand," J.P. said, unsure why he was so riled by the absurdity of it all, given that it didn't affect him in any way.

"I keep my Mr. Coffee pot and paper filters in the breakfast nook in the master bedroom. I rarely use that kitchen. Or any of the gadgets in it. Those fancy toys are for guests and visitors to enjoy. I'm happy you found them and dusted them off."

"Now would be a good time to change the subject." J.P. shook his head, attempting to prevent another tangent in the form of a history lesson, dissertation, or tutorial about the evolution of coffee pots. "Looks like the weather is going to cooperate for Employee Appreciation Weekend. I peeked at the schedules for the clubhouse employees and the teams did a good job of rotating their hours so everyone can enjoy the festivities and ensure all shifts are adequately covered."

"Good. I continue to be impressed by the ship you run inside the clubhouse and on the golf course. Maybe I need my hearing aids fixed but I never catch wind of any drama or gossip at Liberty Oaks. It's refreshing," Mr. Cunningham commended.

"Thanks, Boss. I know you sent the email to the entire Low Country Hospitality enterprise but, since you were gone, I took the liberty of checking in with housekeeping and reservations to ensure they got the memo and were working on coverage plans. Miss Luana and Hailey confirmed they would take charge of coordinating schedules and send you a copy when the plans are finalized."

"Excellent. I'm quite satisfied with the leadership that Hailey shows for such a young woman. She exhibits significant potential in ways she can add to the growth and future of Low Country Hospitality," Mr. Cunningham said matter-of-factly.

"I couldn't agree more," J.P. said with a wide grin. "She continues to go above and beyond her duties and responsibilities."

"Any chance Miss Luana is going to make those key lime pie cookies? The Hilton Head Ice Cream van is going to park at Marlin Manor for a few hours tomorrow, but I know people will be asking about those darn cookies."

"Yes. There will be a few dozen key lime pie cookies on hand. Miss Luana didn't set up at the farmers market yesterday so she could stay home and bake." J.P. smiled, pleased that the subject of the cookies arose.

"Miss Luana shouldn't lose any additional income because she was home baking for her own Employee Appreciation Day. I'll make sure she's compensated." Mr. Cunningham scribbled something down in the notebook next to him.

"As long as we're on the subject of the cookies, have you ever stayed at a DoubleTree?"

"Jonathan, I'm a hotelier. What do you think?"

"Sorry, rookie question. Let this serve as a reminder why I'm better suited for golf management than hotel management." J.P. seized the opportunity for a smart comeback. "You know how they give their guests a warm chocolate chip cookie at check-in? If Miss Luana shared that recipe—or maybe *sold* it—than we could give key lime pie cookies to guests at our properties. Southern hospitality at its finest."

Mr. Cunningham sat forward in his chair and rested his elbows on the desk. He slid his glasses to the tip of his nose and peered out the window to his right like he was deep in thought. J.P. didn't know what to make of the awkward silence since Mr. Cunningham always had an immediate follow-up to any question or statement. He had the uncanny ability to be armed with answers on the ready. The confidence in his words and thoughts, and his always swift response times made him an unparalleled businessman.

"I think that is a brilliant idea," Mr. Cunningham said, despite sounding like he was still mulling over the proposal.

"It's just a thought. I don't expect you to have an answer or come up with a business plan, right now, in the moment."

"I find a great deal of value in the proposition. Miss Luana is no spring chicken, in case you haven't noticed; and her work is very physical, extremely labor intensive. She won't be able to keep up that pace for much longer and I've been racking my brain about how to broach a conversation with her. You *know* how she is," Mr. Cunningham referred to Miss Luana's strong-willed and tough-minded personality. "Part of being a good manager, Jonathan, is always looking out for your employees, knowing their strengths, weaknesses and recognizing their needs. Identifying when it's the appropriate time to help them pass the torch."

J.P. hung on every word that Mr. Cunningham expressed and was eager to hear where his boss's mind was headed with this thought. He also wondered if Mr. Cunningham was referring to his own role within his company to some degree. While J.P. wasn't oblivious to the obvious hints and suggestions Mr. Cunningham dropped about J.P. taking on more responsibility, he never thought it could be because his mentor wasn't physically or mentally up to the demands.

"What are you proposing?" J.P. inquired.

"I'll renovate a kitchen for her at one of the complexes. She'll continue to maintain scheduling, hiring, training, and purchasing of housekeeping services, but the role will be restricted to office duties. The rest of the time she can bake to her heart's content. We'll offer the famous key lime pie cookies to guests and golfers, and she won't have to share or sell her recipe to anyone." Mr. Cunningham stood up from his chair and pounded his hands on the desk like he successfully closed a hard-fought deal. "And tell that lady friend of yours, 'thank you.'"

"What?" J.P. asked, his head still spinning from his boss's quick and assertive restructuring of one of Low County Hospitality's most relied upon arms of the business empire.

"That wasn't your brainchild, was it? I'm assuming this was the idea of your friend, Kenny." Mr. Cunningham asserted.

"Yes," J.P. answered dumfounded.

"Don't give up on the idea of her too easily, Jonathan. Your face lights up when you talk about her. That's a rare phenomenon these days," Mr. Cunningham lectured.

"I did ask her to go for dinner." J.P. shook his head at the rare phenomenon of Mr. Cunningham *always* getting in the last word. "I made a reservation at Charlie's for next Wednesday." He made his way to the door and indicated to Cliff that it was time to go.

"Attaboy! Excellent choice," Mr. Cunningham smirked.

Thirty-Seven

More than sixty miles of bike paths snaked through Hilton Head, and most were sparse on Saturday mornings. Vacationers were either ending their tropical get-aways and begrudgingly vacating the island or were just beginning their periods of respite and were still in transit. Locals stayed close to home and steered clear of anxious visitors who clogged incoming and outgoing traffic.

Kenny seized the opportunity of empty trails and ventured on a longer, more leisurely bike ride than her usual loops around Sea Pines. She wandered out the Ocean Gate on the south side of the plantation and rode down South Forest Beach Road, a mile-long stretch of land that was busier with vehicles and pedestrians than the roads of Sea Pines, but still primarily populated by resort complexes, clusters of villas and tennis courts. The character of the island remained the same, whether inside the confines of one of the eleven plantations that comprised a bulk of Hilton Head, or passing along one of the major thoroughfares that connected them. The earth-colored buildings and structures were constructed of stucco, wood, and brick, and protected by lush vegetation that made everything blend in natural harmony. There were no bright lights or neon signs, and even fast-food chains toned down their trademark, eye-popping logos to adhere to the tranquility of the sanctuary that preferred to fly under the radar off the coast of South Carolina.

She peddled until she arrived at Coligny Plaza. What began as Hilton Head's first grocery store blossomed into a downtown that accommodated boutiques, restaurants, and entertainment venues. Since she hadn't bought anything new to wear in months and hadn't been on a date in nearly as long, Kenny decided to take Colby's advice and freshen her wardrobe. She locked up the bright orange beach cruiser near a huddle of outdoor, round kiosks that looked like tiki huts and popped in and out of the stores that were tucked away throughout the maze-like plaza.

Partially fearful of buyer's remorse but mostly conflicted about what kind of outfits she should be trying on, she didn't take any items into the dressing rooms until her second round of perusing through all the boutiques that sold women's clothing. While browsing the racks, she realized J.P. had only ever seen her in workout clothes, bathing suits, and the loose-fitting maxi-dress she reserved for days she went for a sunless spray tan since the tent-like frock was less likely to smudge her damp skin. She started meticulously examining and closely scrutinizing what hung from every hanger, was folded on every table, and was dressed on every mannequin.

She enjoyed the one-woman fashion show. She had no idea what number would calculate on a scale if she were to step on one, but she felt comfortable in the clothes she was stepping into. The skin that peeked out from under the dresses, tanks, jeans, and shorts she modeled had a healthy glow. Although she could've purchased any number of the fashions she tried on, she over-analyzed and talked herself out of all of them.

She loved the chic red jumpsuit that was tied in a big bow at the lower back but that would be too complicated to wear and reassemble if she had to go to the bathroom. She went crazy for the linen orange shift dress with hot pink embellishments but knew the material would be wrinkled beyond repair before leaving the bedroom at Pelican Pointe. She paired an elegant silk sleeveless black halter top with a pair of wide-legged white jeans, but the top made her boobs look like a shelf; and the "no white after Labor Day" rule floated through her mind. She tried on a trendy pair of light blue denim capris but thought the wash and frayed ankles made them too casual.

She had a fleeting appreciation for early phase dating in Manhattan when most meetups took place after work over drinks, which occasionally progressed to post-work dinner and drinks. Kenny had plenty of "office cube to cocktails" ensembles for those occasions. She had a little black dress and sexy pencil skirt for all seasons, but nothing in her closet at Pelican Pointe or back at The Dollhouse ever gave off a first date at the beach kind of vibe.

After she was certain that she overstayed her time in the dressing room and was satisfied that she had tried on every date-worthy piece of clothing at her last stop, she went to the register to ring out a black camisole and white camisole that were buy one, get one half off and a cardboard sleeve of three silk scrunchies because her favorite blue one was losing its elasticity due to overuse. She didn't really need the tank tops or the hair ties but chalked them up to pity purchases for blowing through the store like a Category Three hurricane, leaving trails of sloppily folded and poorly hung clothes in her wake.

She didn't work up a sweat on the bike ride to Coligny Plaza but could feel herself start to glisten after the physical and mental endurance challenge that she braved running from store to store trying on clothes. She equated what happened in a women's fitting room to a high impact sport. Ladies squat, stretch, suck in, stand on tip toes, and move limbs in contortionist ways, all to zip, button, tie, wrap and snap themselves into an effortless look.

Tired, Kenny unlocked the beach cruiser, slightly disappointed she wasn't going home with something dazzling to wear to Charlie's but planned to ask Hailey for additional shopping suggestions the following night when she met her new friend for a drink. Kenny would still have a day and a half to put together the perfect look for her much-anticipated date night.

When she got back to Pelican Pointe, she was pleasantly surprised to find that the porch furniture for Villa #5 had been delivered. There were four black metal swivel chairs with tan waterproof cushions around a square black metal table that had a glass top. A matching black metal lounge chair with a long tan waterproof cushion accompanied the set. There wasn't a need for the recliner on the small patio since there were so many around the perimeter of the pool that was steps away, but she wasn't complaining. If nothing else, it'd be a good place to dry out her bathing suits and other personals she didn't like to put in the dryer or hang over the patio wall on display for all her neighbors to see.

Thirty-Eight

Around 9:00 a.m. the sun began to break, to Kenny's relief. Heavy rains had pummeled the island the previous twelve hours and gale force winds gusted as loudly as the thunder that rumbled during the marathon of overnight storms. Lightning illuminated the sky shades of red and purple, and with each bolt she wondered if there was a flashlight hidden somewhere inside the confines of Villa #5. She was certain that Pelican Pointe was going to lose power.

Kenny weathered a lot of storms recently, both tangible and cerebral, so was surprised that this one perturbed her as much as it did. There was something foreboding about it. That fear lasted a few minutes before her practical journalist's mind set in and she decided that the lesson in the meteorological event was to stick with the true crime beat at WBS and not attempt to transfer to the weather team. She often envied her colleagues who traveled from continent to continent to report on penguins in Antarctica or cover the hottest-ever recorded temperatures in Australia, but this storm confirmed that she wasn't cut out to produce any live shots from the eye of a hurricane or base of a wildfire.

She grabbed a roll of paper towels from under the kitchen sink to wipe down the furniture on the patio and assess any damage. The ground was covered in fallen pine needles, the waterproof cushions felt like they'd be saturated for a week and two of the chairs had blown over, but nothing catastrophic happened to the quaint outdoor seating area. The pool, however, looked like it needed a whole team of skimmers to clean up the debris that floated on the surface. The deck around the perimeter was in disarray. The lounge chairs and tables, always uniform, were strewn across the concrete. There were no women wading in the pool, anticipating water aerobics to begin; and there were no gentlemen huddled around the coin-operated newspaper boxes to collect copies of *The New York Times* or *The Sea Pines Sentinel.*

Despite the heavy, thick air and streaks of gloomy colors that lingered overhead, it was only a matter of time before the rest of Pelican Pointe slowly awoke and ventured outdoors. While she waited for neighboring signs of life, she swept fallen debris that dropped from the canopy and protected the exterior of Villa #5 to the top of the patio stairs with an old broom she found in the hall closet when she searched for a flashlight.

Kenny squeezed the excess water out of the chair cushions and strategically placed them around the patio in areas where they would receive direct sunlight. She had just finished drying off the arms and legs of the table set and lounge chair when she heard a *buzz buzz* from the other side of the opened glass door. She saw her phone light up next to the percolator on the counter.

FaceTime from Colby.

She normally would've hesitated to answer a call from Colby on a Sunday morning, for fear it was an accidental dial and unsure of the company he'd be keeping; but after hunkering down alone during the recent apocalypse, she welcomed a familiar face whether the call was intentional or not.

She picked up her right arm, tilted the phone down and cast up her gaze. She cocked her head to the right and opened her eyes wide.

"Morning, sunshine," she chimed as she picked up the percolator with her left hand and poured a cup of coffee into one of the whale-shaped mugs from the cabinet.

"You're alive, thank God!" Colby gasped with a sigh of genuine relief, though he still sounded half asleep.

"I am. It appears you are, too. Kind of, anyway," Kenny said noting his tousled hair, squinted eyes and puffy face indicting he had a late night and hadn't strayed from under his covers, yet. "What do I give this early-morning pleasure?" She shuffled back to the patio and reclined on the lounge chair.

"I love your place, doll! That yellow couch is fabulous," he said twisting his head.

From the other side of the screen, it appeared like he was repositioning himself and the phone in the hopes that doing so would give him a better view of the interior of the villa that was now behind Kenny as she walked outside.

"It's not the most comfortable but it fits the space, and the color makes me happy. I'd give you a tour of the rest of Pelican Pointe, but the complex is recovering from a minor natural disaster. I'll give you a call later when things are cleaned up and dried out."

"That's why I'm calling. I was scrolling though my phone to see who I drunk-dialed and texted last night and to assess whom I should actively avoid the next few weeks or, *worse*, owe an apology to." Colby nonchalantly shrugged his shoulders at his Sunday morning ritual, "and all my news apps are reporting biblical flooding in the Carolinas. Powerful waves, high tides, whipping winds, it's a vocabulary lesson in scary words that city-dwellers like me don't have to worry about."

From the way he elaborated, she suspected he was trying to make the point that he thought it was time for her to come home.

Kenny rolled her eyes. "Wasn't it just last month that your 'friend,' the 'best barista in Chelsea,' was arrested for making bombs in his apartment and had wallpapered his bedroom with maps of the subway system? I think you have your own set of problems, Colby."

"I'm sure that was all a misunderstanding," he laughed. "Now that I know you weren't whisked out to sea, tell me about yesterday's shopping trip! This is the first I'm *seeing* you in a few weeks and it's obvious you've shed those pesky pounds. What kind of ensemble did you put together to drive this golfer out of his mind?"

Kenny recounted every detail of her charades in the dressing rooms at the boutiques around Coligny Plaza, complete with commentary about why each outfit would and would not work for her date with J.P. She missed having Colby on the shopping spree. He had a ruthless critical eye, but it was offset with a keen sense of style that she relied on. He had a vision for fashion that she was blind to.

He was in the middle of analyzing the risk factors associated with wearing white jeans after Labor Day, he was particularly hung up on the shade of white, when Kenny abruptly *shooshed!* him.

"Don't. Say. A. Word." Kenny firmly directed as she quietly placed her mug on the patio and slid down the lounge chair like she was hiding from someone.

The stucco wall that enclosed the patio was high enough that there was no chance anyone on the other side of it would be able to see her. Even when Kenny stood vertically, the wall came to her ribs, but she wasn't taking any chances.

"What's going on? Are you okay?" Colby whispered.

She picked up her finger and *shooshed!* him again like she was a grade-school teacher trying to corral a room full of rambunctious third graders.

Colby's squinted eyes grew wide, and he obeyed.

"I'm not worried about it; you shouldn't be either. I think Mr. C will be thrilled when he finds out. And to have you here, full-time, he might be more excited than me!" Kenny heard a familiar voice exclaim.

"I hope so. The last few summers have been great, and I thought I was okay with it being a warm weather fling. But this last month has been hard. I realized I had deeper feelings than I knew or wanted to have," a female's voice said softly, sounding both optimistic and hesitant. "Last night confirmed what I secretly hoped for a long time, that there *is* something real between us."

Kenny's insides tumbled and her head spun. She lost feeling in her right arm and dropped the limb and her phone to her waist. The undeniable, smooth-talking voice was J.P. She didn't know if she wanted to throw up, disappear, or confront the sappy couple who presumably were still basking in whatever happened between them the night before.

"Relationships are never easy, and I'm told the good ones rarely make sense. We have to work on them," J.P. encouraged. "What do you say we grab breakfast?"

"I'd love that. You know breakfast is my favorite meal," the female voice giggled.

By now Kenny was on all fours and crawling on her hands and knees, phone in hand, across the patio to the glass door. She palmed the door with her left hand, slid it open and dragged herself inside.

What is going on? What are you doing? Colby silently mouthed with exaggeration and alarm.

Once she was safely inside, she sprung to her feet, ran to

the front of the villa, and flipped the camera around on her phone so she and Colby could peer out the window together.

"*That* is J.P.!" Kenny shouted, directing the phone to a couple who were walking toward a red Wrangler. "And *that* must be last night's hook-up! What a slime ball! And look at her! Of course she's gorgeous. I should expect nothing less. He looks like a movie star."

"They both look pretty disheveled to me," Colby said in what seemed to be a feeble attempt to reign in Kenny's outburst. "*You* would *never* go to breakfast looking that way. Her hair looks like a bird's nest and those gold sweatpants look like they came from the lost and found box in a high school boy's locker room. That color wouldn't flatter anyone's complexion," he spoke in disgust.

"I can't go there. I don't want to think about why they look disheveled. Look at him now, trying to act like a gentle-man," she spewed as she watched J.P. help the tall blonde into the passenger seat of his Jeep. "My God, her legs are a mile long. She doesn't even need help getting into the car. Her hair looks like it was professionally pinned into an up-do, not a bird's nest."

"She looks like an Amazon woman. If that's the type this J.P. is interested in, you never stood a shot, Hunny," Colby lamented from inside the phone.

"She looks like a runway model, not an Amazon woman. But you're right, I should've known J.P. would never be inter-ested in someone like me. What was I thinking?" Kenny's voice trembled.

She was on the verge of tears.

"Stop that right now, Kennedy Sloane!" Colby scolded. "Do you know how many men would drop everything to be with you? How many men have tried?"

"I don't understand, Colby!" Kenny broke into full blown sobs. "How can I keep misinterpreting my life like this? I really thought this was something special. I thought the connection was mutual. Was this all a dream, too? Did I dream up him kissing me? Did I dream up him asking me to dinner?"

"Oh, Love. It wasn't a dream. I heard it in your voice, and I saw it in your face when you answered the phone this morning," Colby comforted. "He was just a bad seed."

"I thought he was different. I felt different when I was around him," Kenny cried.

"I know it's hard. I hate that you're upset, and we can't lay in bed and watch *Sex and the City* reruns all day and get fat from Levain cookies together. But if there's one thing this loser did, he brought you back to life. He made you realize you don't want to be alone. You need more than me and WBS in your life, Kenny," Colby lectured.

"It never would've worked anyway," she sighed as she watched the red Jeep pull away. "Maybe that's why he pursued me in the first place. He was lonely and needed a quick fix of something. What better way to temporarily satisfy yourself than prey on a girl you know is going back up the coast in a few weeks." Her tears slowly dissipated. "He also alluded to commitment issues, although *that* didn't sound like a guy with hesitation. He probably feeds that line to all the girls to preemptively justify his future actions," she rambled.

"We are getting you back on the dating circuit when you come home. You're going to make dates and keep them. If you like a guy, you're going to answer his calls when he tries to make plans to see you again," Colby instructed.

"It just doesn't make sense. If J.P. *is* averse to relationships or commitment, why would he chase a standing summer fling with someone he works with? Someone he won't be able to avoid?"

"I don't know, Kenny. I'll never understand what makes a

straight man's brain tick. *Thank God.* But don't allow this guy to let you fall back into a slump," Colby warned. "What are you going to do about Wednesday's date? Will you still go if he doesn't cancel? I think you should go and screw with the bastard's head."

"I don't know, yet. I'm meeting a new friend for drinks tonight. She's young, still in school, but seems like a cool girl. I'll get her take on the situation. These Gen Z'ers can be brutal. I'm curious what her recourse would be."

"Yas, Queen! I love it! Now go cut up a cucumber and de-puff your eyes from the tears. We don't want you going out with ugly mourner face."

Kenny flipped the camera on her phone, so she was again looking at Colby.

"Thanks. I'll talk to you later." She sighed, knowing the exact look he was referring to.

She wore everything on her face—fear, sadness, excitement, stress, anxiety, anger—and no makeup could cover it up. To look fresh for her night out with Hailey, she would need to start with a clean slate.

"Love you, mean it, bi-yee!" Colby chimed.

Thirty-Nine

Kenny fell asleep on the uncomfortable yellow couch with slices of vegetables on her face, and woke up from the unplanned, lengthy nap when her phone vibrated from under the pillow her head rested on.

Text from Hailey: SP (Emoji: sand with umbrella) Club bar @ 5? Will b in red (Emoji: pink bikini)

It was already 3:00 p.m. and Kenny couldn't believe she slept most of the afternoon. She was also surprised that Hailey wanted to meet so early in the evening. She assumed her age would make her a night-owl. But Kenny didn't mind. She was grateful that Hailey proposed meeting at the Sea Pines Beach Club and not one of the establishments at Harbour Town or the Salty Dog. The risk of running into J.P. significantly increased if she had to wander around one of those waterfront villages.

Text to Hailey: Perfect! See you soon (Emoji: smiley face with sunglasses)

Meeting at the beach bar also took away some of the pressure of deciding what to wear. In theory, Kenny liked the idea of "No Shower Happy Hour," but she couldn't justify putting on a bathing suit to meet a stranger for drinks if she wasn't technically coming from a day at the pool or the beach. Though coming from a lazy Sunday afternoon spent in pajama pants and her new white tank top, with her hair tied up in a new scrunchie, wasn't an option either.

She woke herself up with a hot shower and put on a short, strapless floral tunic that could pass as a sundress or a bathing suit cover-up. It seemed like the perfect solution to the late afternoon, early evening engagement. She laced up her white canvas platform sneakers and decided to walk to the Beach Club, rather than wait for the plantation trolley.

She took a leisurely stroll down Lighthouse Road to North Sea Pines Drive and admired how quickly the landscape bounced back from mother nature's brutal assault the previous night. The trees and shrubs that had been weighed down from the wind and water bounced back to life; the walkways and roads that pooled with water had receded; locals and vacationers who holed up in their homes and rental units, found their way back to the golf courses and bike paths. She found parallels to her own day in all of it. Instead of sulking in despair and darkness about the conversation she overheard between J.P. and his assumed lingerie model girlfriend, she pulled herself together, went on with the day and didn't cancel her plans.

Kenny walked up the brick steps to the entrance of the beach club and reached for her phone.

Text from Hailey: Got 2 stools! In red (Emoji: baseball hat)

Kenny was nervous and excited. She imagined this is what blind dating felt like before the time of the internet. Just as Kenny didn't Google J.P. while she was getting to know him—although she now regretted that decision—she hadn't Googled Hailey either.

Text to Hailey: Just got here! In a floral dress.

Kenny walked down the extra-wide pathway that dead-ended into the dunes. She passed the entrances to eateries and a gift shop before reaching an open deck that was set with several square seating tables and was situated adjacent to an elevated covered deck with a large square bar in the middle of it.

Oh my God.

Kenny's heart sank. She turned the corner and immediately saw the back of a tall, skinny woman with blonde curls piled high on top of her head.

Text to Colby: OMG. She's here.

Text from Colby: What?

Text to Colby: J.P.'s girl from this morning. She's at the bar where I'm meeting my friend for drinks. What do I do?

Text from Colby: Dear God. Stay calm. Find a seat away from her and keep your back turned. Your new friend will have to keep tabs on her.

Kenny held her breath while she anxiously watched the little bubbles at the bottom of the screen bounce up and down while Colby typed another reply. She briefly took her gaze away from the phone to scan the decks for any sign of J.P. and when she looked back down, she had a text from Hailey.

Text from Hailey: I c u silly! Look (Emoji: up arrow)

Kenny cautiously lifted her head, afraid of who she might see. What she saw was worse than anything she could have imagined. The tall, skinny woman with the golden curls had turned around. She wore a red visor that hovered over her eyes and an unbuttoned, oversized white blouse draped over a tiny red bikini that drew attention to her washboard abs. The girl enthusiastically waved her hands like she was being reunited with a best friend whom she'd been separated from for years.

Shit. This isn't happening.

Kenny turned around, again, desperately hoping that the long and lean lady was motioning to someone standing behind her. No luck. There was no one there. Kenny turned back to face the bar. The girl giggled like a schoolgirl, pointed to her visor, and mouthed, "red hat!"

"That's a visor, not a hat," Kenny mumbled under her breath as she faked a toothy smile and tried to practice pranayama breathing. She knew she didn't have the luxury of time on her side, it would be a matter of seconds before she ended up in a full-blown conversation with her new friend turned foe. Any gasps of air she could muster on her short walk over to the bar—or before the excitable creature pounced over the railing—would have to do.

Inhale. Hold. Exhale. Inhale. Hold. Exhale.

"Kenny! You're even more adorable than I envisioned! I am *so* excited to meet you!" Hailey wrapped Kenny in a tight bear hug.

"Hailey, hi! It's great to meet you, too," Kenny lied through her clenched teeth, feeling pathetic and insignificant as she looked up, barely coming to Hailey's shoulders.

The red visor that kept Hailey's bouncy curls out of her face had the letters "O-H-H-I-O" scrawled across the front in white embroidery. The "I" was the Hilton Head lighthouse and Kenny knew that the play on letters was a nod to the state who proudly sent hordes of residents to vacation on the island every year.

"Cute visor!" Kenny forced sincerity, having a gut feeling it was on J.P.'s head hours earlier.

"Thanks, it's adorable, isn't it? I acquired it this morning," the bubbly girl laughed. "I knew the shade of red would match this bathing suit perfectly! I spent most of my childhood in West Virginia, but I am originally from Ohio."

The only thing that annoyed Kenny more than Hailey wearing a hat that surely was J.P.'s was that Hailey was instantly likeable. In a juvenile, sorority girl kind of way, but that's who she was, and it worked for her. Kenny had been in Hailey's company for less than two minutes, but she could tell Hailey had one of those magnetic personalities that people were attracted to. Her physical appearance only enhanced her endearing demeanor, and Kenny doubted she had a mean bone in her *Sports Illustrated Swimsuit* body.

Hailey talked as fast in person as she did on the phone a few weeks ago and used as many abbreviations and acronyms in her spoken English as she did in her texting prose. Hailey did most of the talking while Kenny listened and sipped a frozen pina colada. The irony of the whole scenario made it too hard to truly focus on anything and she wondered if the self-induced brain freeze was a subconscious attempt to numb herself to the conversation and the inner commentary that buzzed around it. The longer Haiely spoke, the more Kenny enjoyed her company and the greater her anger toward J.P. grew.

"Have you met any hotties since you've been down here, Kenny? I notice a lot of eye candy," Hailey coyly winked. "I bet southern men are different than the guys in New York. I love boy talk with girlfriends!"

Kenny took a deep breath and stirred the plastic, red and white bendy straw in her drink while she debated how to respond. She wasn't sure who the villain was in the J.P and Hailey dalliance. Maybe there wasn't one at all and Kenny was simply collateral damage. A victim of being in the wrong place, at the wrong time, with the wrong person. Although if there was a villain, it had to be J.P. since he was a decade and a half older than Hailey. He could mold her into a world-class trophy wife and proudly display her alongside his numerous golf career accomplishments. There was a slight possibility that Hailey could be the villain, though. Perhaps she was a gold digger playing the part of a naïve and innocent "good girl" from the gateway to America's heartland, who's mission was to find her way into the heart of Hilton Head's most eligible bachelor.

"No, Hailey. I've learned men are all the same regardless of geographic location. I did meet one charmer, but it turned out he was already with someone." Kenny kept it short and simple, deciding it wasn't her place to insert herself into the affairs of others. Especially people she planned to never see again.

"I'm sorry, Kenny! That's terrible. What happened to morals? I'm so happy to be out of that rat race," Hailey began, and Kenny looked at her with wide eyes.

Please stop talking. Make her stop talking. How can I shut her up?

It was too late. The curtain had been drawn, and Hailey was about to storm the stage with a stream of conscious monologue. Kenny didn't know if the soliloquy was going to be a romantic comedy, drama or erotica but she knew it was going to force the butterflies that fluttered in her stomach when she used to think about J.P., to shrink back into their cocoons. Quite possibly, forever.

"Hold out hope, Kenny! Your Mr. Perfect is waiting for

you somewhere. Sometimes it just takes a while. You'll never believe what happened to me last night," Hailey opened her performance.

I can't believe this is happening.

"Three years ago, when I started working down here for the summers, I met this guy who worked at Liberty Oaks Golf Course. Liberty Oaks is part of Low Country Hospitality. Did you know that?" Hailey stopped long enough to notice Kenny's acknowledgement. "We bumped into each other a lot because of work."

There it is, Kenny thought. *J.P. is a master of manipulation. He "bumps" into women; he plays down "working" at the golf course.*

"We got close, quickly, and spent every minute together when we weren't working; but there was always a blurred line between friends and more than friends. We stayed in touch throughout the year and there was undeniable chemistry when we were together; but we never put a label or set boundaries on our relationship. Mostly because I was still in school at WVU, and he didn't think I ever wanted to live here permanently. He knows how close I am to my mom and since she doesn't have any family back in West Virginia he didn't think I'd ever leave her. But guess what?" Hailey gave a you're-not-going-to-believe-this look and acted like she was waiting for a drumroll.

"What?" Kenny asked, raising her brows and faking enthusiasm.

"I'm crazy about this guy, and he told me last night he's crazy about me! I dated lots of boys during high school and college, but none are quite like *him.* I can't explain it. The conversations come easy. I know it's cliché, but I get butterflies. Plus, I really like working for Low Country Hospitality. Mr. Cunningham, the owner, offered me full-time employment after graduation in the Spring! My mom is optimistic about both opportunities," Hailey sang. "I thought the high-light of this last-minute trip was going to be meeting you, which I'm still excited about," she laughed. "But I never thought I'd be flying home with a boyfriend and full-time job! My life is a fairytale right now!" Hailey got louder and more animated with each thought.

"Wow, congratulations, Hailey! That's great about the job. And whoever the guy is, he's the lucky one." Kenny faked a smile.

Kenny couldn't bring herself to say Hailey was a lucky girl. She hoped Hailey was offered the job because of her work ethic and performance, not because of performances that stemmed from being romantically involved with the eventual second in command at Low County Hospitality. As for Hailey getting into a relationship with that second in command, she still couldn't wrap her head around J.P. being a two-timing cradle robber. However, if Kenny learned anything from a decade of producing news, it was that truth is often stranger than fiction.

"Thanks, Kenny! We're going to Charlie's tomorrow night to celebrate our 'official first date,' and me accepting Mr. Cunningham's offer," Hailey said dreamily.

That comment hit Kenny like a ton of bricks. She nearly fell off her stool when she reactively jerked her knee and her right sneaker got caught behind the low rail that was attached to the bar where most people rest their feet.

"Oh my God! Are you okay?" Hailey squealed.

"I'm fine," Kenny quickly recovered, trying to not draw attention to herself. "Clumsy me! I thought I felt a bug on my leg," she lied. "The other day I saw a palmetto bug on the pool deck," she lied again, "and I've been jittery since! In New York we call those ugly insects cockroaches!"

"Oh yuck! Thanks for the warning. Mr. Cunningham is letting a few of us employees stay at Pelican Pointe this weekend, so I'll be on the lookout," Hailey said while she furiously pounded at her phone.

Kenny was impressed by the speed at which Hailey fired off text messages. She knew Hailey was a rapid responder but couldn't believe her fingers could keep up with the thoughts that swirled through her head. Kenny found it difficult to determine which smiley face emoji was appropriate to attach to certain messages; so, she admired Hailey's effortless approach to scrolling through the keyboard of emojis to construct meaningful phrases.

"Guess what!" Hailey dropped her phone and popped her eyes back to Kenny. "My *boyfriend* got out of work early! *My boyfriend!* That has a nice ring, doesn't it?" she giggled. "Mr. Cunningham is hosting an Employee Appreciation Weekend, that's why I'm down here. The last few days have been filled with unexpected perks!"

Some are getting bigger perks than others, Kenny thought.

"He's on his way over for a drink. I'd love for you to meet him! And I told him to bring his boss. I think you two would hit it off," Hailey winked and lightly tapped Kenny on the knee.

Abort! Abort!

Kenny could feel her airwaves constricting. Her head felt like Marilyn's metaphorical clock, the spiral springs were about to snap and shoot all over the Sea Pines Beach Club. The Wheel of Emotion spun in chaotic motion in her brain. She felt like she was on the Tilt-a-Whirl at an amusement park and the ride didn't stop long enough for her to get off.

Breathe in, two, three, four. Hold two, three, four. Out two, three, four. Breathe in, two, three, four. Hold two, three, four. Out two, three, four.

Kenny was angry. She was angry at J.P. for leading her on. She was angry at Hailey for being the type of girl that J.P wanted. She was doubly angry at Hailey for suggesting she would "hit it off" with J.P.'s boss. Kenny didn't care how wealthy or generous Mr. Cunningham was, she would never consider a man who was old enough to be her grandfather. But Kenny was mostly angry at herself, for letting her guard down.

"Wow, um, yea. That would be nice. But speaking of work, I forgot I have a deadline to meet. Tonight. I need to compile research for one of my correspondents," Kenny tried to cobble together a plausible excuse. "I can't believe I forgot. I meant to do it this morning but got distracted. I wish I could stay!" she lied one final time.

Kenny fumbled in her purse in search of a twenty-dollar bill while she calculated in her head how long it would take J.P. to travel from the golf course to the beach club. She scanned the entrances and tried to guess which would be the *least* likely path he would take. Suddenly she heard dogs barking everywhere. They could have been there the whole time and Kenny didn't notice them, but she convinced herself otherwise. She was certain the last bark she heard was Cliff who picked up her scent and was sniffing her out.

Kenny popped up, threw her cash on the bar, and fixed her eyes on a narrow, nondescript ramp on the side of the building that looked like it was designated for restaurant employees.

"It was great to meet you, Hailey! Thank you for all your help while I've been down here," Kenny cautiously hugged her new "friend" and sprinted for the ramp.

Kenny made a clean escape out the service exit, through the parking lot and to the path that lined North Sea Pines Drive. She walked about five hundred feet and made a left into a hidden development so that she was no longer visible by cars, pedestrians, or bikers who were traversing the main road. She wandered along Beach Lagoon Road and when she came to the end of the stretch ambled down a long, wooden pathway between two homes, up and over the dunes, and found herself back on the beach.

It had been a weird day. Since overhearing pieces of J.P. and Hailey's conversation that morning, Kenny felt like every hour played out like a slow-motion film. Unlike the day that sparked her hiatus of life, when her world instantly popped like someone poked a balloon with a pin, today's unraveling was a slow leak. She felt like a beach ball that was deflated a little more with each disappointing detail she learned.

The easy conversation, the "bump-ins" around the island, the butterflies, the dinner at Charlie's.

Those were supposed to be Kenny's things. They *were* Kenny's things until she woke up that morning. Unfortunately, this time Kenny wasn't waking up from a dream that was never real. This time she woke up to a reality that wasn't genuine or true.

The entire length of the beach on Sea Pines was only five miles long but by the time she left the shore and made her way back to Pelican Pointe, she felt like she had walked at least double that. The sand was flat and still compact from the heavy rains, so the walk wasn't overly exerting, but Kenny felt physically tired. She kicked off her sandals and sat down on the pool steps to check-in with Colby, who had texted and called numerous times since her initial S.O.S.

Text to Colby: The plot thickened. My new friend IS J.P.'s girl. Don't wanna talk now but I'm coming home early. I'd like to catch a flight before Wed. night.

Text from Colby: What?!?! What a pair of skanks!

Text to Colby: I completely misjudged him, really missed the mark. Verdict is still out on her.

Text from Colby: Let me know what you need. LYMIB!

Kenny watched tiny drops of water, increasing in size and frequency, fall to her screen as she scrolled through various sites looking for flights from Hilton Head back to New York. When her vision became blurry and she noticed the droplets weren't splashing anywhere else, she realized it wasn't raining. The water was tears flowing from her face. She picked up her shoes and went back to the villa. It was only a matter of time before the other guests returned to their temporary homes at Pelican Pointe.

Direct flights between Hilton Head and New York were practically nonexistent and the few seats Kenny found were astronomical in price. After ruling out a trip home sans layover, Kenny's options were to choose between an extra-long stop in Washington D.C. or a reasonably short ground break in Charlotte. After too many horror stories of cancelled, delayed, and diverted flights over the course of her traveling career, Kenny always opted for a layover at the airport that was in closest proximity to her destination. Flying failures led her to rental cars and subsequent solo road trips back to Manhattan from Raleigh, Pittsburgh, Cleveland, and Ottawa. While she didn't usually mind being behind the wheel, any driving portion of this return trip didn't sound nearly as appealing as the joyride down. It sounded unbearable. At least if she got stuck in the nation's capital for any unforeseen reason, she could fall back on Amtrack.

Forty

Kenny's flight was a little before noon and she wasn't expected to touch down at JFK until after 9:00 p.m. Being that it was Wednesday, date night at Charlie's, she didn't mind wasting the day in airport terminals eating comfort junk food and being largely unreachable due to poor or temperamental cell service.

Kenny's Uber driver pulled up to a sign labeled "Drop Off" on Hilton Head Island Airport Terminal Drive and discarded the bags Kenny didn't ship back via UPS on the curb. The usual painstaking process of checking luggage and passing through the security line took less than seven minutes; and that included Kenny being pulled out of line and patted down by a TSA agent because the underwire of her bra set off a metal detector. She was a full two hours early to the quaint, glorified helipad that looked more like the lobby of a boutique hotel, with its white wooden rocking chairs and vending machines, than the busy and headache-inducing airports Kenny was accustomed to running through.

She found an empty rocking chair and pulled out her phone.

Text from Unknown: Hey Kenny, it's J.P. Looking forward to dinner tonight. I'll pick you up @ 6:30? Reservation is for 7.

Kenny stared at the phone in disgust. Hailey couldn't have been back in Morgantown for twenty-four hours and J.P. was already up to his shenanigans. She wondered if he had standing reservations at Charlie's on several nights of the week or just Mondays and Wednesdays.

Text from Unknown: Hope you don't mind that I pulled your contact from the hospitality reservation log. Can't believe we never exchanged numbers!

J.P. was relentless. Kenny couldn't conceive how a man could have so little shame. It was bad enough to sneak around on your girlfriend and lead on other women. But to surreptitiously secure the cell numbers of said other women through information your girlfriend collected, that was next level. Kenny rocked back and forth in the chair and contemplated if it would have been better for her psyche if J.P. stood her up; or the actual scenario, the one where the serial dater attempted to keep the evening of deceit.

When she couldn't come up with a reasonable answer, she remembered she had to let Hailey know that she was checking out of Pelican Pointe early. She deliberately sent the message via email rather than text. Text messages indicated friendship, and a friend was someone Kenny couldn't be to Hailey. Knowing that Hailey and J.P. were romantically involved was the obvious reason Kenny couldn't be friends with her. The deeper reason, the harder one for Kenny to admit, was because she felt a slight sense of guilt that she wasn't warning Hailey she could be going down a potentially hurtful path by pursuing a relationship with J.P.

From: Kennedy Sloane
To: hailey@lchospitality.com
Subject: Pelican Pointe Villa #5

Hi Hailey,

I hope you enjoyed your dinner at Charlie's on Monday night. I wanted to let you know that I had to cut my trip short, and I am flying back to New York today. I left the plantation passes on the island where I found them. It was nice meeting you on Sunday, and I wish you all the best in the future.

—Kenny

The drawn-out travel day was largely uneventful. The three hours and fifteen minutes Kenny spent in the air were easy and smooth, absent of bumps, turbulence, or hard landings. During the six-hour layover, she completed three *New York Time's* crossword puzzles, ate at two fast-food joints, and read the latest editions of *InStyle* and *Vanity Fair*, cover to cover. Despite the low-stress, anxiety-free trip, Kenny breathed a long sigh of relief when her plane was finally taxiing on the tarmac at JFK.

When the aircraft reached the gate, Kenny reluctantly turned her cell phone back on. While all the passengers around her scrambled to pull down their carry-ons from the overhead bins and barreled through the center aisle to get off the jet, Kenny sat back down in her seat.

Missed call from Unknown.

Text from Unknown: Was just calling to say I'm running early. Will hang by the pool if you're not ready. Take your time!

Text from Unknown: Hey! It doesn't look like you are home.

Maybe we said we'd meet at Charlie's? I probably messed that up. See you over there!

Missed call from Unknown.

Text from Unknown: Here! I'm at the table in the corner at the end of the porch.

Missed call from Unknown.

Text from Unknown: I'm not sure what happened tonight but I hope you're okay.

Kenny pulled a tissue from her pocket and wiped the tears that were streaming down her face. She was hurting but she'd made the right decision to leave without saying goodbye *or* confronting J.P. If she could have such strong conflicting feelings—sadness, anger, confusion, hope—about him after such a short period of time, she couldn't imagine how she'd feel if she let her guard down further.

After the last person deplaned, Kenny rolled her international-sized carry-on down the aisle of empty seats, briskly walked to the baggage claim area where she wrestled her oversized, overstuffed, and overweight large suitcase off the carousel and hustled to the taxi line.

Her hiatus was over.

Forty-One

Four months later.

"Is this really necessary?" Colby asked as he pulled the black fleece neck warmer that hugged his chin up to his lower lashes.

"You are so dramatic!" Kenny scoffed. "I'm sure temperatures got colder than this in South Dakota during the month of January. Keep walking."

It was a Sunday afternoon and they were power walking along the Hudson River. There were signs of sunshine hiding somewhere behind a thick grayish-blue blanket that covered the sky but the cold, crisp air and chilling winds that blew off the water made it feel like it was going to snow. The city lingered in the quiet and sleepy state that occurred when the holiday season tourists, who invaded Manhattan from the weeks leading up to Thanksgiving and loitered until a few weeks after New Year's, had finally gone home; and lasted until early February, when locals who had hibernated long enough in their tiny apartments began running and biking outside with proper layers of Polartec and dined on sidewalks under heated lamps and restaurant provided blankets.

"Why can't you be like every other single girl in New York? Curled up under a blanket on your couch with a glass of wine and swiping left and right through the catalogue of men who live on the apps in your phone. This is prime cuffing season, and you could be missing spectacular matches. *Your* Mr. Right could've just been snatched up by some undeserving chick sitting in that apartment, right there." Colby pointed to a random window of a high-rise building on Riverside Drive. "All because you're out here in the elements. You can't burn *that* many more calories by exercising in the cold, can you?"

"If you keep talking, I'm going to pick up the pace," Kenny said, her breath becoming more visible. She was frozen to the bone but wasn't going to give Colby the satisfaction of letting him in on her secret.

He surprisingly obeyed. She planned to turn around and allow him to speak again when they reached the Pier i Café around West Seventieth Street, so she embraced the silence for a few more moments. During the warm months, this was the spot she would come to write and watch sunsets. While she had been furiously writing the romantic comedy since she returned from Hilton Head and was close to submitting the manuscript to Muffin Evans for review, Kenny realized that she hadn't watched or noticed a sunset since the night she ran into J.P. at the Harbour Town Lighthouse. She had a sudden yearning to see one, but the root of the yearning was hard to decipher. Was she craving a beautiful production by Mother Nature or was she still thinking about J.P.?

"What is cuffing season anyway?" Kenny asked as she pivoted on her heels, queuing to Colby that they had reached the halfway point in their workout and invited him to converse.

"It's already halfway through, so you best hop on the bandwagon soon, Queen. According to the *New York Post* it's the time between October and March when people look for cold-weather partners to keep them warm. Relationships usually peak around Valentine's Day." He jumped on the chance to engage once again.

"So, it's like a socially acceptable, casual hook-up period?" she interpreted, like she was interested.

"Yass, you get it, girl! It's a generational movement. That same article also said that airports are the hottest places to meet people, which is perfect for your lifestyle. Maybe you can add Mile High Club member to your long list of travel credentials this cuffing season." He excitedly clapped.

"Colby!" Kenny snapped.

"National Car Rental Executive Club, Delta Gold Medalion Status, Marriott Bonvoy Ambassador Elite," he rattled while ticking off his fingers.

"As much as I would love to be a success story profiled on *Page Six* for heeding their profound dating advice, I'm not participating in cuffing season *or* adding anything to my travel resume. But I was *thinking* about texting Ed," she cautiously said. "He's a nice guy. I should've given him a second chance." She gazed out over the water wondering if she could be fair to Ed or herself on a second date; or if her mind would be somewhere in South Carolina.

"You are full of surprises today, you little minx! You finished the manuscript for your romantic comedy *and* you're ready to date again. I love it! I love it all!" Colby threw his left arm around Kenny's neck and kissed her on the cheek. "I'm proud of you."

"You're just saying that because you know those two actions will make your boss and cube mate happy, paving the way for manageable days at the office for you," she nudged his side from under his headlock.

He halted and gripped her shoulders with both of his hands. She was slightly taken aback.

"I mean it, Kenny. I'm proud of you. I don't know what happened down in Hilton Head; I don't know what was in the water or what was in the air, but it agreed with you." He hugged her tightly.

Kenny stood still, and let Colby embrace her while a few soft tears slid down her face.

Forty-Two

<u>To-Do Monday, January 22</u>

- Confirm dinner date/location with Luke + Lonnie Locke (propose week of 2/5 in Stamford)
- Arrange travel for Boise, Idaho trip (Dr. Love's codefendant arraignment, 2/14)
- Hand-deliver manuscript to Border Books before 4:00 p.m.
- Text Ed

Kenny ripped the daily to-do list from the pink Post-it pad and stuck it under the appropriate date in her new planner. She unplugged the percolator, tossed her Swell bottle in her black Longchamp bag, and popped in her earbuds so she could listen to the Network Editorial Call on the commute to the office. She was passing Amsterdam Books when she felt the phone vibrate in her bag. The morning was bitter and blustery, and she was bundled up for her walk; the last thing she wanted to do was take off her mittens and expose her hands to the cold while she dug around for her phone. But she did. She reverted to the life of being available to the world on demand, the minute she turned on her phone while taxing on the tarmac at JFK four months ago.

She dug around the deep bag for a few seconds and when her numb fingers couldn't locate the phone, she stepped inside the bookstore whose front door welcome sign hadn't even been flipped to "Open." She took off her left mitten and found the phone with the hand that still had some feeling in it.

Text from Hailey: I'm rly worried abt Uncle Johnny. Can u pls call me?

Kenny's stomach dropped. Seeing the name "Hailey" startled her.

She had a busy day and few weeks ahead. She couldn't get sidetracked by going down any rabbit holes or games of "let's catch up" that Hailey would inevitably propose. On the other hand, Kenny could easily nip that in the bud with a simple, "Sorry, wrong text!" response. Given the formality of the message compared to Haileys's usual text speak, Kenny thought whatever the situation was, it must've be serious and warranted a reply.

Text to Hailey: Hey Hailey! I hope everything is okay with your uncle. I think you have the wrong number. This is Kenny from NYC.

Text from Hailey: No, I'm hoping to talk 2 u. Uncle Johnny hasn't been the same since you left w/o a goodbye. And Mr. C dropped dead of a heart attack soon after that. Pls call me.

Kenny fell back against the wall of books she was standing next to, and her bag slid down her arm and *clanked!*

to the ground. The message was short but so much information was packed into it that Kenny's brain didn't know where to begin processing. The news of Mr. Cunningham's death was heartbreaking. Although Kenny didn't know the man, personally, she knew the impact he had on so many people and the void his death would leave in the community. Before Kenny could analyze what she *thought* the other part of that message could mean, her phone lit up again.

Text from Hailey: J.P. is my uncle. I call him Uncle Johnny.

Kenny's legs nearly gave out, and her lean sank to a squat, until she found herself completely seated on the dusty floor of the bookstore. When she peeled her eyes up from her phone, she realized she was in the children's section and was eye level with the *Clifford the Big Red Dog* series. She burst into a fit of laughter and whimpers. None of it and all of it suddenly made sense.

All but her trembling fingers regained composure, and Kenny picked up the phone to call Hailey.

"Oh, Kenny! I'm so happy you called! I've thought about reaching out to you for a long time. Uncle Johnny would *kill* me if he knew I was doing this, but I can't stand to see him so sad. I hope everything is okay with you, and I don't know what caused you to leave, but he was devastated when you did. He regretted and second guessed everything he did or didn't do," Hailey launched into one of her signature dialogues. "He even bought a plane ticket to go to New York and track you down. He had to know where things went wrong and if you two could work past whatever it was. But then Mr. C abruptly passed away, which, of course, tore him apart. And, Kenny, Mr. C left J.P. *everything*. Aside from mourning the loss, Uncle Johnny's overwhelmed. I went down to the funeral and then, again, over winter break. I'm back at WVU now until graduation. I'm worried about him. He cared for you, Kenny. He really cared for you. Do you think maybe you could talk to him?" Hailey vented without taking a breath.

Kenny was speechless. The thoughts in her head swirled like flakes in a shaken snow globe. But this time, instead of falling into a scene of chaos like they usually did, they seemed to fall into a place they had been longing to land.

"Hailey? Can I be honest with you?" Kenny asked sheepishly, embarrassed by what she was about to admit and how juvenile it could sound.

"Of course!" Hailey welcomed.

"I thought you and J.P. were a couple," Kenny said softly.

"What!" Hailey laughed, "I know I live in West Virginia but don't believe everything you hear about us Mountaineers, Kenny!"

"Oh my God, Hailey. I can't believe how badly I screwed things up. I fell fast and hard for your uncle and it terrified me. Before I met you for drinks at the Beach Club that day, I saw the two of you at Pelican Pointe. I heard you talking about a relationship and moving down there permanently. I saw he had his arm around you. That afternoon, you were so excited about the long-awaited commitment between you and your boyfriend. You were wearing the new OHHIO visor that I assumed was J.P.'s and you were talking about your date at Charlie's. J.P. and I were supposed to go to Charlie's that week, too. I concocted this whole story in my head. My version of the story was too much for me to handle or face, so I left. I feel like such an idiot."

"Ouch! You thought Uncle Johnny was a liar and a cheat? And me? You probably had a few different scenarios playing out about me, right? That's a terrible story," Hailey said sympathetically.

It perplexed Kenny that Hailey could be so nonchalant,

understanding even, about the scenario that she construed and involved unflattering portrayals of her and her uncle; but she was relived Hailey viewed it has as reality TV soap opera and was able to move past it without thinking twice.

"I like my view of the story better. Uncle Johnny is the closest thing I have to a dad. He's been alone for a long time and deserves a great girl. From the little bit I knew about you and the conversations we had, I was hoping the two of you would run into each other. When I came down for Employee Appreciation Weekend, I told him I had someone I wanted him to meet. He told me he wasn't interested; that he had met a woman and was taking her on a date that week. But I tried to get him to come with Matt—that's my boyfriend—to meet us at the Beach Club for drinks, anyway. I had a feeling about the two of you. Earlier that day, I asked Uncle Johnny to come over to Pelican Pointe because I wanted to talk to him about the job offer and getting into a relationship with Matt. Lastly, Uncle Johnny *did* give me the visor, he said it was too small for his head; and I think Mr. Cunningham recommended Charlie's to everyone," Hailey chuckled.

"I am at a complete loss for words, Hailey," Kenny said as she stumbled to her feet, noticing droves of mothers, nannies, and au pairs parking their snow covered UPPAbaby and Bugaboo strollers on the other side of the glass windows, ready to storm the door for story time.

"It wasn't until a few weeks after you left that I made the connection. He told me he was flying to New York for the weekend, but I could tell in his voice it was for more than the work trip he tried to pass it off as. After I forced him to share a few details, a light bulb went off! What are the odds that the girl my uncle had fallen in love with was the same girl I wanted to set him up with?" Hailey's enthusiasm grew.

Kenny lost her breath but caught her body on a wobbly bookshelf when she heard the word *love*.

Forty-Three

Something slowly drew Kenny out of a deep sleep but before she fully opened her eyes, she observed from behind closed lids that the sun was shining. She saw a canvas of yellow and could feel the warmth on her skin.

"Miss Sloane. Excuse me, Miss Sloane." Kenny heard a gentle voice in the distance.

She lazily blinked open her eyes and through squinted lenses pieced together her surroundings. She jolted to an upright position. The voice wasn't echoing from the distance; it was coming from the mouth of the patient flight attendant who hovered over her. The plane was empty of passengers and the overhead bins cleared of any luggage.

"I'm so sorry! I hope I didn't keep you too long," Kenny exclaimed, shoving the manila envelope that was resting on her lap into her black bag.

"No worries, Dear. You were sound asleep before the cabin was fully onboarded back in New York. You must have needed your rest. Even the older gentleman who sat next to you commented on how peaceful you looked. I hated to wake you," the soft-spoken attendant whispered.

Kenny gingerly walked down the plane's steep, shaky metal steps that led to the tarmac, through the small airport and back outside to a rocking chair at the entrance of the terminal where she called an Uber. She pushed her sunglasses off her face and looked around at the palm trees while the breeze waved across her skin. It was cooler than when she left in October but warmer than the plunging temperatures and accompanying blizzard that she narrowly escaped back in Manhattan. The familiar smell of pine, oak and sea salt permeated the air and Kenny's eyes were drawn to the vibrant colors that blossomed from the trees and flowers and brought the landscape to life.

Kenny quietly slid into the backseat of the Uber and immediately started to second-guess the rash decision to raid her savings account and jump on the first direct flight out of New York to Hilton Head. The voices in her head started to chatter. She should have called or texted or emailed J.P. before dropping everything to rush to the island. There were countless scenarios that Kenny didn't evaluate or factor into her plan. J.P. could be out of town on business. Perhaps he wouldn't be as forgiving as Hailey when Kenny told him the truth about what prompted her to leave without warning or regard in October. Maybe he wouldn't understand at all, and her sheer presence would make this already difficult time even worse. There was the chance that the major events that unfolded in his life over the last four months left a version of him that she wouldn't recognize.

Kenny was so engrossed and distracted with her internal dialogue of weighing the pros and cons of the plan she didn't have in place and deeply regretting not balancing them before she left the confines of The Dollhouse, that she didn't realize how close she was to Sea Pines. She was grounded back to the present when the small, black compact car pulled up to the Greenwood Gate and Derek the gatekeeper popped out of the tan hut with his Hawaiian shirt, toothy smile, and overstated welcome wave.

"You can roll down the windows, ma'am," the reserved Uber driver suggested. "It's too warm to turn on the heat and too cool to turn on the air conditioner, but it's a beautiful day for fresh air," he winked at Kenny from the rearview mirror.

"That's a great idea, thank you," Kenny replied.

As she rolled down the rear windows and slid the sunglasses to the bridge of her nose, she brought her attention back to her senses. She fixed her eyes on the beauty of her surroundings, felt the fresh air hit her skin in the form of a light breeze, and smelled the ocean that was only a few hundred feet away. Behind the flapping of the wind, she heard a soulful tune coming from the speakers in the front seat. They were the wise words of Billy Joel. The same reflective lyrics that started her on this journey.

In that moment, as the car pulled around Fraser's Circle, Kenny had all she needed. The last four months of her life were about to come full circle. They started and were going to end here, in her Vienna.

She anxiously pounded the four-digit code into the keypad at Villa #5 and pushed open the heavy, beige door. She left her suitcase in the foyer and walked to the back of the airy room to open the blinds and back door to the patio. There were no swimmers or waders in the pool but the pickleball courts were brimming with players. The pavilion was free of construction equipment and busy with people lunching, reading, and playing cards.

She walked back into the villa that looked the same as when she left it in October and noticed a small white cardboard box, tied up with a green ribbon, on the counter next to the plantation passes. She untied the ribbon, opened the box, and found a business-card sized note with three perfectly shaped and frosted cookies.

"We hope your stay with Low Country Hospitality is as refreshing as Miss Luana's famous key lime pie cookies!"

Her eyes welled with tears for the hundredth time in the past two days and she took a giant, savory bite out of one of the cookies. Tasting the cookie, hearing the song, noticing Derek at the guardhouse, all made Kenny's life seem real and right. The last piece of the puzzle was to find J.P. But before she rehearsed any more scenarios in her mind, she took a long, hot shower to clear her head and wash away the ragged look and disheveled appearance that accompanied even the most well thought-out and planned travel excursions, which this trip certainly was not.

She dried her hair and applied makeup to her translucent skin; aside from the peaks of light that shone through the plane windows, she hadn't seen significant sun in months. Kenny paired skinny jeans with a fitted white blouse and threw a tan suede jacket around her shoulders. She pulled up a pair of tan wedge boots and looked in the mirror. The person staring back at her looked happy. She looked like the person she saw four months ago.

Since there was no food at the villa and Kenny needed to walk off pent-up nervous energy, she started ambling down the bike path with the intention of stopping for food somewhere, be it a grocery store or restaurant. Without any thought behind her chosen course, she found herself lost in the comforting sense of calm and serenity that overcame her every time she ventured around Sea Pines. She also found herself taken up with a lone monarch butterfly that she followed all the way to Harbour Town. The fluttering of bright orange wings with tints of red caught Kenny's eye somewhere around the intersection of Plantation Drive and Lighthouse Road. The sight of it released the kaleidoscope of butterflies that were unleashed in her belly the first time she laid eyes on J.P.

It also took her back to the day that she and J.P. ran into each other on the beach. When one landed on her sunburned belly, he explained that monarchs were the smartest of all butterflies; because, just like the bottlenose dolphins, they stayed in Hilton Head year-round and didn't fly south for the winter like the rest.

Stepping onto the red brick walkway that circled the marina suddenly made her hyperaware of her surroundings. Every tall man with dark hair or a baseball hat that she saw up close or in the distance caused her to take a double look. Every dog that she heard bark, halted her in her tracks. She sat down on one of the red rocking chairs and tried to calm her mind, but anxious thoughts had her back on her feet and walking toward the lighthouse. The top of the landmark was J.P.s favorite spot on the island and the colors that illuminated the sky would arguably make a picture-perfect sunset within the hour. She debated climbing the tower but wondered if that would be too much like playing with kismet. Then she thought about the butterfly that led her to the marina in the first place and threw that logic and overthinking out the window.

She took a deep breath, craned her head to look up at the observation deck she would soon be standing on and reached for the door. As she was about to push it open, someone tapped her on the shoulder, causing her to shriek and nearly jump out of her nervous skin.

"Sorry, ma'am! Didn't mean to startle you," apologized the young kid whom Kenny recognized from her last jaunt up the lighthouse. "They're predicting some nasty storms this evening, so I've been asked to close early in case the heavy rains roll in earlier than forecast. Sorry!"

"Oh sure, okay. I understand," Kenny said hoping the grim weather wasn't a foreshadow of how her night or the trip would go. "I'm sorry I was so jumpy, I probably scared you, too!"

Her stomach growled and she remembered the purpose of her evening walk was to eat something, so she visited the Maître d at the Quarterdeck and requested a table by the windows on the second floor. It was the next best spot on the plantation to catch a view of the sunset and if she had come this far, she thought she ought to enjoy the light show.

While she waited for her salad and scallops, she got up from the table and stepped onto the deck that circled the second floor. She never snapped the photos of the picturesque scene she promised Colby four months ago, so decided to make good on her word. She carefully captured breathtaking views from all around the deck; and as she scrolled to identify the best pictures to send, and the sun slowly slipped out of view, her phone buzzed.

Text from Unknown: This is my favorite part.

Without thinking, Kenny slowly turned around and found J.P. standing so close to her that she was certain he could hear her rapidly beating heart. She cast her gaze up and he gently cupped her face with both of his hands. Neither of them spoke and he lowered his head closer to hers. J.P. delicately kissed her forehead and then her nose. Kenny's legs trembled with each touch.

"I should have done this a long time ago," he said before kissing her on the lips.

"I missed you." She smiled, when he lifted his head back up and slid his hands to her waist. "What happens now?" she timidly whispered.

"Now, we give it a shot. We give us a shot and we see what happens." He winked and pulled in her for another long, slow kiss.

After a few moments, Kenny took a small step back and pulled out a manila envelope from the bag that was on her shoulder and handed it to J.P.

"What's this?" He released her lower back and opened the clasp of the paper sleeve.

"It's my manuscript. It's going to be published and should be on bookshelves by the end of the year," Kenny said with a smile.

"That's amazing! You're amazing. Which storyline did you choose?" J.P. excitedly asked.

"None of them. It's about a girl. And a guy. Who accidentally meet on the sandy beaches of South Carolina and fall a little more in love every day." She shrugged and lifted her arms to hug him.

"I hope this guy and girl live happily ever after." He grinned and scooped her up and into his arms.

Acknowledgments

While at times writing and editing an 85,000 word novel seemed daunting, those tasks paled in comparison to when it came time to write this section of the book.

Those who know me know I like to know what I'm doing. I like to have a plan. I like to understand the way and why things work. I like to have deadlines and I *love* to cross tasks off of my daily Post-it notes. I'm the ultimate planner and overthinker (Some call it Type-A, I call it efficient and practical!)

So . . . diving headfirst into the world of fiction writing was completely unchartered water for me and *way* outside of my comfort zone. I didn't know the first thing about creative writing or the publishing industry. But I knew when I sat down to write, I couldn't stop. It made me happy.

When I shared this secret with people I admired and loved and received their full support and confidence to pursue this passion, I knew it was time to take a risk and put my work out there.

When I had enough written to start sharing my story, I knew I needed to have a mixed bag of seasoned, critical readers and those who hadn't picked up a novel since a high school book report. The one requirement: these people would have to be brutally honest with me. I knew that if I could intrigue them, there was a chance that my novel would find an audience. Ashley Leighton, Christoher Klaiss, Jimmy Dunleavy, Jill McGlynn, Colleen Doyle and Dakota Brown—

thank you for adding beta-reader to your already impressive resumes! Thank you for taking the time to critique my pages, offer your opinions and point out my glaringly obvious mistakes. Like incorrectly spelling Snoop Dogg. I may or may not have forever lost credibility with my brother for that one.

A huge thank you to the faculty, staff and other writers at the Kauai Writers Conference. Aside from having the opportunity to gather in paradise to read, write and practice yoga on Kalapaki Bay with the best in the industry, the experience and connections I made changed the trajectory of my writing career. Little did I know on the first day of the conference that the woman on the yoga mat next to me would become my publisher!

I'd be remiss to not give a huge shout out to my ABC family. The day I walked through the revolving doors on West Sixty-Sixth Street and Columbus Avenue, as a naïve Junior in college, I knew I had endless possibilities at my fingertips. I was excited, terrified, and eager to take it all in. I went on to stay seventeen years and truly feel like I grew up there, figuratively and literally. To this day, I rely on the lessons I learned—particularly, you can choose to sink or swim—and the friendships I made. My crew at *20/20*, you impacted my life in more ways than you'll ever know. There's no other team I would have ever wanted to be in the trenches with.

To all of the instructors and yogis at Melt, thank you for keeping me physically, but more importantly, mentally fit. I love sweating with you! To my friends who are up as early as I am, thank you for always hearing me out when most people are still sleeping! Many thanks to the Wilkes University Small Business Development Center for helping me navigate the business side of this crazy publishing world.

Holly Kammier and Acorn Publishing, thank you for taking a chance on me and Kennedy Sloane! It has been an absolute pleasure to work with your brilliant team. Jessica Hammet, Jessica Therrien, Marci Clark, and Jaelan McCloud, thank you for guidance, support, expertise and keeping me on track!

To my family. I am the luckiest niece, goddaughter, cousin and godmother to be yours! The Leightons, the Michael Dunleavys, the Jimmy Dunleavys, the Hunters, and the Davidsons, thank you for the unwavering support throughout my life. They don't come any better than you! I wish every day that I could have one more conversation with Nanny and Poppop, and Grandma and Grandpa, but I know they are beaming down with pride at our families and the continued devotion to family, faith and work ethic that they tirelessly instilled in all of us.

Thank you to Christoper for being the best little, bigger brother a girl could ask for. And thank you for bringing Erica into the family. Erica, you are the wife I would have chosen for my brother and the sister-in-law I would have hand-selected for me! There are no words to express how grateful I am to both of you for always sharing Charlotte. No one brings me more joy, happiness, and occasional attitude than my sweet, smart, and sassy niece. My favorite role is Cai Cai.

To my parents, Michele and Jan, you deserve so much more than a dedication at the beginning of a book. Thank you for the relentless support, not just on this writing journey, but in life. Through the high and lows, ups and downs, you have always been there. And I truly would be lost without you. There were several occasions throughout this process when I doubted myself, and for reasons I still don't quite understand, you never did. If I had a dollar for every time in my life you said, "start your book," I'd already have that house on Sea Pines! Thank you for encouraging, challenging and pushing me to travel this road. But more importantly, thank you for the constant love, support, and patience when I thought I should just turn around. To my self-proclaimed momager, you've gone above and beyond, as you always do. I hope you've had as much fun getting to this point and learning these ropes as I have. To my crisis communications advisor, thank you for always lending an unjudgmental ear and having the best advice. Neither Caila Klaiss nor Kennedy Sloane would be anywhere without the two of you!

To my readers, thank you for supporting my debut novel and "Kenney Sloane Gets Scooped." When I conceived a plotline, it was a sunny October afternoon and I was lucky enough to be sitting on the beach at my happiest of places . . . Sea Pines on Hilton Head Island in South Carolina. The story could have gone many different directions. But looking around and thinking about my own family and generations of women, I wanted to write a novel that ladies and girls could pass down the row of beach chairs when they were finished. I wanted to write a happily ever after with emotional depth that grandmothers, mothers, daughters, granddaughters, aunts, and nieces could relate to and talk about. I hope you find a piece of yourself in Kennedy Sloane and I hope you think about your Vienna along the way.

- Kennedy felt that her entire world crashed down in a single day. She made the bold, perhaps unintentional and unconventional, move to temporarily leave chaos behind. Do you agree or disagree with how she handled her series of disappointments? How do you cope after a particularly bad day?

- When Kenny first meets J.P. she views him as allusive, mysterious, and quite handsome. Do you think she initially had preconceived notions about him? Have you ever encountered someone in your life who exudes confidence but you later learn they're battling their own insecurities?

- When Kennedy spots J.P. and Hailey walking around Pelican Pointe, she assumes they are a couple. Have your own doubts ever caused you to misinterpret a situation or relationship?

- Colby withheld information from Kennedy that he knew would crush his best friend. Do you think he betrayed her trust and confidence? Or do you think he was trying to protect her feelings? What would you have done?

- When Kennedy picks up the pen to write again, the first thought that comes to her mind is, "Luck is when preparation meets opportunity." What are your thoughts about this quote? When tasked with making big life decisions, what comes first for you? Luck, preparation, or opportunity.

- Kennedy Sloane (maybe, accidentally?) put her professional life ahead of her personal one. She made the brave, yet difficult decision to retrieve and freeze her eggs to protect a future she always hoped for. Have you or a friend ever pursued this path? Or is there someone in your life you'd like to have this conversation with?

- Muffin Evans asked Kennedy to go out of her comfort zone when she asked her to write a romance novel. How willing would you be to undertake an assignment that was outside of your wheelhouse? Even if it might help you achieve your dreams and goals?

A graduate of Fordham University, Caila Klaiss is an award-winning network news producer who spent seventeen years crisscrossing the country to cover breaking and developing stories for platforms across ABC News. The bulk of her career was spent producing true crime documentaries for *20/20*.

Since making the difficult decision to leave a career she loved, Caila has pursued her other lifelong dream of becoming a writer. When she is not reading, writing, or researching, Caila recharges by practicing yoga.

Born, raised, and currently living in northeastern Pennsylvania, Caila is a New Yorker at heart whose happy place is a warm sandy beach, under a palm tree.